Malarkey

Other Lark Dodge Mysteries by Sheila Simonson

Meadowlark
Mudlark
Skylark
Larkspur

Historical Novels

Love and Folly
The Bar Sinister
Lady Elizabeth's Comet
A Cousinly Connexion

Malarkey

S<small>HEILA</small> S<small>IMONSON</small>

St. Martin's Press
New York

A THOMAS DUNNE BOOK.
An imprint of St. Martin's Press.

Permission to reprint from the following is gratefully acknowledged:

"The Hosting of the Sidhe" from *The Poems of W. B. Yeats: A New Edition,* edited by Richard Finneran (New York: Macmillan, 1983).

"Long-Legged Fly" and "Under Ben Bulben" reprinted with permission of Simon & Schuster from *The Poems of W. B. Yeats: A New Edition,* edited by Richard J. Finneran. Copyright © 1940 by Georgie Yeats, renewed 1968 by Bertha Georgie Yeats, Michael Butler Yeats, and Anne Yeats.

"Meditation in Time of Civil War" reprinted with the permission of Simon & Schuster from *The Poems of W. B. Yeats: A New Edition,* edited by Richard J. Finneran. Copyright © 1928 by Macmillan Publishing Company, renewed 1956 by Georgie Yeats.

Design by Nancy Resnick

Library of Congress Cataloging-in-Publication Data

Simonson, Sheila
    Malarkey / Sheila Simonson.
      p. cm.
    "A Thomas Dunne book."
    ISBN 0-312-15168-3
    1. Dodge, Lark (Fictitious character)—Fiction. 2. Ireland—Fiction. I. Title.
PS3569.I48766M34   1997
813'.54—dc20   96-44923
                                                  CIP

First Edition: February 1997

10 9 8 7 6 5 4 3 2 1

Special thanks are due to Anne McCaffrey, for her generous hospitality and good advice, and to Richard Woods, for his cottage. Needless to say, nothing unpleasant happened there and much that was pleasant did. This book is for my husband, Mickey, who shared an Irish adventure with me, though it wasn't Lark's adventure.

Malarkey

1 ༦

I'm a rambler, I'm a gambler,
I'm a long ways from home . . .

—Irish folk song

KEEP LEFT. I entered the roundabout under the indignant nose of a lorry approaching from the right.

"Did you say something, Lark?" My father leaned forward against the seatbelt the better to read road signs. "Should be the second exit. Ah."

I eased the car around the tight curve. Was that sedan going to ram me from the left? No, I had the right-of-way. I shifted to second, left-handed.

The roundabout decanted my red Toyota hatchback onto a major street, two lanes each direction, moderate traffic, lights, and, oh God, a sign warning of another roundabout. I kept the car in second gear.

"The Southeast!" Dad announced, triumphant. He was the navigator. "Left lane."

With a premature sigh of relief, I flipped on the windshield wipers and entered the correct lane to head south on the N11. It took me a second or two to turn the wipers off.

It was not raining. The problem lay with the car. The turn signal lever was in the windshield wiper slot and vice versa. The effect unnerved me. No doubt it unnerved the drivers following me, too. I shifted into third.

It was five years since I had driven on the left, and that had been in England. Driving in Ireland was different in ways I was only beginning to comprehend. I had just come south from Dublin airport and, jet-lagged though I was, I hadn't bumbled into the heart of the city. With Dad's help, I had negotiated the Eastlink—a route along major streets that led to a toll bridge across the Liffey and, ultimately, to the Irish Ferries terminal. Since we didn't need a ferry, we were now trying to make sense of the road map the man at the car-hire desk had given us. It was not easy. For one thing, some of the signs gave place names in both Irish and English. Does *Ath Cliath* look anything like Dublin? A rhetorical question.

Dad squinted at a street sign posted high on a shop. "Stillorgan Road—I think this is right."

"It should turn into a freeway, I mean a motorway, fairly soon." I braked as the traffic halted for a stoplight. So far the N11 was just another four-lane street. At half-past two of an April afternoon, the traffic was still moderate. The light changed. I shifted appropriately and kept to the slow lane. Cars went on passing me on the right. They were *supposed* to pass on the right, I reminded myself. I was gripping the wheel too hard. I flexed my fingers one by one.

We putted through the southern suburbs of Dublin for a good quarter of an hour before the street evolved into a motorway. A van and two cars zoomed past on my right. At last I worked up the courage to overtake the Morris Mini I had been tailing at thirty-five miles an hour—and flipped on the windshield wipers. "Damnation."

"Are you all right?"

I turned the wipers off again and shifted rapidly into fourth, pulling back into the slow lane ahead of the Mini. A red *L* in the window announced that the driver was a learner. "I can manage the left-handed gear shift, and paranoia is keeping me on the left-hand side of the road, but I can't seem to get the hang of the turn signal. How far do we go on the N11?"

"About a hundred kilometers."

The speed limit (seventy) was posted in miles per hour, but distances on the signposts were given in kilometers. I kept having to make arithmetic conversions, no easy task for an English major.

"Uh, sixty-five miles?"

"About that."

I decided I could relax and drive for a while without watching for the turnoff. BRAY, a blue and white road sign announced, and, in parenthesis, BRÉ. I had the vague notion that Bray was a resort town.

I whizzed past the exit. "Nice weather."

"Yes. It's been raining." Dad had spent the previous ten days doing historical research in Dublin. He and his luggage had taken a taxi out to meet me at the airport. "Are you groggy?"

"A little. But my body's at seven in the morning, so I'll be okay for a while." I live in the Pacific Northwest and that meant an eight-hour time difference on top of a twelve-hour flight. I had slept a little on the plane.

"It was good of you to come, Lark."

"Now, Dad, you promised you wouldn't cover me with gratitude. I needed the break." I was driving my father because he had suffered a mild stroke the previous summer.

Dad was only sixty-eight, and he had made an excellent recovery. Still, he didn't trust himself behind the wheel, and neither did the State of New York. It had suspended his license until his physicians and the folks at the DMV were ready to give him their blessing. So far he hadn't asked for it. My mother fretted over that. She thought he should try, but I figured it was *his* body. Besides, I wanted to get away—from what, exactly, wasn't entirely clear to me.

My father is an emeritus professor of history at a small liberal arts college in upstate New York. His field of expertise is the American Civil War, specifically Confederate finance. However, he comes from an old Quaker family and had done considerable personal research into the Society of Friends over the years.

When Dad decided to get back to his roots and research the Irish Friends, everyone thought his interest was a sign of returning vigor. He could study the records of the Dublin Meeting easily enough without a car—and had done so before I arrived—but he wanted to visit the Quaker settlements in the southeast, villages where the Dailey family had lived and flourished before they emigrated to Pennsylvania at the beginning of the nineteenth century. For that, he needed a car and a driver. I was the driver-elect.

"Watch out," Dad said. "I think the freeway's going to end."

Sure enough, the road narrowed—to two slim lanes with lots of curves and no perceptible shoulder. We passed through hamlets set in glens of an intense green rendered more intense by contrast with dark rock outcroppings and brilliant flowering gorse. Traffic piled up behind me, but there was no way I was going to push the Toyota beyond fifty on those curves.

At last the road widened again to four lanes. A sign announced that we were approaching Newtownmountkennedy. Now there was a place name that would have been simpler in Irish. About five miles farther south, the N11 gave up any pretense of being a motorway. Then the sky clouded over. A patter of rain encouraged me to turn on the wipers. I managed to do it without hitting the turn signal first.

The road wound upward and down again through at least forty shades of green. Sheep dotted the high hills, and sleek black and white milk cows browsed the lower reaches. One field had been mown in stripes as neatly as a lawn. I was used to huge unbroken expanses with an occasional barbed-wire fence. Here I saw, for the first time, the magic of Gerard Manley Hopkins's landscape—"plotted and pieced—fold, fallow, and plough." Hopkins was an Englishman, but his years as a priest had mostly been spent in Ireland.

4

Had I come to Ireland for poetic insight? I didn't think so. It stopped raining. I flipped the turn signal. "Tell me about our landlord," I murmured, correcting my error. A car passed.

"Alex was a student of mine for a couple of years. He thought he might go into history, but he was impatient about details."

"Tut tut." I didn't actually say that, but I made a sympathetic sound. For Dad, history *was* details.

"He and his wife, Barbara, and a friend started a little company, Stonehall Enterprises, in their garage. It's the classic success story. They wanted to make CD–ROM disks for university libraries. One disk can hold all of ancient Greek literature . . ."

"Or the Dead Sea Scrolls?" The road was winding through steep hills and there was no shoulder. I gripped the wheel.

"Yes, now that they're in the public domain. A team of computer experts has recorded the texts of Tibetan Buddhism, too."

"Using an electronic scanner? How did they know the scanner hadn't scrambled the texts?" I had used scanners and was familiar with their eccentricities.

"They hired monks."

Copy-editing monks. Why not? I wondered if anyone had scanned the *Book of Kells*. Speaking of monks.

"Watch out."

I hugged the shoulder as a lorry heaped with squashed car bodies wobbled past, going north. A portent? Keep left, I told myself, keep your eyes on the road. "So did the Steins' scholarly disks pay off?"

"Of course not." Dad gave a mild snort at my innocence— or at the innocence of his former students. "There's no money in history. Alex and Barbara were going bankrupt, so they took on a partner, an idea man. They started making entertainment disks—albums of unusual images, multimedia things. . . ." His voice trailed off. Dad's interest in multimedia could be gauged by his vagueness. He was an old-fashioned man in many ways, though not a fuddy-duddy.

The road wound on. I drove through the village of Ashford

without incident, but at Rathnew, a few kilometers along, I had to negotiate a right turn of 110 degrees at a three-way intersection. And all I was doing was following the N11.

"So what happened to Stonehall Enterprises?"

"They made lots of money and decided to move the plant to Ireland for tax reasons."

"And they bought a castle."

"It's a Victorian Gothic manor house. An investment, Alex tells me. They're renovating it."

"Busy little bees."

Dad chuckled. I drove.

The highway rose into rolling hills with a "climbing lane" that permitted the half-dozen cars stacked up behind me to pass. The Toyota chugged along in fourth. It was a tight little car with plenty of power. I could have gone eighty, but not on that road. The climbing lane disappeared.

My father is six-foot-three-inches tall and I am six feet, so our knees came perilously near the dashboard, but I hadn't gone a kilometer before I understood the wisdom of Dad's choice. A larger car would have been useless on streets and roads designed for donkey carts. Even the highway, in those stretches without a shoulder, was too narrow for, say, my husband's Honda Accord—not a huge car but not small, either. The Toyota was just right. Too bad it didn't come with automatic transmission.

"Not far now," Dad murmured.

"A right turn?"

"Alex said west from the N11."

"All right." I was driving due south. "What the hell?"

An oncoming Mercedes had flashed its lights. It began to pass the van ahead of it—in my lane. I swerved onto the shoulder, which was wide and paved, and the Mercedes swept by unscathed. A miracle.

Then the cars behind *me* began to pass in the face of oncoming traffic. I clung to the shoulder. When the last car squeezed between the Toyota and a coachload of tourists bound for Dublin, I gave up. I hit the emergency blinker, rolled to a stop, and set the hand brake. Two more cars surged past. Then it was quiet, the road empty in both directions.

I laid my head on the steering wheel. "Wow."

Dad cleared his throat. He hadn't made a sound from the moment the Mercedes flashed its lights until the rear window of the coach receded northbound. When I looked at him, he gave me a tentative smile. "All right?" He was rather pale.

I swallowed hard. "I may live."

"I think there's a pattern."

"A giant game of Chicken?" I sat up and fiddled with the rearview mirror.

He said seriously, "The car that wants to pass flashes its lights, and both the vehicle it's overtaking and the oncoming vehicles move onto the shoulder."

"To make a passing lane in the middle?" I shuddered. "They leave a lot to faith."

"An Irish habit."

I drew a long breath. "It's going to take some getting used to. Thank God for the paved shoulder."

"The cars behind you didn't pass until there was one."

"So there are rules."

He rubbed the bridge of his nose. "A pity the car-hire people don't hand out pamphlets with driving tips. It would save unnecessary anxiety."

Anxiety? Terror was closer to the mark. When my pulse slowed, I eased back onto the road and raised the speed to fifty-five. "Now, about this turnoff."

He dug in his jacket pocket—quite a feat with the seat belt firmly in place—and found the printout his student had sent him describing the cottage we were renting. He read it to me.

Ten minutes later he said, "We just missed it."

"Oh, no, I'm afraid to leave the N11." We were approaching Arklow. I knew from my English experience I couldn't just drive around the block to correct my error. There were no blocks.

The highway curved past a school and a stretch of shops, then crossed the River Avoca on a narrow bridge. I glimpsed a pretty boat harbor to my left, but had no time for rubbernecking. A sign announced that an experimental traffic light lay ahead. I could see where the road ended in a T. The light wasn't working. I wondered if the experimenters had noticed.

At the T-intersection, I did my head-twisting trick, checking for traffic in the wrong direction, then turned right onto a narrow street. Cars parked on both sides allowed one and a half lanes for traffic. I inched up the long hill at the head of another impromptu parade.

"It's the High Street," Dad observed.

"High but not wide." I avoided knocking the mirror off a parked car as a lorry boomed past me.

The street wound upward, full of shops. I spotted banks, hotels, a scattering of restaurants and news agents, a bookie, and the post office, if that was what *An Post* meant. A gray church loured on the left. The dominant color of the stonework in Arklow was a somber gray, but many of the buildings had been stuccoed in cheerful pastels.

At the top of the High Street we came to a roundabout. I negotiated it with grim concentration and retraced our path back to the nonfunctioning traffic light. A left turn took us across the Avoca—swans drifted on the slack tide—and we escaped the town. It looked well worth exploring, but not then.

"Turn left at that brown sign."

Obedient, I dodged onto a one-lane paved road. As I shifted to third, a van careened toward me going flat out. I scraped onto the nonexistent shoulder. We didn't die. "I don't know if I can take much more of this."

"You should see the view from the passenger seat."

I glanced at Dad. "I'd rather drive."

"I keep wincing at gateposts," he admitted.

There was now no margin for error. A stone wall six feet high and overgrown with vines hung right on the edge of the asphalt. I breathed again as the wall gave way to a white-railed fence and

8

four inches of weedy shoulder. A small car whipped past on its way to town. "How much farther?"

"About half a kilometer. Alex said there was a church tower on the right."

"I see it." I gripped the wheel and aimed for the tower. As we approached, I saw that it rose above a roofless Protestant church and a neat graveyard, walled, with tall marker slabs. "Next road left?"

"Toward the river."

I turned onto a graveled lane, and we jounced and rattled between bramble hedges. The trees that towered over the hedges had not yet leafed out. Patches of blooming gorse brightened fields full of incurious cows. A rook rose from the ground with an angry flap of wings.

"Oh, my word," Dad murmured.

I braked and gaped. Below us lay an enchanted palace, a fandango of turrets in a green, green field. Stanyon Hall.

"A remarkable structure," Dad said. "I can see why Alex wants to save it."

I put the car in first gear and rolled on. It wasn't a palace, of course, or even a castle. It was just the residence of an Anglo-Irish landlord with more money than sense, a monument to foolish display. Dad had told me the history. The Stanyons were long gone, and the place had been used as a T.B. hospital and, briefly, a convent. Then it had stood derelict until the Steins bought it two years before. No longer dazzled, I could see scaffolding, patched stucco, a tarp draped over one of the battlements. A mundane metal shed sat on the far edge of the grass.

The road branched in a Y. One lane led down to Stanyon Hall. The other curved past a clump of rhododendrons at least twenty feet high. They were budding out. I nosed the Toyota around the curve.

The graveled surface thinned. There were potholes. The car jolted along. Conifers closed in, some overhanging the lane. After perhaps five minutes, we emerged into a clearing. There

9

on a fresh patch of gravel stood our goal, the cottage my father had leased from the Steins, a neat stone box with white trim and a slate roof. I had been expecting thatch. Yellow and scarlet tulips glistened in the weak sunlight.

I drew up by the varnished front door, set the brake, and killed the engine. A ceramic plaque on the stone wall announced BEDROCK COTTAGE. Cute. "I can't believe we made it."

Dad had already opened the door and released his seat belt. He swung his long legs out and pulled himself from the car slowly, like an old man. By the time I extricated myself, though, he had found the key to the cottage and was at the front door.

"Wait! The alarm . . ."

He glanced back in the act of opening the door. "Oh, dear."

I dashed past him, found the alarm box, and punched in what I hoped was the right code. If it wasn't, we were due for a visit from the local Garda. However, no bells sounded. After a panting moment, I decided I had disabled the security system.

Dad said, "Sorry. I need to use the loo." He was on diuretics, blood-thinners, and analgesics. He headed through the door to the right.

The front door opened into the kitchen. I looked around. It seemed larger than it was because of a high ceiling. A trestle table took up most of the center of the room. Directly behind it lay the Rayburn cooker—a heater fired by kerosene—that was supposed to warm the house, heat water, and cook our meals, all in one. From the chill in the room I deduced that the Rayburn was not working. Light came from a high window to the left, above the sink, and another slim window beside the door. I found the light switch and flipped it on.

By the time Dad returned I had my head in a broom closet that concealed the thermostat and the switchbox as well as a backup electric water heater with yet another set of switches.

"The plumbing works."

"Small blessings. I turned the Rayburn on and nothing happened." Two buttons, obviously controls, lay just below eye level. I squinted. One was marked RESET. I pressed it and the cooker rumbled.

"It's coming on," Dad said.

"That's good. This place is colder inside than out. Shall we unload the car?"

"Yes. Then I have to take my medication and lie down for a while, I suppose. Nuisance."

I yawned. "I may nap, too. Is there any food?"

Dad opened the door of a small refrigerator that was tucked into the corner next to a heroic sink. The sink had to have come from a dairy. It was deep enough to hold a steel milk can. The drainboards were varnished wood. "Bread, milk, eggs, cheese, ah, and some real Irish bacon."

"You're not supposed to eat bacon."

"Nonsense. There's a microwave, too, coffee and tea in this cupboard, and a cottage loaf in the bread box."

"Then we're in business." Except that I could have used a beer.

"Smithwick's Ale in the fridge." Dad took a bottle from the refrigerator and rummaged through a drawer below the sink.

"Lead me to it." Someone should do a study of the merits of beer as a tranquilizer. I skirted the table, took the tall brown bottle from Dad's hand, and pried the cap off with the opener he'd dug out. "Cheers."

Dad smiled but didn't follow suit. He doesn't like beer. "This is cozy. I can work here. There's a desk in the next room."

"Excellent. Is there a telephone?"

"In the desk, Alex said."

I took another swallow of beer and headed through the door. I found the telephone and plugged it into the jack. When I lifted the receiver, it emitted a noise I decided was a dial tone. I dug my address book from my purse, found the code for international calls, and dialed home. I got our answering machine. In a way, that was a relief. I left a message to the effect that I was alive and well and would call later. Then I hung up.

11

Dad poked his head through the door. "How's Jay?"

"I got the message tape." Jay was my husband. He was fine. At least I hoped he was. Whether our marriage was fine was another question. I handed Dad the phone, finished my beer, and went exploring.

The layout of the cottage was rather odd. We had entered the main floor at ground level. The whole floor was taken up with two big rooms: the kitchen; and a large living room, a corner of which held the desk and telephone. It was a handsome space, high-ceilinged, the stone walls offset by blond woodwork and comfortable-looking Danish furniture upholstered in warm shades. A batik wallhanging of a stylized dragon hung against the fireplace wall. A bucket full of little black cubes stood on the hearth. Turf. I thought about starting a turf fire.

At the far side of the living room, a flight of stairs led downward. I went over to the window above the sofa and looked out. The land behind the cottage sloped steeply down to a terrace that looked as if it had been planted in grass that day. Beyond lay stone outbuildings and a pond surrounded by willows. The cottage was going to be a splendid investment for the Steins when the landscaping took hold. Right now it had a raw look. Below the window, a small slate roof jutted out into the embryo lawn. A tool shed?

I trotted downstairs. Two bedrooms and a bath. The bedroom below the kitchen held twin beds, a tall wardrobe, and, concealed in what had once been a closet, a tiny *en suite* bath—toilet, sink, and shower. The larger bath stood in the center of that story with a front-loading washing machine against its outer wall. A narrow hall led to a door that had to open onto the lawn. I twisted the lever-style handle, but the door was locked. Scuff marks on the floor suggested that workmen had been in and out of the house recently.

The other bedroom held a double-bed futon folded into couch configuration on a blond frame, a chest of drawers, and a closet. The bedside reading table looked low enough to serve with the futon laid flat. My relationship with futons is ambivalent. I sleep well on them, but not long. After about six hours, a futon repels the human body. This is a fact. Dad needed access to the *en suite* bathroom, however, so the futon was mine, like it or lump it.

I mused for a moment on the oddity of Japanese-Danish-Irish style. Then I strolled back upstairs to find my father wrestling his luggage—an old-fashioned leather portmanteau and a modern wheeled suitcase full of books—through the open front door. I took the portmanteau. "How's Ma?" He had called my mother.

"Mary's fine." He jerked the handle of the book bag up and pulled the bag into the living room. "I wish she wouldn't fuss."

I didn't comment. Dad's stroke had frightened my mother. Ordinarily she doesn't fuss, but she had been as fluttery as a hen with one egg over the Irish trip. She was scheduled to run a major poetry workshop that spring, and Dad had not allowed her to cancel it when he decided to do his research. She would join him later.

It was Ma who had convinced me to leave my bookstore in the hands of my very competent clerk and fly to Dad's rescue. Watching him drag the heavy suitcase across the polished oak floor, I could see Mother's point. He was not jet-lagged, but he was gray with weariness.

I lugged the portmanteau downstairs after him and installed him in the room with the bath. "Time for a nap?"

He didn't even argue.

I helped him stow his clothes and switched on the electric space heater. "Do you have a key for the door that leads to the back lawn?"

He fumbled in his jacket. "Where? Oh, yes." He handed me a key ring with two keys, ordinary Yale locks. "Here, madam. I dub you chatelaine." The words were jaunty but his pronunciation blurred. A muscle on the side of his face had contracted—not obviously, but enough so I noticed.

13

"Keeper of the keys?" I stood tiptoe and brushed his cheek with a kiss. "See you in a couple of hours."

"But your bag . . ."

"I'll get it."

I had a suitcase and a carry-on. I brought them down and unpacked, yawning as I began to relax from the strain of the drive. When I had flattened the futon and made it up with linen, a duvet, and pillows from the closet, I came close to collapsing into a nap of my own. But I knew that the longer I stayed awake, the quicker I would adjust to local time, so I fished the keys from my pocket and went to the locked door.

It opened easily onto a flagstone patio. A stone shed sheltered the patio from the east. I supposed some of the nastier weather must blow in from the southeast. The shed looked unfinished. I stood for a while admiring the masonry, but I could see that the door was unpainted. There was a hole where where the lock and knob should have been. The door stood open a crack.

Though the pond across the way looked interesting, I didn't want to walk to it over the newly planted lawn, so I yawned and stretched and decided to go make tea. On impulse, I shoved the door of the shed open. It caught on something. I stuck my head in to see what the obstruction was and found the body.

For a brief moment I thought one of the workmen was taking a nap on the flagstone floor. A man, well-fleshed, as they say, and about thirty, lay on his back with his arms folded across his chest. He was wearing combat fatigues and boots, and his toes pointed out at equal angles. Someone had closed his eyes. A round red circle marred the center of his forehead and trickles of red had run down over his eyelids.

After a frozen pause, I cat-stepped around him and bent down to touch his neck. No pulse. He was cold, dead for some time. Close up, the "wound" in his forehead looked phony. It was too red. When I touched it, it felt slick. Some kind of paint. Apart from the red mark I could see no sign of violence. With a shaking hand, I took a tissue from my pocket and wiped red off my finger.

14

I must have made noise. I did not feel cool and collected, but at least I didn't scream. By the time I had reentered the cottage, I was capable of thought, and the thought that was foremost in my mind was that I must not do anything to shock my father. A tall order, under the circumstances.

2 ❧

Isn't it grand, boys, to be bloody well dead?

—Irish music hall song

I STOOD IN the narrow hall and listened. I heard a bedspring
creak, then slow, even breathing, so I crept upstairs and headed
for the telephone.

A neat printout on the blotter listed useful phone numbers.
I could, I saw, dial 999 in an emergency—police, fire, or medical. Or I could call the local Garda station, the one connected
to the cottage security system. I tapped out that number.

Irish phones ring twice—*brrng brrng*—while ours ring once.
I waited.

"Garda. Sgt. Kennedy."

I pitched my voice low. "My name is Lark Dodge. I am a visiting American. I'm at Bedrock Cottage on the Stanyon Hall
estate. Do you know where that is?"

"Sure and don't we have it on our security list?" He sounded
good-humored.

"I've just found the body of a dead man in the tool shed."

"What are you saying?" His voice sharpened.

"Please listen to me. There's a corpse in the tool shed. My father is here in the cottage with me. He's recovering from a
stroke, and I don't want to shock him. Can you come quietly,

without sirens? Dad's napping. I'll take you down and show you the shed, then wake my father and explain, but I don't want him disturbed until he's had a chance to rest."

Silence. "You're very calm, Miss Dodge."

"Mrs.," I said. "No, believe me, I'm not calm. I'm a seething cauldron of emotion, and suffering from jet lag and driver-shock on top of that, but I am not going to do anything to upset my father. Can you come quietly?"

After some hemming and hawing, he agreed that he could. He questioned me about the condition of the body and told me not to touch anything in the shed. I promised. He said he'd tell the ambulance not to use the klaxon. That was a relief. There are few sounds more horrible than an emergency siren.

When Sgt. Kennedy hung up, I looked at the printout again. Then I dialed the number listed for Stanyon Hall.

An impatient female voice responded. "Stonehall Enterprises."

"May I speak to Alex Stein?"

"Who shall I say is calling?"

I swallowed a wild urge to laugh. "My name is Lark Dodge. I'm George Dailey's daughter. We're at the cottage . . ."

The voice warmed to cordiality. "Welcome to Ireland, Lark. You're the book dealer, aren't you? This is Barbara, Alex's wife. I'll tell him you and your father are here."

"Thank you, but I think you ought to know that I just found a dead man in the shed at the back of the cottage."

Squawk. "Did you say dead?"

"Very. I called the Garda."

"My God, who is it, one of the workmen?"

"I have no idea, Mrs. Stein."

"I'll be right over."

"I wish you wouldn't." I explained about Dad's stroke. It was news to her. I wondered why he hadn't discussed his illness with the Steins. Dad was the soul of honesty.

"I'm so sorry." It wasn't clear whether she was sorry about

17

the dead man or sorry about Dad's stroke. "Alex is in London. He's due back this evening. I'll call him, then I think I'd better come over."

"Well, don't knock or ring the bell." Was there a doorbell? I hadn't noticed. "I'll be watching for you." I hung up. And waited and shivered while the Rayburn hummed away, radiating warmth.

Barbara Stein showed up before Sgt. Kennedy did, though she walked. By that time, I was peering out the small window beside the front door and checking my watch every ten seconds. I let her in.

She was a tiny, intense woman of about thirty with frizzy red hair, freckles, and snapping brown eyes. She wore jeans and a red sweatshirt with the Stanford logo. We shook hands. Before I could launch into an explanation, she began asking questions.

I said, "Do you want a cup of tea?"

"Tea? No. I want to see the body."

"We shouldn't enter the shed until the police say it's okay, and, besides . . ."

Her eyes narrowed. "It's my house." She moved toward the door to the living room.

I intercepted her. "No, really, you shouldn't. I don't know if it's a crime scene, though I doubt that the man just lay down on the floor and expired. He's too neat." Except for the red paint on his forehead. I didn't mention that. If I had known Barbara Stein longer I would have, but her manner provoked caution.

"Who is it?" She made as if to dart past me.

I blocked her. Not for nothing had I played basketball for Ohio State. "I'm bigger than you are." I spoke in my mildest voice. "I don't know who the dead man is. I don't know anyone here. I've been in Ireland less than three hours, and it's my first visit."

Barbara stared at me, then shrugged and sat on the nearest kitchen chair.

I stayed in the doorway. "I started to tell you that my father's asleep downstairs. I'll have to wake him when the police come, but I don't want to until I have to. If we tromp downstairs and fumble around and whoop and holler, Dad will hear us. So we're going to wait for Sgt. Kennedy. Here."

"Kennedy? Oh, Joe Kennedy at Killaveen." She made a face. I deduced that she didn't think much of Sgt. Kennedy. "Well, okay, but describe him for me—the corpse. Maybe it's Toss Tierney." She brooded. "I hope so, the sucker. That's our contractor—builder, they say here. If he doesn't finish the workroom by Saturday, I'll kill him myself."

I didn't rise to the bait, but I was briefly amused. Contractors must be contractors the world over. I went to the sink and filled what looked like an electric tea kettle, but I kept an eye on Barbara. I was ready to tackle her if need be, and she must have known it. She stayed seated.

The tea water heated up. As I hunted out mugs and tea bags, I thanked her for the groceries and chatted about the Rayburn's eccentricities.

"It keeps things warm," she muttered. "Where is that cop?"

"Is the Garda station very far away?"

"Half a mile northwest. He should be here by now, but I suppose he had to feed the chickens or something. He lives above the station."

I considered. "He was going to call for an ambulance, and he probably talked to his superiors, too. That would take a while."

"All the same . . ."

The kettle shrieked. I poured hot water. Tea ensued. We sipped, eyeing each other.

"How was your flight?"

"Fine."

"If George is doing research on Quakers . . ." She cocked her head, listening.

A car crunched on the gravel and a door slammed.

I set my mug on the table and went to open the front door.

The quintessence of Irish cops came toward me around the back of a white car marked GARDA. Black hair, rosy complexion, blue, blue eyes, wide shoulders, and a trim body beneath the dignified blue uniform. He was as tall as I am. "Mrs. Dodge?"

I nodded, momentarily bereft of speech. I am susceptible to male beauty.

"Ah, you're only a lass! I was picturing an older lady."

The sheer meretriciousness of that brought me to my senses. He was playing a role. Why?

I shook hands. "Come in, Sergeant. Barbara Stein is here."

The smile faded. The blue eyes searched my face. "And how's herself?"

"In the pink," Barbara said from the door, rather waspishly, I thought. "Cut the blarney, Joe. This is serious."

"Certainly, madam." He bared his teeth—very white, very even. He did not like Barbara. "Are you here in your landlord capacity then, himself being off in the big city?"

"Alex is flying back from London tonight."

They glared at each other.

I said, "I'll show you to the tool shed, Sergeant. My father's still asleep, though, and the bedroom's downstairs, so please be quiet."

Kennedy nodded and followed me into the living room. He knew the layout, he said, because he had inspected the cottage when the security system was installed. Barbara snorted.

At the head of the stairs, I paused and turned. "There were scuff marks on the floor inside the downstairs door. I noticed when I went out."

He whistled softly through his teeth. *Whhst.*

"And I don't think the lock was forced."

"Then it may be we should go out the front door and walk down the slope."

"The lawn did look undisturbed. Surely footprints would show on that fresh a surface, and I didn't see any. Of course, I didn't go all the way around the shed." An idiotic comment. My thought processes were fuzzy. There was only one door into the shed. Whoever had hauled the corpse in and placed it on the flagstones had used that door.

"When was the grass sown, missus?" Kennedy turned to Barbara.

"The gardeners finished yesterday." She was standing, hands on her hips, in the middle of the living room rug, a nice gray and white striped affair with white tassels.

"Who?"

She named names—Irish-sounding names—and added, "Toss Tierney promised to finish the shed yesterday. I didn't see him, though."

I said, "It's not finished. There's no door latch and the window doesn't have a pane." Briefly I considered the window. It was too high for easy access and too small to fit the body through. The dead man was bulky.

"I'll have a word with Toss." The sergeant rubbed his nose. It was his least interesting feature, short and uptilted. He hesitated, as if he were uncertain what to do next.

Barbara cut him no slack. "Afraid you'll screw up?" What was wrong with the woman? She was taunting him.

His eyes narrowed, but he ignored the gibe. "If you'll come out with me now, Mrs. Dodge. You . . ." He nodded to Barbara. ". . . can wait in the kitchen."

Her lips compressed. "Maybe I'll be able to identify him. Lark can't. She doesn't know anybody."

"Sure, and it may be I'll know him myself," Kennedy rejoined. "If he's local."

"Fat chance. You wouldn't know . . ." She bit her lip.

Your ass from your elbow? I thought that if I were a foreigner living in Ireland I'd try for a little more tact with the authorities.

Kennedy turned to me. "Will you come out now and show me the body?"

I nodded. Jet lag had me by the throat and I was fading fast. Woozy, I led him out the front door and around the living

21

room end of the cottage. We descended the slope on flagstone steps that ended at the edge of the house. The raked ground looked untouched. I stepped onto the soft surface carefully and Kennedy followed in my footprints, but my suede ankle boots sank in. The area would have to be raked and replanted after us—and after the ambulance crew.

When I stopped at the patio, reluctant to enter the shed, Kennedy paused beside me. We had tracked the Irish equivalent of bark dust onto the flagstones. "There's no latch," I repeated. "The door was ajar."

"So I see. Tell me what you did."

I described my movements.

"And he's in there on the floor?"

"He looks as if somebody laid him out." All that was missing was a lily in his hands, or a rosary if they didn't do lilies in Ireland. I have no idea why I didn't warn Kennedy about the red paint mark.

"Laid out, do you say?" He pursed his mouth. "A shock, was it?"

I stared at him.

He gave a slight smile of apology. "Let's have a look at the feller, then, shall we?" He nudged the door open with his foot, as I had, and entered. "Jaysus, if it's not General Duffy, God rest him."

I thought of the paint splotch and the man's combat fatigues, and my memory played one of the tricks it plays when I'm tired. When the sergeant emerged from the shed—and he didn't stay inside it long—I asked, "The Blueshirt? You said Duffy."

Kennedy stared at me. His black-fringed eyes were suddenly very shrewd indeed. "Well, now, what do *you* know of Gavin Duffy and the Blueshirts?"

"Senior seminar on William Butler Yeats," I muttered. A good fifteen years ago. I didn't mention that. "In the thirties, Yeats had a flirtation with a group of fascists. Duffy was the local *Duce*." I gestured toward the shed. "Are you saying this guy was a neo-Nazi?"

22

"T'was just my pet name for him. He liked to dress up like Rambo and play little war games with his mates. They shoot at each other with polythene guns full of paint."

"Squirt guns?"

"Yes." After a moment he added, "Neo-Nazi? His politics was no business of mine."

"But his games were?"

"He recruited some of the lads from the high school. I had complaints."

"Wonderful." My mind drifted back to my own situation. "Then you can identify him?"

"And so could herself." He jerked a thumb upward toward the cottage. "Slade William Wheeler, thirty-one, U.S. passport. Queer names you Yanks have."

"Like Lark?" I am hypersensitive about my name.

He didn't comment. "Wheeler was the bursar—as you might say, the business manager—of Stonehall Enterprises."

"The business manager! He's . . . he was too young."

"They're all unhatched chicks," he said sourly. He was about my age. He met my eyes and we exchanged wry smiles. His faded. "You called Stanyon Hall. Who else did you telephone?"

A damp gust ruffled my hair. I smoothed it. "Since I found the body? No one. The Steins own the cottage. I thought they should know, but I didn't describe the dead man to Barbara, and I didn't bring her down here either. I thought that might compromise the physical evidence. My husband was a policeman," I added when his eyebrows rose.

"Was? Are you widowed, then?"

A chill ran up my spine. "No! I mean he was a policeman for many years. Right now he runs a college-level police training program."

He frowned.

"I called Jay, my husband, that is, before I found the body. I left a brief message. My father also called home." Horrors, I was going to have to tell Jay I'd stumbled into another crisis. I shuddered.

23

"Are you cold?"

"No, it's just reaction." The wind was damp and had an edge, but I was wearing wool pants and a heavy pullover.

"We can go in now. You need a cup of tea. I'll take it as a favor, Mrs. Dodge, if you say nothing of the red paint for the time being."

I nodded.

"It's the sort of detail newspapers love to exploit."

I thought of the English tabloids. Was there an Irish equivalent? I shuddered again.

Kennedy cocked his head the way Barbara had when she'd heard his car drive up. "That'll be the ambulance coming." He led me back up the slope to the front entrance. By the time we reached the door, the square white ambulance was jouncing down the lane toward the cottage. I wondered if I ought to have my hearing tested.

"Poor devils," Kennedy murmured as the driver set the brake and the doors opened.

"Why so?"

"They'll have to wait, won't they, while I send for the boys from Dublin."

I made tea for the paramedics and Kennedy called his equivalent of the CID. I wondered how Criminal Investigation Department translated into Irish.

The crisp air outside temporarily revived me. Barbara Stein was still waiting in the kitchen. She kept asking me questions and I kept temporizing. Perhaps the medics read her suppressed hostility—the air was charged with it—for they took their mugs outside with mumbled thanks.

I sat down at the table.

Barbara declined another cup of tea. "Why won't you tell me what's going on? Did that block of a policeman know who it was?"

"It's your man Wheeler," Kennedy said from the doorway. "Dead as a mackerel and laid out on the floor of the potting

24

shed." He didn't mention the paint. "When did you last see him alive, Mrs. Stein?" He was watching her intently.

She turned the color of Devon cream, the freckles standing out in bold relief. Her mouth opened and closed. I thought she was going to faint and half-stood to catch her if she fell over.

Kennedy took a notebook and pen from his breast pocket. He pulled the chair opposite Barbara's and sat with his back to the front door. He repeated his question.

"I . . . uh, Saturday, I guess. Sunday was Easter. That's right. The staff were on holiday. Alex and I drove down to Wexford Sunday, to the Boltons', and stayed overnight." She gulped. "S-Slade said he'd check the answering machine for us. We were expecting a big order. But he was taking Monday off. He'd scheduled one of those stupid role-playing games for the Bank Holiday . . ." She broke off.

Kennedy raised his pen and his eyebrows. He had been taking rapid shorthand notes.

"Was that . . ." Barbara's voice trailed. An odd expression crossed her face. Relief?

The pen hovered.

She went on in a cooler voice, "When Slade didn't show up yesterday I was annoyed, but I had to drive Alex to the airport. What with one thing and another, that took most of the afternoon. I called Slade's girlfriend, Grace Flynn, this morning. She hadn't seen him since Sunday evening."

"Had she expected to see him?"

Barbara wrinkled her nose. "Slade's games were for boys only." She deepened her voice. "Men's business."

"And you didn't like that?"

She shrugged. "He was about twelve emotionally. I found his obsessions tiresome, but he was an efficient manager and a genius with software. If he wanted to run around Stanyon Woods with a bunch of teenagers . . ." She hesitated. "I suppose he quarreled with one of them."

"Why do you say that?"

25

"Isn't it obvious? One of them must have killed him."

"Killed him," Kennedy mused. "I wonder why you say that."

She sat up, eyes wide. "But you said . . ."

"There's no evidence of foul play, Mrs. Stein, apart from the attempt to conceal the body. He may have died of natural causes."

Barbara stuck out her jaw. "He was only thirty. People that young don't just pop off."

"Barbara, my dear," said my father from the doorway. "How thoughtful of you to call. It's a grand place, just the thing for a decrepit scholar." He looked at Kennedy.

I cleared my throat. "Sgt. Joseph Kennedy, Dad."

Kennedy had risen.

My father held out his hand. "I'm George Dailey. I do apologize, Sergeant. It's all my fault, as Lark will tell you."

Barbara and Kennedy gaped at him.

I said, "It wasn't the security alarm, Dad. I disabled it in time. It's something else. Will you sit down?"

His hand fell and he frowned at me.

"There's a stone shed attached to the cottage," I began. "You gave me the keys. I went outside for a moment and saw that the door of the shed was open a crack. When I looked in, I found the body of a man lying on the floor. He was dead."

Dad sat slowly in the chair at the end of the table. "Dead, you say?"

I nodded. "I called Sgt. Kennedy."

"And you didn't wake me?"

"Dad . . ."

"Upon my word, Lark, that's the outside of enough. I may have had a little stroke—not a serious one, mind you—but I'm not a child or a fool. You should have called me at once. What were you thinking of?"

"I'm sorry," I said miserably.

He slammed both hands on the surface of the table. "I will not be wrapped in cotton wool."

The display of temper was so out of character I forgot to defend myself.

"I beg your pardon." Dad gave Kennedy a regal half-bow. "This is a bad business, Sergeant. How may I assist you?"

Kennedy looked from my father to me to his notebook. He fiddled with his pen. I think he was embarrassed. "I'll need a statement from you, sir, and from Mrs. Dodge. Sure, it's just a formality. I've sent for Chief Detective Inspector Mahon and his investigation team, though I may have jumped the gun. As I was after telling Mrs. Stein, there's no sign of violence. The dead man is an American, though, a foreign national, and the death is at least questionable."

"I see. Do you know who the man was?"

"Our business manager," Barbara said glumly. "Slade Wheeler."

"Wheeler. I don't remember a Wheeler in your class . . ."

"Alex and I met him later at Stanford," she interrupted. "You don't know him, George."

Dad looked relieved. "I see. I'm sorry, my dear."

She blinked hard. "So am I."

The telephone rang.

Kennedy started to rise.

I said, "I'll get it." I reached the desk by the fourth ring and picked up the receiver. "Bedrock Cottage. Lark Dodge speaking."

"Who?" A male voice, tenor.

"We're leasing the cottage. Who is this?"

"Mike bloody Novak. Where is everybody? I want to speak to Barbara Stein or that prick, Slade Wheeler."

"I'll call Barbara. Just a moment."

The voice grumbled on.

I set the receiver on the desk and walked to the doorway. "Barbara, someone named Novak."

She jumped up. "Oh God, Mike! We're supposed to be holding a staff meeting!"

"Convenient." Kennedy made squiggles in his notebook.

"Please tell your people Inspector Mahon and his colleagues will want to interview them."

Barbara said something rude under her breath.

"I beg your pardon?" His face was bland.

"I said 'when?' "

"When CDI Mahon and the boys make their way south through the purlieus of Dublin," he murmured, dulcet, "like the salmon itself lepping down the weirs of the Shannon."

"Oh God, it's rush hour."

"It is."

She edged between Dad and me and dashed for the front door. "And I have to meet Alex's plane."

I said, "The telephone."

"Tell Mike I'm on my way," she called over her shoulder.

Kennedy made no move to stop her. He was smiling to himself. When I went back to the telephone Novak had hung up. I reported that.

The sergeant clucked his tongue. "An impatient lot, aren't they?"

"Like the darling nags itself gnashing at the bit," I murmured, taking a tentative step in the direction of Kennedy's style. "Or the hogs shoving at the swill bucket."

Both men gaped at me, then Sgt. Kennedy laid down his notebook and whooped.

When he had subsided into the occasional chuckle, I said mildly, "I thought salmon leapt *upstream.*"

"You've twigged me." He wiped his eyes on a large white handkerchief. "I can't help it, you know. She's so sure I'm an idiot, I have to pull her leg." He said "idjit" without affectation. I had been half-convinced by his verbal imposture because the lilting accent was genuine.

"I'll admit Barbara's a tempting target, but your diction is strictly ersatz."

My father said plaintively, "Will someone tell me what's happening?"

Kennedy smiled at him. "I beg your pardon, Mr. Dailey.

Your daughter caught me in a bit of unprofessional persiflage. I'll take your statement when you're ready, and Mrs. Dodge's too, if she's speaking to me. I'll need your passport numbers."

When Dad volunteered to go downstairs for our passports, I restrained myself from jumping up and saying I'd get them. I told him where to find mine.

The idea of anyone going downstairs raised the problem of the scuff marks. They might or might not be evidence of an intruder, and, if so, the whole basement area would be part of the crime scene.

Kennedy went down to inspect the marks and Dad trailed after him. I fell asleep. I dozed with my head on the kitchen table and dreamed I was driving. When I woke with a snort the two men were at the table talking quietly.

". . . and I've known both of them for years," Dad said. "They're fine young people from good families. Manny Stein was general counsel for the AFL-CIO until Clinton appointed him to the federal bench, and Alex's mother teaches mathematics at Columbia. I believe Barbara's father is a neurosurgeon. Alex and Barbara met in my seminar on Southern Reconstruction, so I like to think I brought them together. They come to see me whenever they're in Childers." Childers was my hometown in upstate New York. "So few students trouble to do that."

"I see." Kennedy's hand paused. "You've been very helpful, sir. Thank you. Back with us, Mrs. Dodge?"

"Mmmm. Like a salmon lepping into the net."

He smiled. "I'll just take you through your version of things the one time. I already have a fair idea of what happened." And so he did, crisply and efficiently. He read what I'd said back to me. Then he rose. "I've a phone call or two to make now, if you've no objection."

"Help yourself," Dad said cheerfully. "Hungry, Lark?"

"Ravenous." I'd eaten an airline breakfast hours before and it was now nearly six, local time. So I fixed scrambled eggs on the Rayburn. The bacon was salty but lusciously lean and the

29

eggs tasted like eggs. Dad chowed down, too, which made me feel guilty. I was going to have to find a market and buy some healthy food. As we ate, he apologized for losing his temper. That also made me feel guilty.

"I really wasn't trying to hide anything from you, Dad."

He sighed. "I know."

"I promise to be open and direct from now on, but *you* have to promise to rest when you're tired. And not to blame me for fussing if I remind you."

He sighed again. "I think the role reversal is part of what's troubling me. I'm your father. I'm supposed to take care of you, and here you are driving for me and carrying my suitcase and summoning the police."

"And wrapping you in cotton wool. I'm sorry." I blinked back tears. I was still very tired.

He looked away. "Sgt. Kennedy thinks the investigators will be here all night."

"Oh, no!"

"I have the name of a hotel on the N11."

I groaned, remembering the one-lane road past the church tower. Was I up to driving along Suicide Lane in my feeble condition?

Fortunately, I didn't have to. Kennedy returned to the kitchen and suggested that we spend the night at his sister's bed-and-breakfast. She was sending his nephew over on a bicycle, and the young man—he was a university student home for the Easter break—would drive us to her farmhouse in the Toyota.

I barely had time to toss Dad's shaving kit and pajamas into my carry-on before a bright-eyed kid wheeled up on a rickety old black bike. His name was Cieran and he didn't talk much. I do not remember the drive.

The sergeant's sister turned out to be a comfortable, gray-haired woman in her fifties. She took one look at me and said, "Ah, the poor thing." Clearly the sergeant had laid on the explanations. "Show the two of them up to their rooms, now,

Cier. There's a hot water bottle in the bed, lass, and breakfast at half eight. I'd tuck you in meself but I'm serving dinner."

I could have wept on her neck, she sounded so kind, but I was too sleepy. The stairway looked like a cliff. I scaled it. We had separate rooms. Dad retrieved his gear from my carry-on. I think he said good night.

As soon as the door closed on him, I crawled into the pink sweats I sleep in in a cold climate, slid under the duvet, hugged the water bottle to me, and passed out. Naturally, I woke up at two A.M. I would have called Jay but there was no telephone in the room. For about half an hour I tried to coax myself to sleep but my eyes remained obstinately open. I pulled from my purse the thick paperback of *Phineas Finn* I'd been reading on the airplane, and resigned myself to nineteenth-century politics.

3 ～

His friends assembled at the wake,
And Mrs. Finnegan called for lunch . . .

—Irish music hall song

SOMEBODY WAS SCRATCHING at the door. I surfaced from a
nightmare that involved four cars abreast on a two-lane road.
The cars, camouflaged in jungle green like tanks, kept flashing
their lights.

Scratch. "Lark?" It was my father.

I pulled my limp arm loose from the water bottle and looked
at my watch. Nine o'clock. At night or in the morning? Had
to be morning. I had fallen asleep again at five A.M. "Just a
minute, Dad." I slid from the bed and staggered to the door.

"Are you all right?" His tone was anxious but his color was
good. He must have slept.

"Mmmm."

"Mrs. O'Brien is serving breakfast."

"Why don't you go down? I'll join you when I've had a
shower. Where's the bathroom—down the hall?"

Dad laughed. "You *were* tired, weren't you? Look around.
Bathrooms in all the rooms and unlimited hot water. Quite a
change from the guesthouses of my salad days. I'll see you
downstairs."

He was right. Two steps up, in a corner of the pleasant room and concealed behind what looked like a closet door, was a sparkling, state-of-the-art bathroom. No claw-footed bathtub. No chain-pull toilet.

British fascination with baroque plumbing had extended across the Irish Sea, though, and manifested itself in the shower controls. I decoded the mechanism after a minor scalding, showered, and woke up. It had been, horrors, thirty-six hours since my last shower. Fortunately, my hair is short and curls when it's wet. I threw on my emergency jeans, the grungy pullover, and the suede boots, gave my hair a perfunctory brush, and went out into the hallway. Fifteen minutes.

My memory of having to scale the stairs was hazy but accurate. As in many old houses, even the hall presented several levels, and the requisite hairy plant on a small table sprawled out onto the landing of the steep stairway. The floors were carpeted in thick British Floral, the wallpaper was fresh but traditional, the woodwork shiny white.

When I reached the ground floor I hesitated. A long hall strewn with furniture—a coat rack, a table covered with brochures, a stand full of no-nonsense umbrellas—led toward the back of the house. Five doors, one on the left and four on the right, presented more choices than I was ready to cope with in my pre-coffee state.

I peeked in the first door on the right and startled a German couple dressed for hiking. They were sitting in front of the unlit hearth with a map spread between them. The room was done in plush and mahogany. I decided it had to be the lounge. A television, fortunately off, stared back at me. The woman hiker said something in German that sounded friendly. I smiled and withdrew.

My second guess—the last door at the end of the hall—hit the mark. As I entered the large room, a party of four hikers, Dutch or German, broke off their conversation and stared at me. I smiled again.

Tables covered with pink cloths seated two family groups and another set of hikers. I spotted my father in the far corner behind a pillar. The hikers resumed their discussion. Tableware clattered. I squeezed past a teenaged boy helping himself at the cereal bar and slid into the chair opposite Dad.

He had reached the bacon and egg stage. Toast was cooling to crispness in a metal rack by his plate. A basket held soda bread wrapped in a pink cloth. Dad smiled and waved a piece of toast. "Want to share my tea?"

"I'll wait, thanks. Do they do coffee?"

"I believe so." He attacked his black sausage with gusto. I thought of clogged arteries.

"Good morning, Mrs. Dodge. Sure, I didn't hear you come down." The sergeant's sister materialized at my elbow.

I said, "You have a lovely house, Mrs. O'Brien. Especially the shower."

She laughed. "A grant from the farmhouse association. Didn't we have four new baths installed this winter, and Toss Tierney in and out with his great muddy boots? He started at New Year's and said t'would be done in six weeks, but he finished the last one on Holy Thursday itself." Her eyes flashed at the thought of Mr. Tierney. She heaved a dramatic sigh. I wondered if role-playing ran in the family. "But all the rooms is *en suite* now."

"And very nice. I slept . . . er, well." I was going to say "like the dead," but caught myself. I didn't mention the hours I had spent reading Anthony Trollope in the middle of the night either. My bout of wakefulness was not her fault.

"Grand." She indicated an aproned sprite at her side. "This is my daughter, Eithne. She'll take your breakfast order when you're ready."

I wasn't, quite, except for the caffeine lust, but I made my selections from a bewildering list of choices. Eithne, who looked sixteen, rejoiced in hair the color of a bonfire. When she had jotted my order on her pad, she and her mother bustled out the service door and back to the kitchen. I must have been the last guest down.

"I hope Mrs. O'Brien didn't have to turn people out to accommodate us." I eyed Dad's soda bread.

"No, but we took the last two rooms." Dad mopped egg yolk. "Free-range hens."

"Is that an explanation?"

"Now, Lark, you promised not to fuss. This is a grand place."

Grand seemed to be the adjective of choice. "I spent more than an hour in the lounge last evening talking to young Cieran and a charming couple from Birmingham. They're hiking the Wicklow Way. Cieran says there's a Quaker museum at Ballitore. He's reading history at Trinity, you know."

"Is he?" I felt a flicker of amusement, but I was pleased that my father had found himself a history student. He attracts them. The sprite reappeared with bread and a cafetière. I inhaled coffee scent. "Where's Ballitore?"

Dad sawed bacon. "Not far at all on the back roads."

Back roads. I suppressed a groan.

"It's in Kildare. Cieran got out the AA atlas and showed me the best route."

"Then let's go there after breakfast."

"Do you feel up to it?"

Not really. I shied from the thought of driving at all, but I was in Ireland as Dad's chauffeur. "Of course."

"Splendid." Dad poured a last cup of tea. "I suppose we ought to check with the Gardai first."

I shoved the plunger of the cafetière down and poured myself a cup of coffee. While I laced it with free-range cream and sucked down half a cup, I considered the prospect of another police interview. Inspector Mahon was bound to take us over the ground Sgt. Kennedy had already covered.

I almost said, "What a bore," but bit the remark back unspoken. My father would not have approved. A man was dead. It was our duty to cooperate with the police.

I was a little surprised that Dad didn't seem depressed over the incident—I was trying to think of it as an incident. Evidence of violent animosity horrifies him. He broods over tiny news items. In a sense, his entire academic career had involved brooding over the Civil War. And here was a corpse on his doorstep. It was true that Dad hadn't seen the body, as I had, and also true, though I had doubts, that the victim might have died of natural causes. Still, Dad's jolliness in the face of sudden death seemed as far out of character as his display of temper the day before.

I buttered a chunk of soda bread and heaped it with marmalade. I drank my orange juice. I meditated. Was my father's cheerful demeanor evidence of a personality change? I had heard that stroke victims sometimes underwent such a change. I hoped not. I liked the old Dad.

When Eithne brought my egg and bacon, my father asked for more hot tea water. Then he rose. "I'm going to get that road atlas and show you the short cut to Carlow. From there it's a straight run up the N9."

I gave him an absent smile and dived into the pool of cholesterol. I would eat cereal tomorrow. Dad returned as Eithne was bringing him a fresh pot of tea. She also offered to get me more coffee, but I declined.

The road atlas was rather large for the table. Dad disappeared behind it as I addressed my bacon and fried egg. Free-range eggs did taste better than the supermarket kind. I dipped buttered toast in the warm orange yolk. Luscious.

"We could drive through Avoca and Woodenbridge," he mumbled.

I buttered another morsel of toast and dipped. "Did you call Mother last night?"

"Hmm? Yes, briefly. She's leaving for her workshop tomorrow."

"I ought to call Jay."

"Isn't it the middle of the night there?"

"True." The thought cheered me. I did not want to explain to my husband that I had entangled myself in yet another police investigation. I polished off my egg.

36

Dad found Ballitore. He showed me a map crisscrossed by what looked like tiny lanes. He gulped tea and told me about the museum, his eyes sparkling. I warmed to his enthusiasm.

We left the breakfast room replete. I watched Dad's progress up the stairs. He didn't leap upward like a goat, but he was moving faster than he had the day before. When we reached the top of the stairs, I said, "I suppose we ought to pack and check out."

He looked guilty. "I booked us for another night."

"But you're already paying for the cottage!"

"I like it here."

A new, willful father. I regarded him with a mixture of bafflement and affection. "Well, okay, but I'll have to get some clothes from the cottage." After another day of driving, my sweater was going to stick to my skin.

We reached the cottage without incident, though it was a good thing Dad navigated. I had no recollection of the road I drove on. A patrol car and an anonymous sedan sat on the gravel by the front door. The ambulance had gone, I hoped with the remains of Slade Wheeler.

As we emerged from the Toyota, a uniformed constable stepped through the door and held up his hand, palm out. "Crime scene."

I introduced Dad and myself as the lawful tenants of the cottage and explained that I had found the body.

"Wait here." He disappeared inside.

A damp wind was blowing from the southeast. After a chilly five minutes, a man in a rumpled gray suit came out to greet us. He told us he was Chief Detective Inspector Mahon, and he commiserated with us on the unpleasant start of our holiday. We shook hands all around.

Dad said crisply, "We're not on holiday. I'm here to do historical research. And I've been here—in Dublin, that is—for ten days. My daughter and I intend to visit a museum in Kildare this morning, if you've no objection. However, we're entirely at your service."

Chief Inspector Mahon frowned. He was a balding, heavy man of about fifty. "Come in, come in. It's cold out here, and I need to clarify a few matters."

We followed him into the kitchen where there was evidence of tea drinking and fast food. If the police had been there all night, they were entitled. Mahon sat us down in the living room, offered us tea, which we declined, and took us through our statements. Someone had typed them. The constable took notes. I wondered where Sgt. Kennedy was but didn't ask. I could hear voices belowstairs.

Mahon seemed awfully interested in the scuff marks I'd found inside the doorway. I was unable to elaborate on what I'd seen, a mere impression.

"You walked all over the marks, I take it."

I kept my voice mild. "I didn't anticipate finding what I found."

"I daresay not." He looked depressed.

I did want to cooperate. "I'm wearing the boots I wore yesterday. Why don't you take them down and eliminate my footprints?"

That cheered him a little. He vanished down the stairs. More rumbling and scuffling. I contemplated the toes of my socks. Hadn't Barbara Stein said something about workmen's boots? No. What was it?

Toss Tierney. I was telescoping Mrs. O'Brien's comment about the great muddy boots and Barbara's similar exasperation with Tierney. I wriggled my toes. Should I say something to Mahon? According to Barbara, Tierney was supposed to have finished the tool shed. Obviously, he hadn't. If he had tried to, wouldn't he have found the body? I squirmed, uneasy. On the other hand, Sgt. Kennedy had said he was going to question Tierney anyway. If the man had entered the shed in the past few days Kennedy would find out.

The telephone rang. My father answered it, though the constable made a move to cut him off. I gathered from what Dad said that the caller was someone from Stanyon Hall. I glanced at my watch. Eleven-fifteen. Three in the morning at home. Still too early to call Jay, thank God, though he could advise me about Tierney. I decided to speak to Jay before I said anything to the Gardai.

Dad hung up and came over to the couch. "That was Alex. They want us for dinner tonight."

The funeral baked meats? I felt little enthusiasm but could think of no reason to object.

"His . . . er, the dead man's sister is flying in from London."

"London?"

"She lives there."

"And the Steins want moral support?"

He frowned. "Something of that nature. He said it would be an informal buffet—nothing fancy."

"I imagine we'll be back by dinner time."

"Heavens, I hope so. Ballitore can't be more than sixty miles from here."

Less, I thought, as the crow flies. More on those little wiggling lanes. But I didn't object. I wanted to be elsewhere, though I wished we could make the trip to Ballitore by train or helicopter.

Mahon returned. "Forensic will want to keep your boots for a day or two, Mrs. Dodge."

"That might prove inconvenient."

He gave an apologetic shrug.

"You'll have to allow us to retrieve our bags from the bedrooms, then. I need shoes right now and we'll both need a change of clothes for this evening."

He didn't want to allow us downstairs and finally agreed to have the constable bring the luggage up to us. I wished him joy of Dad's book bag. It weighed a ton.

As it turned out, Mahon also wanted to search our suitcases, though it wasn't clear why. A matter of routine, he said. Since we had nothing to hide, we didn't object, and the search was perfunctory. The constable's ears turned red as he riffled through my undies. He copied out the titles of Dad's books.

The Republic had been known to censor books. I trusted my father had not brought anything salacious. It seemed unlikely. I replaced the suede boots with my ancient sneakers.

It was one o'clock before Mahon finally allowed us to go. He had been relieved when Dad told him we intended to stay another night with Mrs. O'Brien. "That'll be Ballymann House," he murmured, looking faintly envious. The constable squiggled a note.

"Will we be able to use the cottage tomorrow?" I asked.

He said something polite and diplomatic. I gathered he wasn't sure.

The long-suffering constable helped us load our luggage, including my father's book bag, into the Toyota. I strapped in and looked over at Dad. "Where to?"

He checked his watch. "It's late."

"It's lunchtime." I thought of the O'Brien breakfast. "On the other hand, I may never eat again."

Dad smiled. "Why don't we postpone the trip to Ballitore until tomorrow? I'm not sure how long the museum stays open, and it will take us at least an hour to get there."

"More like two."

Dad nodded. "I have some reading to do. You could drive in to Arklow. There's a famous hand-weaving establishment at Avoca, too."

I cheered up. "I need to cash a couple of traveler's checks and buy some real food for the cottage."

"Black pudding."

I looked at him again.

He gave me a puckish smile.

"Just yanking my chain?"

"Something like that."

I deposited him and our bags at Ballymann House. Then I drove without major mishap to Arklow. It was a pretty town with an almost idyllic setting, but I could see that I was fated to regard it as a shopping center. Oddly enough, I found an

American-style supermarket, Quinnsworth, at the top of the town near the roundabout, so I accomplished my shopping in jig time. I even bought a bottle of decent French wine for the Steins. The bank took a bit longer. I drove to the cottage and, watched by the suspicious constable, bestowed the groceries suitably. By three, I was free to wander.

I think I suffered a residual spasm of jet lag. I got lost along the seacoast. The road wound between stone walls with glimpses of steep headlands and golden sand far below. Except for one cramped-looking park, the beach was in private hands, a disappointment. Ocean beaches in Washington State, where I live, have public access. I wanted to run on the sand. I needed a good run.

I gave up on that idea somewhere between Arklow and Wicklow. It was time to go back to Mrs. O'Brien's for a shower and a change of clothes. After half a dozen false starts, I pointed the Toyota west and drove until I hit the N11 north of Suicide Lane. From there it was plain sailing, but I was a little frazzled when I drew up at Ballymann House. Which may explain why I forgot to call my husband.

Mrs. O'Brien had an instinct for succoring distressed tourists. She greeted me at the door and asked if I fancied a pot of tea in the lounge with my father. I could have kissed her feet.

Dad and I drove back to Stanyon at half past six. Alex Stein wanted to show us the house before dinner.

Alex was a good-looking man with dark hair and eyes and an endearing cowlick. He was short, by Dailey standards, but half a head taller than Barbara, and, like Barbara, he was intense. He so clearly idolized my father I was inclined to like him.

Alex took my bottle of wine, shook hands, and gave me a brief smile. Then he turned to Dad. "This is a bad business, George."

"The dead man?" Dad shook hands, too. "If he was your business manager, I imagine his death does leave you in fix."

Alex led us into a foyer that was in the throes of restoration.

41

"I'm more concerned about the legal situation. The police are talking as if Slade was killed by one of the kids who were role-playing in the woods Monday."

"An accident?"

"Maybe."

Or manslaughter. That was interesting, though not surprising. I said, "How was he killed?"

"The Garda inspector used a lot of technical jargon. What it boils down to is that they think somebody used a choke hold on him."

I blinked. "Do people use choke holds in Ireland?"

"Somebody did. Slade liked to think of himself as an expert on the martial arts. He may have showed the kids how to use the choke hold to subdue an attacker."

"Those are fast results for an autopsy," I observed.

Dad stared at me as if he found my knowledge of autopsies distasteful. Perhaps he did.

Alex said, "They're not sure that's what happened. Preliminary findings. They're going to hold a coroner's inquest."

That was consistent with British law. American courts rarely require an inquest. "And you're worried about liability?"

He sighed. "The Irish are not as litigious as Americans in these situations. I suppose I'm worried about moral liability."

Dad nodded, approving.

Alex went on, "I didn't like Slade's little games. They smacked of hate groups and white supremacist militias. He swore his had no political overtones, but everything has political overtones, especially in Ireland."

My father said gravely, "If there's anything I can do to help you, Alex, don't hesitate to ask. I spoke with Chief Inspector Mahon this morning."

Alex gave Dad a dazzling smile. "Thanks, George. We need all the support we can get. Do you want to see the house first or have a drink?"

"The house." Dad didn't hesitate.

I was less enthusiastic but I tagged along.

The interior of Stanyon Hall in its heyday must have caused a sensation among the landed gentry. Most Irish manor houses were reputedly Georgian. Stanyon looked as if it had been generated by a cabal of Black Forest gnomes.

When I was an undergraduate I went on a six-week European tour between basketball clinics. Among the *chateaux* and galleries and cathedrals we visited, I recalled the stately home of a German industrial family, folks who helped bring us World War I. The house had been built in the 1880s, when the fake-Gothic craze was already in decline, and it looked much like Stanyon. The interior of the monumental German house was done in stained wood and wood paneling with clots of tormented wood carving to liven things up. It felt like an overdose of Wagner.

Stanyon wasn't quite that bad. For one thing, the carvers had been Irish, so harps and shamrocks and Celtic curves lightened the angst. At some point most of the wood had been covered with institutional gray enamel. As a rule I dislike gray enamel but it took the curse off all that dour paneling. The Steins were in the process of stripping the wood. I had done a bit of that myself, so I sympathized with the process if not with the goal. The substance you use to remove stubborn paint has to be classified as toxic waste.

Up an intricately carved stairway we went and through a maze of Toss Tierney's hurdles and tarps to the library. "The muniment room," Alex said. He sounded half-ironic, half-impressed.

"Lots of wood," I said feebly.

"Yeah, in a country that was deforested by the seventeenth century."

I live in a region where the big lumber companies are busy exporting the last temperate-zone rain forest to Japan in the form of logs. I didn't feel competent to criticize. "I like the stained glass."

That was a subject Alex could enter into with untainted enthusiasm. He told us all about the local artists he had hired to replace missing panes, and the small crest he had commissioned for the tallest window—with the company logo picked out in gold and rose.

My father admired the glass-encased bookshelves, empty now, with their little pointy windows. The Stanyon book collection had been sold off long before.

"Volumes of Debrett's and leather-bound copies of horse periodicals," Alex said wryly, "and the occasional seventeenth-century divine. I looked at the catalogue."

All the same, I would have liked to see the books.

Alex checked his watch. "Barbara should be home from the airport by now. She went to pick up Slade's sister. Shall we rescue her?"

Obedient, we followed him downstairs, though my feelings toward Barbara Stein were not warm enough to warrant a rescue mission.

Downstairs, Alex ushered us into a room the restoration had not yet touched. It was vast and gray, with an industrial carpet and an angry-looking parlor stove in which a fire was burning. None too soon. The huge house was cold. Barbara and her guest had not yet appeared.

Alex must have seen my raised eyebrows. "We're still camping here," he said defensively. "The staff uses this room as a lunchroom."

"The staff?" I was confused. Did he mean housemaids?

"Our mass production and packaging facility is in Arklow, but the design staff, the brains of the outfit, work here in what was the drawing room. I'll show you the computer stations later, if you like."

Dad said, "Did you have to rewire?"

Alex gave a hollow laugh. "We're still rewiring."

"Thanks to Toss Tierney?" I ventured.

He stared. "You must have talked to Barbara."

I explained.

His face clouded. "The man has never, not once, brought a job in on time."

"Why don't you fire him?"

"Because old Toss is everybody's friend—or everybody's cousin. The sucker must have invented networking. The quality of his work is good," he added, grudging. "When he gets around to doing it."

"Has he talked with Sgt. Kennedy yet?"

Alex was pouring wine, white for me, red for my father. "Nobody's seen Toss since Monday."

"Though how that dolt Joe Kennedy could overlook a daffodil-yellow van is a little hard to imagine," Barbara said. She had crept in through a side door. "Hi, George. Lark. Red for me, Alex."

He handed her a glass of burgundy. He was pouring from a rather nice teak drinks-trolley that looked about a hundred and fifty years too recent for the house. All the furnishings were modern, Scandinavian, and somewhat the worse for wear. When the company moved to Ireland, Alex explained, they had shipped their own furniture. He had an agent scouring the antiques shops for Victorian tat.

Barbara took her drink to a couch that resembled the one in the living room of the cottage. She collapsed onto the cushions. "My God, what a ride. They have got to extend DART to the airport." DART was the Dublin transit system train. "I will not drive through Dublin at rush hour again, Alex. I swear it. And never with Kayla Wheeler."

"How is she?"

"Obnoxious." Barbara tossed back half a glass of wine. "At the best of times, Kayla whines. It is not the best of times. Considering that she and Slade couldn't stay in the same room without bickering, I'm a bit surprised at the display of grief."

Alex frowned. "Barb . . ."

She made a face. "Yeah, I know. Have a little respect. I notice you didn't volunteer to make the airport run."

"Damnit, I had to deal with the Netweaver contract . . ."

"Says you."

They glowered at each other.

I drifted to a window and sipped wine to cover my irritation.

45

I hate it when married couples rend each other in public. The window overlooked an expanse of lawn and the river—the Avoca, I supposed. It was still light out and would be until almost nine. I reminded myself we were as far north as Juneau, Alaska.

Dad said, "This is a nice burgundy, Alex. A European Community perk? Are the French going to start using varietal labels one of these days?"

Alex allowed himself to be led into oenological speculation and the tension eased. I ought to have engaged Barbara in similar chitchat. I was trying to come up with a neutral topic when the doorbell rang. Barbara jumped up, muttering something about dinner guests, and left the room.

Alex said, "We asked our friend, Maeve Butler, to dinner to meet you. She's an archaeologist. And Mike Novak's coming, I think. Mike, and Liam McDiarmuid from the design staff. And Tracy Aspin—you remember Tracy, George. She was a year behind Barbara and me."

Dad's face brightened. "Of course. Tracy did a paper on Elizabeth Cady Stanton."

Barbara ushered in a thirty-ish woman who had the spare elegance of a greyhound. She was tailed by Sgt. Kennedy. He was not in uniform.

Alex took a startled step forward.

The aristocratic lady smiled at him. "Hullo, Alex. I brought Joe to even your numbers. I knew you wouldn't mind."

Alex swallowed visibly but shook hands with the sergeant, who listened to his escort's graceful apology with the bland expression I had learned to distrust.

Barbara looked grim. "You know George and Lark already, Joe, so I'll introduce Maeve. Maeve Butler, our favorite history professor, George Dailey, and his daughter, Lark."

Maeve held out a long, aristocratic hand, first to me, then to Dad. "A pleasure. I read your article on cotton-smuggling through Liverpool and the western ports, Professor Dailey. Very solid."

46

"The one in *Economic History Review?*"

"To be sure. I'll look forward to your work on the Quakers."

"I'm not certain where it's leading," Dad murmured. A becoming flush tinged his cheekbones. My father is the most modest of men, but scholarly ego is a wonderful thing. I left him to feed it and turned to Sgt. Kennedy.

"Alex tells me the coroner is going to sit on Mr. Wheeler— is that the correct terminology?"

He took a glass of wine from Alex. "Thanks. Strange you should mention that, Mrs. Dodge."

"Oh, do call me Lark."

He set his wineglass on an end table and withdrew a slim manila envelope from the breast pocket of his heathery gray tweed jacket. He looked good in tweed. He handed me the envelope.

I fingered the paper. "What is it?"

"A subpoena."

"*What?*"

"For the inquest. It's set for Monday morning." He glanced over where Dad was having a reunion with a young person, probably Tracy Aspin. Two men had come in, too. I wondered which of them was Mike Novak, the man I had spoken to on the telephone. Alex poured wine. An unmuffled engine sounded in the distance.

"...and I thought the old gentleman might prefer not to testify." Kennedy was frowning at me, intent.

I drew a long breath. "Thank you for that. Since I found the body, I'll have to testify. I should have thought of it."

"Routine," he murmured.

"Did you wangle the invitation tonight in order to slip me this little party favor on the sly?"

He picked up his wineglass. "I'm, how d'ye say it, socially challenged?"

I spluttered into my wine. "No, you are not. You're socially slinky."

"Sure, I could have had me sister Connie serve it to you with your breakfast." He drooped over the wine, melancholy.

"The whole family is playboys entirely."

His teeth flashed in a grin.

It was a long time since I had read *The Playboy of the Western World* so I gave up mangling the idiom. "Have you found Mr. Tierney?"

"Toss? He'll turn up like a bad penny." Kennedy sipped. "I spent the day at St. Malachy's, that's the high school, talking to lads with attitude. T'was wearing. Maeve took pity on me."

Outside, the engine—motorcycle, I thought absently—neared and stopped. There were few noises other than birdsong in the Irish countryside. The mechanical sound was almost comforting.

Possibly the archaeologist heard her name. She detached herself from a low-voiced conversation with the Steins, strolled over, wineglass in hand, and took Kennedy's arm in a way that was not quite possessive. "I'm peckish, Joe. I deduce we're waiting for Miss Wheeler. Roast lamb or chicken, Miss Dailey? What odds? The Stanyon cook is temperamental and quite splendid."

I was about to explain that I had been Mrs. Dodge for a number of years when the doorbell rang. Alex and Barbara exchanged looks. Barbara shrugged and slipped from the room.

Maeve Butler's long mouth quirked at the corners. "Poor darlings, they're besieged."

"Isn't it the stroke of good fortune they've a castle to hole up in?" the sergeant said. "Now, Maeve, I explained that Professor Dailey's daughter is a married lady."

"Oh God," I blurted. "I forgot to call my husband."

Both of them looked at me with expressions of benign concern.

"You can't go in there!" Barbara's voice rang sharp.

The drone of conversation stilled and we all turned to the door to the hall.

A young woman, blond and rather short, pushed into the

room. A man in black leathers had slunk in behind her, followed, like a worried terrier, by Barbara Stein. The blond swept us all with a scornful glance. "Where is she then? Where's Miss Wheeler?"

"In her room, Grace. I'm won't have her disturbed." Barbara's tone was cold but indignation reddened her cheeks.

The young woman's eyes flashed. "Sure, and why not? I've every right to disturb the grand Miss Fucking Wheeler." She said "fooking." "I'm Slade's woman, aren't I, and I'm carrying his child."

4 ❧

And I hope that the next generation
Will resemble old Rosin the Beau.

—Irish folk song

"GRACE!" ONE OF the men—Alex or Novak or McDiarmuid—said the name in a choked voice. My father and Tracy Aspin broke off their conversation. The Steins froze where they stood.

Grace Flynn—I recalled the full name of Wheeler's girl-friend—looked defiant but embarrassed. Her face flushed, but she kept her chin up and her eyes wide open. If she hadn't been trying to project another image, I would have said she looked cute. Her escort, who was not cute, slunk after her.

I heard Maeve draw a startled breath and felt, rather than saw, Joe Kennedy move beside her. The rest of us shifted from foot to foot and gawked. Whatever Grace's object may have been—and it was, at least in part, dramatic, she certainly had our attention.

As for me, I felt as if someone had hit me in the stomach, and I remembered, again, that I had not called Jay.

For several years we had been trying to have a baby. Both Jay and I had undergone every possible fertility test with the result that we knew his sperm count—so-so—and my basal temperature—unreliable. I had read articles about women who failed to conceive because they postponed childbearing beyond the optimal years. There was some disagreement as to what those years were, but Grace Flynn was clearly more optimal than I.

I had finally conceived a child the previous April. Six weeks later I miscarried. It was all very well for the doctors to assure me that spontaneous abortions were common in mothers of a certain age. I was not consoled. My grief and fury extended well into summer, until Dad's stroke jolted me out of my self-absorption.

Jay had borne with me. I realized I ought to be grateful, but what I felt was a kind of shamefaced resentment. Hence my desire to escape. Hence my flight to Ireland.

And here was the fecund Miss Flynn confronting me with my inadequacy.

"The poor child," Maeve murmured.

My cheeks burned as if she had heard my selfish reaction.

"Do something, Joe."

Kennedy cleared his throat. "Gracie darling, should you be riding on a motorcycle in your condition?"

"Joe!" Maeve's tone was stern.

"Come and sit down, lass." Kennedy walked across the long room to Grace and led her back to the couch. She looked less dramatic sitting down. The leather-clad man, who was younger than I had thought at first glance, circled and stood behind the couch. His eyes kept darting around the room like a cornered animal's.

Alex hovered at Kennedy's elbow. "I'll get her a drink, shall I?"

"Juice or water," Kennedy pronounced. "We can't have the baby suffering from fetal alcohol syndrome." He said "babby."

Grace blinked. She looked as if she wanted to protest.

Alex brought her something fruity. She took it and sat with the glass balanced on one bejeaned knee.

"That's the ticket," Kennedy said kindly. "Now, Grace, why don't you tell us what it was moved you to burst in here without an invitation?"

51

"I want me rights." She took a swallow from the glass and made a face.

"And who is trying to deprive you of them?"

Grace muttered dark aspersions against Kayla Wheeler.

Kennedy straightened. "Ah, I see. You're concerned for your child's rights in the estate of Slade Wheeler." Grace nodded. "His Dublin solicitor doesn't know of a will. If he died intestate, the child stands to come into a share of his property. Time for the lawyers, lass. Isn't it grand that it's so easy to establish paternity these days? I'll alert the doctors . . ." His voice trailed.

Possibly he decided taking tissue from a dead man for genetic analysis was an indelicate subject in the presence of the dead man's putative child. Or he may have wanted to work on our imaginations—and Grace's.

Grace's eyes widened and she shifted on the couch. Her bodyguard stared. Somebody gave a choked laugh. Maeve frowned.

I wondered if Grace was sure who the child's father was. She looked alarmed. Of course, she might have been puzzling over the word intestate. I hoped she had some instinct for self-preservation, because she had just handed the Gardai a motive for murder.

Kennedy was saying soothing things. He expressed no doubt that the child was Wheeler's. "You'll want to talk the legal situation over with your da, Gracie."

"He'll kill me."

"Does he know you're with child?" Maeve interjected, sharp.

Grace shook her head no and her eyes brimmed tears.

Barbara took a step forward. I edged toward the couch, too. Both of us, I think, were moved by an impulse of protection, but it was Maeve who expressed it.

"I'll come home with you, Grace. So will Joe, if you think that will help. And you should ring up Caitlin Morrissey in Arklow."

"The solicitor?" Grace looked awed.

Maeve said, "Shall I telephone her for you?"

"Oh, please, Miss Butler, I'm that upset I don't know what I'd say to a lawyer at all." She burst into tears.

Maeve sat beside her and held her quivering shoulders. Grace's henchman looked as if he would have burst into tears, too, if he hadn't been covered with leather and tattoos. They were just kids, and Grace, at least, had suffered a loss, though I had to wonder about the depth of her grief for Wheeler if her mind was on property rights. It occurred to me that Wheeler had probably owned shares in the company, and I remembered what my father had said of Stonehall Enterprises. On the verge of bankruptcy, the Steins had brought in another investor, an idea man. If that investor was Slade Wheeler, Wheeler's interest in the company had to have been substantial.

When Grace's sobs began to subside, Kennedy jerked his head toward the open door. "Hop it, Artie. We'll take Grace home."

Artie slunk out. We heard the motorcycle cough to life and roar off.

Maeve helped Grace to her feet, made an imperious gesture to her own escort, and led the girl toward the door. Kennedy followed without protest.

As they passed her, Barbara said, "We'll wait dinner for you, Maeve."

Maeve frowned. "We'll be some time."

"That's okay." Barbara's intense brown eyes glinted. "I want to know Grace will be all right. And whether she needs money for a solicitor."

Maeve smiled. "Very well. Thanks. I'll phone if we're running too late."

Grace's departure, with Maeve holding one arm and Kennedy the other, let loose a burst of conversation. I moved to my father's side.

He looked well enough, if a trifle distracted. "Ah, Lark, do you remember Tracy Aspin?"

I admitted I didn't and he introduced us. Tracy offered her hand and shook briskly. Crisp and cheerful, she wore her hair in a short crop that suggested an eye for style as well as convenience.

"Gosh, what a scene!" Tracy's shrewd hazel stare was bright with interest. "I didn't know Slade had it in him."

The dark man at her elbow gave a snort of amusement. "You can say that again. I'm Mike Novak, by the way. Sorry I yelled at you over the phone yesterday, Mrs. Dodge. We had a crisis. We always have crises, though maybe not so many now that Wheeler's out of the picture." He had the wisp of a beard and a malicious glint in his eyes.

"Mike!" Tracy made a face at him and so did Barbara.

He flushed. "I'm sorry, but I'm not going to pretend I liked Slade. He was a jerk."

Alex said, "He understood fiscal responsibility."

"And I don't?"

"No," Barbara said without heat. "You don't. Nobody expects you to."

"What do you mean nobody? Slade was always in my face. The sucker counted my fucking paper clips."

The quiet man standing beside him sipped red wine. "Wheeler was a boor and a bully, friends." He raised the glass and took another swallow. "Bad cess to him." He was Irish in his speech. Liam McDiarmuid, I deduced, though nobody introduced us. He was older than Novak and the Steins, in his mid-thirties, perhaps. I thought it was he who had said Grace's name.

Tracy said, "He didn't understand artists."

"He didn't understand people," McDiarmuid shot back. As if he had spoken with too much heat, he added in milder tones, "That business about smoking in the workroom, now."

"Smoking is an unhealthy habit," Barbara said firmly. "I was in full agreement with Slade on that point."

McDiarmuid heaved an elaborate sigh. "We know Stonehall is an American firm and we know Americans are puritans. . . ."

"Hey!"

"Come on, Lee."

"Puritans?"

His mouth twitched at the corners. "Puritans," he repeated. "Sure, it's a wonder you allow demon rum in the house, leave alone the vile weed. It could be worse. If you were Japanese, I daresay we'd have to do physical jerks on the parapet first thing in the morning."

Everyone laughed.

McDiarmuid cocked his head. "I don't smoke myself, as you know, but the data processors are smokers, to a woman, and their productivity sank like a stone the day your man told them no more fags on the job. 'Twasn't so much the idea, mind you, as the way he laid down the law. He gave them a lecture, and two of them old enough to be his mother. It's a miracle they didn't call in the labour council."

Novak groaned. "Or strike. A strike is just what we need with the baroque disk in production." He turned to me and his eyes lit with manic fire. "It's a great disk. Classy."

"Super," Tracy chimed in. "We call it *Going for Baroque* and it's got everything—architecture, sculpture, theater, music, Rubens up the kazoo. Liam did three major gardens, including Blenheim, for the 'Great Creating Nature' bit."

"What do you mean, 'did' the gardens?"

"Photographed them," McDiarmuid said. "Some video. Mostly stills. There are grand gardens at Powerscourt, by the by, Mrs. Dodge. Just up the Dublin road."

"Did you film them, too?"

He shook his head. "Powerscourt's nineteenth-century, too late for the disk."

Liam's a brilliant photographer," Barbara assured me, earnest. "He did combat footage in Bosnia for the Irish *Times.*"

McDiarmuid gave her another ironic salute with the wine glass. "Prepared me to fight off the hordes at Blenheim."

"Lee's film of Blenheim," Tracy said with an ecstatic sigh, "is pure Bach."

Alex smiled at her. "Tracy did the audio, Lark."

Dad said, "I didn't know you were musical, Tracy."

"The disk sounds fascinating." I was having trouble imagining how all those things could fit together. So far neither of my computers could read CD–ROM disks. "Is the disk, er, interactive?" I had at least heard that buzzword.

All five of them hastened to assure me how thoroughly interactive their creation was. Dad listened with an air of bemusement. Alex poured another round of wine.

The Stonehall shop talk, though confusing, was less uncomfortable than hearing them gripe about the late Slade Wheeler. I thought how quickly they had put Grace Flynn from their minds, but my judgment may have been unfair. They didn't know me, and only Tracy and the Steins knew my father. I wondered what they might have said of Grace had we not been there.

My stomach was approaching lunch Pacific Standard Time or a late dinner Greenwich Mean Time. In other words, it rumbled. I wondered whether my father was tired. I was tired, and I needed to call Jay. Abruptly I decided to do just that.

Alex seemed the softer-hearted of the two Steins. I pulled him aside and explained. He led me down the hall to a small office with one of those intimidating devices equipped with fax, voice mail, intercom, and assorted mysterious buttons with asterisks. I have a simpler phone in my bookstore.

He showed me how to get an outside line. "That should do it, if the post office isn't on strike."

"What?"

"All public communications, including the post office and the telephone system, come under the aegis of one government department. The workers are a moody lot. They strike at the drop of a hat. I don't think they're out this week, though. You're in luck."

I may have been in luck at the Stanyon Hall end, but I was out of luck at home. I got our message tape again and said something noncommittal. Jay was probably still at the college. If I had called him there, I would have got the building secretary or his voice mail. Discouraged but relieved, I hung up.

As I made my way back to the salon, a voice hailed me from above. "Who're you?"

I watched a black apparition descend the staircase. It had to be Kayla Wheeler. She wore black tights, a black miniskirt, and a black T-shirt with the logo of some obscure band fading across her not insignificant bosom. Her hair was dyed dead black, and she wore grape-purple lipstick and a lot of black eye gunk against matte-white foundation. Her fingers were loaded with blackening silver rings.

On a ninety-pound, nineteen-year-old waif, the Transylvanian get-up would have been effective if a bit passé, but Kayla was almost as large as her brother had been and the poundage was less compactly distributed. She was also at least five years older. I was too dumstruck by her appearance to respond to her question, so she repeated it.

"Who the bloody hell are you?"

I introduced myself without embellishment, explained that I had found her brother's body, and offered my sympathy.

She wasn't interested. Her watery gray eyes wandered as I spoke. "I got lost down a fucking servants' stair. Some prick in the kitchen waved a butcher knife at me. Where is everybody? I want a bloody drink."

I understood Barbara's reluctance to sit in the same car with the woman. Kayla was wearing a heavy perfume over unclean underwear and stale smoke, and her voice sounded like a murder of crows. Her accent was California flat with an overlay of British punk idiom. The resemblance to her dead brother was striking.

Silent, I led her to the drawing room. She made straight for the drinks trolley and whined at Alex while he concocted a large gin for her. She pouted, she whined, she sneered at my father when Barbara introduced him to her, she lit a Player's and waved it in Barbara's face. I ought to have despised Kayla, but I found I was sorry for her. It was hard to tell how much of her

57

unhappiness was the result of her brother's death and how much was endemic. The others offered polite condolences that made their distance from her obvious.

Kayla occupied the couch, gulped gin morosely, and scattered ashes on her black garments. Alex, who looked as unhappy as his guest, hovered over her. Barbara opened a window wide and left the room to parley with the chef.

I poured myself another glass of wine and drifted back to Dad. He was listening to Tracy tell him about her postgraduate accomplishments. She was, it seemed, a sound engineer. Novak and McDiarmuid were having a low-voiced argument over the work schedule. I pretended not to listen. It was chilly with the window open.

I wondered how Maeve's mission to Grace Flynn's father was progressing. Maeve had the confidence of a woman with a university degree in a country in which relatively few have access to universities. She seemed to know exactly what to do, and it was also clear she had a support system in mind that was not limited to the convent. Things were changing for Irish women, as the election of Mary Robinson as President ought to have suggested. I don't know why I was surprised.

When Barbara returned she announced dinner. Her chef insisted. He was an Irishman trained in Paris and New York, she told me as we lined up for the buffet in the dark Victorian dining room. He had burned out operating his own restaurant in Kinsale and liked the idea of running the Stanyon kitchens while he thought his options over. I gathered he was a formidable personality. He had promised to save something for Maeve and Sgt. Kennedy.

All of us, led by Kayla, loaded our plates, and I was relieved to find a long dining table to sit at. I dislike balancing a plate on my knees. Little touches of fancy cookery let us know the chef could pull out the stops if he wanted to, but the meal was basically plain fresh food cooked just enough. I have never tasted more delicious veggies, but I did wonder at the appropriateness of the main course. The chef's tribute to the late

Slade Wheeler was a large, perfectly roasted capon.

I sat between Kayla Wheeler and Liam McDiarmuid. Kayla ate with morose intensity. She had clearly decided I was no bloody use, so she didn't trouble me with conversation. I asked Liam about his adventures in the Balkans.

He was a slight, mousey man who tended to fade into the background. Close to him, I saw that his eyes, dark gray and thickly lashed, were quite beautiful. He shot me an ambiguous look and the eyelashes dropped. "Ah, the ladies. They always want to hear tales of gore."

Few things annoy me more than generalizations about the ladies. As I spooned a bit of the starter—an artistic mélange of minced tomato, basil, scallion, and lime juice in an avocado half—I considered making a sharp response. I did the next best thing. I fluttered my eyelashes at him and tittered.

He got the point. Not stupid. "Sure, it went over a treat with the girls of County Wicklow."

"Grace Flynn, for instance?"

His spoon clattered on the plate but he said, with composure, "Grace is young for the likes of me."

That was true.

After a moment, he added, "I was a stringer. Do you say that?"

"Yes."

"I'm fond of that part of Europe. I used to holiday in Dubrovnik. As the war began to spread, I saw the opportunity, so I went out to Sarajevo."

"My God."

He nodded. "It was a horror. Still is. I helped document a mass execution of prisoners of war for Amnesty International. A fine time we had of it, digging up skeletons." He took a sip of wine. "So my 'adventure' wasn't entirely self-serving, but it did bring my work to Alex's notice."

"And you took this job."

"I thought virtual reality would be an improvement on the mundane kind."

59

I finished my starter. "And is it?"

He toyed with his spoon. "I've worked in the States, but I needed high-tech credits."

"You should have a substantial reputation in the trade when the baroque disk hits the media stores."

"I hope so."

"You didn't answer my question."

"Ah, you're a hard woman. I'm an artist, trained to present the truth, so to speak. There's all kinds of fakery involved in the images we create. That's one reservation I have."

"And?"

"The game-playing." He shoved his starter aside without finishing it.

Game-playing.

"Interactive disks developed from computer games."

"Nintendo?" Like a great many women, I had found the early computer games boring and faintly repulsive because they seemed to involve little beyond zapping an imaginary enemy.

He said softly, "The corpses we dug up were boys in their teens and twenties playing at war. When I heard of Slade's war-gaming I was appalled. He was writing an elaborate game program whilst teaching Irish lads guerrilla tactics. I'll admit drilling boys in the art of war is not unheard of in these parts, but the Provos at least have a cause."

I recalled that the Provos were the provisional branch of the Irish Republican Army. "Ulster?"

"The six counties." He pulled his plate toward him with the air of a man about to do his duty. His tone was light, mocking. "Ulster is the ancient province. It's not Ulster without Cavan, Monaghan, and Donegal, or so my grandfather would have it. He's a strong Sinn Fein man, is my grandfather."

"The North, then."

"The North, God help it." He shoved at a bit of new potato. "I saw what the Serbs and the Croats were doing to each other. The so-called ethnic cleansing is sectarian slaughter, the Or-thodox killing Catholics and vice versa, and everybody murdering Moslems. There's no end in sight. I kept seeing the obvious parallels. Car bombs are bad enough. I'd hate to see a Bosnian bloodbath in the streets of Derry or the fields of Antrim. It could happen if enough lads were willing to play the game."

"Was Wheeler . . ."

"Political? No. That was the horror of it. He thought he was a conservative, but he'd no philosophy. The man had never heard of Edmund Burke. He was as ignorant as my grandda's dog about Irish history, too." He stabbed a bit of potato. "Of course, most Americans are."

"My father isn't," I said peaceably.

"True for you." He chewed. "T'was the skills of warfare that interested Slade. I wanted to do a photo essay on his game-players, but he told me he'd break my hands if I tried."

"Nice."

He shrugged. "I doubt he could have. He liked that kind of talk. But it made me wonder what he didn't want photographed. And all the while his lads were sneaking through the Stanyon woods zapping each other with paint the color of fresh blood."

"I'll say they were." Neither of us had been paying attention to Kayla Wheeler, but something of what McDiarmuid was saying must have got through to her. "One of those yobboes killed Slade and shot him with a paint gun after he was dead. The Garda inspector told me when he phoned me in London."

She had a penetrating voice. Her remark brought the hum of conversation to a dead stop. My father looked appalled, the others, in varying degrees, avid.

"He had a splash of red paint on his forehead when I found him," I admitted, since Kayla had let the cat out of the bag anyway.

"And you didn't mention it?" Barbara sounded affronted. My father gave me a reproachful look. He was pale.

I felt my cheeks burn. "Sgt. Kennedy told me not to."

Barbara snorted. That seemed to be her ingrained response

to Kennedy in his police role. She turned her attention back to the dead man's sister. "Did they tell you whom they suspect?"

Kayla ripped a piece of bread in half and slathered it with butter. "One of the war-gamers. Mahon didn't name names." She snickered. "Slade was playing around with a local girl. Maybe somebody got jealous."

Universal shuffling and mumbling. Silverware clanked. Nobody was meeting anyone else's eyes.

Incredible as it seemed to me, Kayla had missed Grace's performance. I wondered whether anyone would bother to tell her what had happened. I also thought of the motorcyclist, Artie. Had he been one of Wheeler's toy soldiers? His relationship with Grace was unclear. Protective? Possessive? He could have been a friend, a lover, an old schoolmate, though I thought he must have left school several years before. If he were a significant war-gamer, a lieutenant of some sort, he might have felt a need to protect his dead captain's woman.

"Who's Slade's heir?" Mike Novak drooped over his plate with unconvincing innocence but the question quivered on the air.

"I am." As if aware that her tone registered smugness, Kayla set the bread down. She dabbed at her eyes and left an unappetizing black smudge on the linen serviette. "I'm his nearest relative. Our parents died in a car wreck while Slade was in high school." She sniffled. "Now I'm alone."

I made an involuntary soothing noise which she ignored.

She picked up her knife and fork and attacked a slice of capon with bruising energy. "Whoever did it, I hope the cops nail his hide to the wall. Me and Slade had our differences, but he was my brother." She speared the meat, American style, and poked it into her mouth. "Bloody sods."

We ate in uncomfortable silence. Liam picked at his food. So did my father. I was wondering how soon we could make a graceful exit when Maeve reappeared looking cheerful. She was without police escort.

Barbara and Alex rose in unison and began fussing over her.

Alex poured her a glass of wine. "Where's Joe?"

"I left him at the station. He said he had to finish a report."

"But dinner . . ."

"The man can open a tin of beans," Maeve said callously. "We settled Grace in at the safe house and telephoned Caitlin Morrissey. The old man was drunk."

Barbara said, "I hope Grace will be all right."

"Ah, Flynn's not a bad sort when he's sober. Joe talked with Grace's mother. I think she understands the, er, situation."

Barbara did not look reassured.

"When we left, she was giving Flynn a piece of her mind." Maeve smiled at her. "Send Caitlin a retainer, if it will make you feel better. Grace is resilient. She'll be all right." She sat at the table and dug in.

"Is that Grace Flynn you're talking about?" Kayla's voice rasped.

Maeve raised an eyebrow, fork half-lifted. "I don't believe I know you, but you must be Miss Wheeler. How d'ye do? I'm Maeve Butler."

Kayla scowled at her. "Is it Grace?"

"Oh, yes." Maeve chewed with appreciative thoroughness and took a sip of wine. "We've been seeing to the safety and comfort of your nephew. Or niece." She beamed at Kayla. "What a blessing to know that your brother's, er, lineage will go on."

"If she's pregnant," Kayla said flatly, "the brat is not Slade's. He was a fiend for safe sex."

"Oh, Grace is safe as houses." Maeve raised her wine glass. "*Sláinte,* Miss Wheeler."

5 ❧

If I was a blackbird I'd whistle and sing
And I'd follow the vessel my truelove sails in.

—Irish folk song

ALTHOUGH WE DIDN'T reach Mrs. O'Brien's house until eleven
after the Stanyon Hall Theatricals, Dad and I set out for Ballitore before noon on Thursday. I decided that postponing the
visit to the Quaker museum would be a bad idea. Dad had remarkable resilience, but the revelations of the evening had depressed him. I thought his morale needed a boost. After another
heroic breakfast, we packed and checked out, promising to return for a visit, Dad with my mother when she came.

It seemed strange, given my apprehensions, but I found
driving to Ballitore on the narrow secondary roads easier than
driving south on the N11. There was little traffic, though the
occasional lorry zooming along in the opposite direction kept
my adrenaline flowing. I had to watch out for farm vehicles.

Dad had borrowed the atlas from Ballymann House and dug
a guidebook from his book bag. He kept up a litany of place
names every time we came to a signpost, which was often.
There was no point in trying to follow a numbered route. The
only number to be found on the signposts was the distance in
kilometers.

We passed through villages with lilting names—Avoca,

Aughrim, Tinahely. We should have gone to Tullow as well, but I took a wrong turn and we wound up with an English clank in Hacketstown. I spotted a signpost for Carlow there and followed it.

We drove awhile in silence. In fact, Dad had said very little to me beyond commonplaces since we left Stanyon Hall. I thought he was displeased with me for not telling him about the red paint. I was not going to apologize.

One of the disadvantages of nervous driving is that you focus fiercely on the yellow line—when there is one. The scenery rushed by in a green blur. I wondered why the tourists hadn't discovered the area. There were no B&Bs, which was how I knew they hadn't. The rolling hills and pasture land were as lush as Wicklow, though lower. I crossed the main road to Tullow, still on course. As we rounded yet another blind corner, I spotted the first dolmen.

"My God, what's that?"

While Dad riffled through his guidebook, I heaved the car over a humped, one-lane bridge, pulled onto a wide spot that looked like a turnaround for tractors, and set the brake.

"I believe it's the Haroldstown Dolmen."

"Yes, but what is it?" I got out of the car and walked back over the bridge. My father followed. A van rattled past. The driver waved.

"A megalith. According to the guide, there are more than fourteen hundred of them in Ireland."

The dolmen resembled nothing so much as a huge, three-dimensional rendition of the Greek letter π. It squatted, massive, in the middle of a field full of black and white cows that looked small beside it. Affixed to the stone wall that girdled the pasture, a neat brown sign in Irish and English warned that dire punishments awaited anyone who defaced a national monument. So somebody else had noticed the dolmen's existence. Part of its eeriness arose from the fact that we had come on it unwarned.

I considered leaping the stone fence and slogging through the cowpats for a closer look. The cows seemed amiable. I saw no bulls. I didn't want to curdle some farmer's cream, though, so I just stood and looked. The hair on the back of my neck bristled.

Dad was in lecture mode. "Dolmens were tombs. The stones formed the interior framework for a burial mound, and dirt was heaped over them. There are tumuli all over the country that probably contain similar stonework. Here the earth eroded away and exposed the stones."

A tomb.

We edged back to the car. I had not driven five kilometers when we found another one. Dad identified it as the Browne's Hill Dolmen, the largest in Ireland. The site was clearly marked and featured a graveled lay-by for pilgrims. I parked the Toyota.

The dolmen sat on the brow of a hill on the far side of the inevitable cow pasture. The Office of Public Works had built a tall wire fence that created a safe corridor through the field.

I turned to my father. "Do you want to walk over there? It's quite a distance."

He smiled. "Absolutely."

Close to, the dolmen was even eerier. The builders had heaved vast slabs of stone into the characteristic formation. Smaller stones marked the edge of the sanctuary, if that was the right term for the area surrounding the tomb. A pair of frolicking calves nudged the OPW fence, but the rest of the herd ignored us. The wind freshened.

I walked around the dolmen several times and even stuck my head under the huge capstone. I was searching for meaning, but the symbolism eluded me. When Dad began to shiver in the rising wind, we headed back to the car. As we walked, I kept looking over my shoulder at the massive stones.

Just east of Carlow, a roundabout shunted us north onto the N9 and it began to sleet. I turned the windshield wipers on without messing with the turn signal, a sign of progress. We had a snack for lunch at a pub in Castledermot, a town with Celtic high crosses we didn't pause to investigate. The sleet stopped and the sun peeped out.

We reached Ballitore at two and found the museum. A Quaker academy and meeting hall had been restored as a public library. Museum exhibits—working tools from the village grist mill, items of clothing, ledgers in neat copperplate—ringed the main floor library. Up a flight of stairs from the foyer lay a small meeting hall that was still used for religious purposes.

I looked. I listened while Dad talked to the nice librarian. I followed the two men upstairs and admired the rows of plain wooden pews, two and two, facing each other, in the tiny meeting hall. The Friends who met there had no visual distractions. They would have to look at each other's faces. Not a bad idea, philosophically. I found the museum interesting, but my mind kept drifting back to the dolmens.

What did they mean? How did the dairy farmers who owned the land cope with their daily presence? A Quaker cemetery lay not far from the Ballitore museum. I was looking at a Quaker meeting hall and thinking about neolithic dolmens. The artifacts of religion are sometimes very strange.

We left Ballitore before four-thirty. I believe my father would have stayed until the library closed, but I wanted to get back to the cottage and settle in.

I drove past the ruins of the huge mill around which the Friends had built their settlement, then turned onto the N9, retracing our route as the simplest way to get back. There were any number of one-lane alternatives. I took a wrong turn and we missed the dolmens.

As we left Tinahely, Dad said, "You didn't like the museum."

"I thought it was fascinating!" I braked for a manure hauler, passed it.

"Really?"

"Really. The bride's gray bonnet was especially fetching."

"Edmund Burke was a student at the academy."

"I heard that part, Dad." And Napper Tandy, the nationalist. I wondered why my father didn't mention him.

I met with Napper Tandy and I took him by the hand,
And I said how's poor old Ireland, and how does she stand?
She's the most distressful country that ever yet was seen.
They're hanging men and women for the wearing of the
green.

My father sighed. "I've never asked you what you feel about the Friends." His tone warned me the indirect question was a serious one.

I geared down behind a slow-moving car and tried to focus my mind. "I have great admiration for their courage and patience."

"Did you always feel that way?"

A straight stretch of empty road permitted me to pass. I waited until I had pulled back into my lane, then said, "When I was small, I didn't think about it much. I loved my grandparents and the farm."

My Quaker grandfather had suffered a stroke in his sixties. Unfortunately, he had been driving a car at the time. Like Kayla's parents, he and my grandmother were killed in the wreck. It would be natural for my father to brood about that, given his own stroke.

After a moment, I added, "I remember the funeral service. I've always thought that was the way funerals were supposed to be. 'I will teach you, my townspeople, how to conduct a funeral.' " The quote from William Carlos Williams was inappropriate, but my father didn't object.

We drove for a while in Friendly silence.

Dad eased his seat belt. "I left the Meeting when I married your mother."

"Would the Friends have disapproved of Ma?" My voice squeaked with surprise. My mother was not of Quaker descent, but it was she, not my father, who had participated in the Peace Movement of the sixties and seventies.

"Possibly not. I didn't ask. You know I was a conscientious objector, don't you?"

68

"Yes. Ma said you were drafted after the Second World War."
I took the sharp turn for Aughrim.

"I did my national service with the American Friends Service Committee—in Europe."

"Refugees?"

There was another interlude. At last, he said bleakly, "We interviewed survivors of the concentration camps. When I came home, I found I was still in agreement with the Friends, that coercion of any kind was an evil. Unfortunately, I no longer believed in God."

I glanced at my father. His eyes were closed. I drove along a stretch of green fields. "But you still find the Friends worthy of study?"

"Of course, though their numbers continue to decline and, I suppose, their influence. There were never many Friends in Ireland."

The little I knew of Irish history had come to me indirectly, in an English history course and in bits and pieces in literature classes that focussed on Irish writers. None of my reading had so much as mentioned the Society of Friends, though there was a great deal about religious conflict between Catholics and Protestants. I gained the impression that the Protestants were mostly Anglicans in the south, and that the Scottish Kirk was strong in the north.

"Mary Leadbeater," Dad murmured.

"I beg your pardon?"

"She lived at Ballitore, a granddaughter of the founder. Mary was a poet of some repute, like your mother. She wrote the most lucid account we have of the rebellion of 1798, Napper Tandy's rebellion."

So he had noticed the nationalist connection.

He added, "The librarian showed me one of Mary Leadbeater's manuscripts while you were looking at the display cases."

"1798. The United Irishmen?"

"Yes. It's sometimes called the Wexford Rebellion, though vi-

69

olence occurred in Wicklow, Tipperary, and Kildare, too. It began as a high-minded political revolution, modeled to some extent on ours, and also on the French Revolution. But it degenerated rapidly into sectarian slaughter of Protestants by Catholics and vice versa. An appalling failure."

I shivered, remembering Liam's comments on sectarian killing in Bosnia. "And Mary Leadbeater was an eyewitness?"

"Oh, yes." He sat up straighter and his voice strengthened. "Before the revolt broke out, the Friends had refused to support coercive measures against their Catholic neighbors. During the rebellion, the community at Ballitore nursed the wounded of both sides. There was some looting, and the government hunted the insurgents down ruthlessly, but no one harmed the Quakers."

I said, "No wonder you found the museum interesting."

"It's not academically interesting. There's not much left in Ballitore for a scholar. The records of the Dublin Meeting are more useful for my purposes, but I found the museum touching. The building was restored by the Kildare County Council, even though there are fewer than fifty Friends left in the area."

"That's impressive."

"Yes. The local people want to remember the Quaker community." He sat silent for awhile. "And, of course, they remember the role of the Friends during the Great Famine. That's what I'm studying. Quaker efforts in America to organize famine relief were the genesis of the American Friends Service Committee."

We were approaching Woodenbridge. I slowed and crossed the bridge, bound for Avoca. "I thought you were just studying the Dailey family."

"The Daileys left Ireland after the Wexford Rebellion. The brutality was too much for them. In fact, the whole Quaker population of Ireland began to dwindle from that time on, mostly through emigration to America. There were less than five thousand Irish Friends by the 1840s."

Maybe Quaker women had hereditary fertility problems, I mused, irreverent. "But small as it was, the Dublin Meeting still had enough energy to organize an international famine relief effort?"

"They had help from the London Meeting, from the Committee on Sufferings," Dad said seriously, "but yes. It doesn't take many determined people to make a difference."

We crossed the river into the village of Avoca. The streets had been laid out before the invention of the automobile, so I concentrated on driving. When the Toyota broke through into open country, I said, "Doesn't stumbling on mineshafts of historical fact bother you?"

"I beg your pardon?"

I abandoned my extravagant metaphor. For a man who has been married more than forty years to a poet, my father has a curious resistance to figurative language. "I was thinking of the dolmens, too, not just the museum. There we were, tootling through the countryside, minding our own business, and all of a sudden, wham, we were back in the Stone Age. It was like a time warp."

Dad chuckled. "I'm a historian. I like time travel."

A milk truck loomed, horn blaring. I crunched onto the shoulder. A space warp. Our brushes with automotive disaster were now so commonplace I was almost able to ignore them.

We made it to the cottage without mishap, though I nearly turned off for Ballymann House in a fit of absent-mindedness. At Bedrock Cottage, the Gardai had gone, and the long-suffering constable had even tidied the kitchen before they left. I sent Dad downstairs for a nap while I fixed dinner. As I was, what else, peeling potatoes, the telephone rang.

It was Barbara Stein, wondering whether the police had let us return to the cottage. I assured her of that and thanked her for dinner.

She laughed, a short unhappy sound. "I should have known better than to put Kayla and Maeve at the same table."

"Ah, well, at least no blood was shed."

71

"So far. Who knows what the future may hold? Kayla stormed around for an hour after you left. The drawing room smells like a pub. Fortunately, she drank half a liter of gin and slept until noon. She's been tying up one of the phone lines talking to her lawyer ever since. Is George okay?"

I thought he was in fine shape and said so. I told her about our trip to Ballitore, thanked her again, and announced that I had to go back to my potatoes.

"Right. I just thought I'd mention that we tend to unwind in the drawing room every afternoon around six-thirty. If the thought isn't too repulsive, drop in and let us know what's happening."

That was kind. As I scraped away at the spuds, I reflected that my initial hostility to Barbara was thawing. Alex was easy to like. Barbara just required more effort. I was sorry for Kayla and jealous of Grace. I wasn't sure what I felt about Maeve. I admired her confidence.

I put the potatoes on the Rayburn, which I had switched over to its cooking function. It had no broiler, so I would have to pan-fry the lamb chops. I was rummaging among the pots for a skillet when the telephone rang again.

This time it was Sgt. Kennedy. He sounded rather distant. He was, he said, just checking to make sure the lads from Dublin had left the cottage liveable. Though there were smears of fingerprint powder on the downstairs woodwork, I said everything was all right. The smears weren't the sergeant's fault. I said flattering but true things about his sister's B&B, too. That warmed him up a little.

I asked about Grace. She was safe and talking to the Arklow solicitor. Kennedy reminded me that the inquest was set for ten o'clock on Monday, in the hall of the disused Protestant church just down the lane. Convenient. I promised to be there.

"Ah, sure," he said, "I almost forgot. Mahon said your husband called this morning. Now where did I put the message?" Sounds of rummaging among papers.

If Jay had called around eleven that morning, it would have been three A.M. in Shoalwater. He must have stayed up all night. I felt a twinge of guilt.

"Here it is. He's arriving at Dublin Airport at eleven tomorrow and wants you to meet the plane."

"*What?*" I swore.

"How's that again?"

"I'm sorry." I fumbled in the desk and found paper and pencil. "Aer Lingus, you said. What's the flight number?"

He read me the flight information. Apparently Mahon had given Jay the phone number of Ballymann House and Jay had called there, too. Kennedy said his sister had tried to reach me several times during the afternoon.

"My father and I drove to Kildare." I was so angry with Jay I could barely articulate. What business did he have rushing to Ireland to take charge? He hadn't even talked the situation over with me.

Kennedy was making polite closing remarks.

I asked him, through my teeth, how the case was progressing. He assured me that Mahon had it well in hand, but that Toss Tierney's son had gone missing.

"His son? I thought the father was the one who disappeared."

"They've both done a bunk," Kennedy said glumly. "The lad's been gone since Easter Monday, too, but the missus didn't admit it to me until today. I knew she was hiding something. Tommy Tierney and I had a run-in this winter. He's a wide boy, is our Tommy, and he was one of Wheeler's war-gamers to boot."

I whistled. "A suspicious character."

"He is that, but his da thinks the sun rises and sets in him. Good evening then, Mrs. Dodge." Kennedy rang off without further chat. Perhaps he regretted his openness. I supposed Mahon was giving him some heat for misplacing a suspect.

As for me, I didn't care a great deal about the Tierneys one way or the other, not having met either of them, though the younger Tierney's flight suggested plausible scenarios. My mind was on Jay.

I fumed through the preparation for dinner. The potatoes scorched, an instance of sympathetic magic. By the time Dad appeared, looking refreshed, I had calmed down enough to report Jay's imminent arrival without swearing and throwing things.

"Jay's coming?" My father's face lit like a candle. "Splendid. We can go fishing."

On the surface, the two men had little in common, though Jay's undergraduate degree is in history. Dad had greeted the news of my decision to marry a police detective without enthusiasm. At some point, however, the two men had bonded over fly-fishing.

It was a good thing somebody wanted to fish with my father. My brother, Tod, a stockbroker, loathes wading for hours in frigid streams. He once took a cell phone on a fishing trip with Dad and disgraced himself by beeping. Dad could fish for hours in dead silence. So, apparently, could my husband. I had no idea what they talked about when they did speak. Whenever I thought of him rushing to rescue the little woman, though, my blood pressure rose.

The next morning, I gave myself two hours for what should have been a one-hour drive to Dublin Airport.

In the intervening time I had done a lot of thinking about Jay, and about our marriage, mostly in tight, angry loops. My father's pleasure at the thought of Jay's arrival tempered my fury somewhat.

I passed a dawdling car with vicious effectiveness in the face of an oncoming coach. I was muttering to myself, partly because the only radio station I could find was broadcasting in Irish. "I'll dump the pair of them at a trout stream and leave them while I do my own thing." I wasn't sure what that stale cliché represented. Maybe I'd hang out at pubs. Or explore the used bookstores. Or search out the remaining 1,398 dolmens in Ireland.

The Toyota labored up the wooded gorge beyond Ashford and sped onto the southernmost stretch of motorway. North of Newtownmountkennedy the road narrowed again and twisted through glens that had to be prime trout-fishing country. I was making good time despite the tag-end of the rush-hour traffic.

What I wanted Jay to do, beyond leaving me some space, I didn't know. I realized my anger was excessive. Any husband would worry about any wife embroiled with the law in a foreign country. Jay had a right to worry, but he should have trusted my judgment.

I had once found myself caught in the investigation of an English murder. Jay had flown to the rescue then, too, and his presence had eased my relations with the Metropolitan Police. But this time I wasn't a suspect. I was peripheral to the investigation, a mere witness after the fact. I didn't need to be rescued, and neither did Dad. I was coping.

As I approached the Stillorgan Road, it occurred to me that I could exact a measure of revenge by making Jay drive the Toyota back to the cottage. On the other hand, I had to ride in the car, too, and I hoped to live a bit longer. I wondered what his cop-mind would make of local driving customs.

Possibly because of my preoccupation, I got lost on the East-link and wound up at Malahide Castle. Malahide Castle is *north* of the airport. It was also, that spring, the focus of major road construction. When I finally found the N1 and headed for the airport, I had three minutes to meet the plane. I chucked the car in the short-term parking structure and sprinted down concrete stairs and across a wide asphalt apron to the terminal. I wondered how long Jay would wait for me before he called Interpol.

That was a little unfair. He looked unruffled when I found him. He was standing near the now-deserted arrival gate, frowning at something on his ticket folder the way he does when he isn't wearing his reading glasses. His face looked a little bare without the mustache he had shaved off that spring, but, hey, I recognized him.

When he looked up and spotted me, his face went blank. He was trained to look impassive when revealing emotion might be compromising. I wondered what emotion he was masking.

I said, "I got lost. Sorry I'm late."

He gave me a spousal peck on the cheek, stuck his plane ticket in the breast pocket of his jacket, and hoisted his ancient garment bag from the carpet. The carrying case for his notebook computer hung from one tweedy shoulder by its long strap. I took it by way of being useful. The computer weighed four pounds, but he'd stuffed books and papers in the case, too.

"How are you?" Sagging slightly under the weight of the case, I led him back along the concourse.

"Doped."

That was not surprising. Jay has a well-founded flying phobia and the sensible way to deal with it is prescription tranquilizers. I should have been grateful he'd taken them. "Then I won't ask you to drive."

"Good thing." He swung along beside me. After a moment, he added, "I can't anyway. You couldn't have listed me as one of the drivers when you hired the car."

True. Since I hadn't anticipated his rescue mission, I hadn't listed him. He was at my mercy. I cheered up. Slightly.

I waited until I had negotiated the maze of roundabouts leading from the airport to the N1 before I asked the obvious question.

"Why did you come?"

He flinched as a large tanker sped by on the right. "I talked to your mother. We're concerned about George. Mary thought I might be able to smooth the way."

"There is no way to smooth," I said coldly, thinking I would have a few good words to say to my mother. Nor was I mollified. Jay was capable of resisting my mother's suggestions. "The

Gardai have been very considerate. Dad wasn't called to testify at the inquest."

"But you were?"

"A formality." The tires squealed when I made a sharp left onto Griffith Avenue. I'd almost missed the turnoff. The alternative was O'Connell Street on a business day, a choice too horrible to contemplate, according to the travel experts.

Jay yawned. "Suppose you tell me what happened."

"Okay, fine, I'll do that." I bit back a rude comment about police interrogations. "You'd better rummage in my coin purse for the bridge toll, though. I need fifty-five pence."

As he dug in my handbag and sorted through the unfamiliar coins, I gave him a terse account of my discovery of Slade Wheeler's body. I also went on to describe the scarifying dinner party and the dramatis personae in some detail. Mind you, all the while I talked I was threading my way past the east Dublin docks, flinging the correct change into the toll basket, crossing the Liffey, tangling myself in a major roundabout, and merging onto the Stillorgan Road without ramming anybody. I thought it was an impressive performance.

When I pulled up at a stoplight I looked over at Jay.

He yawned.

"Sorry to bore you."

"I'm not bored, but I'm not tracking either."

"Okay, I understand. But I still want to know why you dropped everything and roared over here at the first hint of trouble."

He stifled another yawn. "I can tell that you're spoiling for a fight, Lark, and I'm willing to oblige when my brain starts functioning."

"What if I'd rather have it out now?" The road had changed to highway. I picked up the pace.

"Hmm. Well, you may want to but I'm pretty sure you won't insist."

"Really? Why is that?"

He yawned again. "Because you always fight fair."

That silenced me as he knew it would. He slouched against the door and fell asleep. I thought about turning on the Irish broadcast at full volume, but I was not supposed to be petty.

My father was waiting at the door when I drew up in front of the cottage. I set the brake and poked Jay.

He started and woke up completely, wide-eyed.

"We're here."

Dad had come out the door. Jay disentangled himself from the seat belt and got out. He gave Dad a hug. That surprised me until I remembered that Jay hadn't seen my father since the stroke.

I popped the trunk lid and wriggled out of the car. My father is about four inches taller than Jay. Arm still on Jay's shoulder, Dad was guiding my husband into the cottage with the air of a squire welcoming the heir to the manor house.

That's your son-in-law, Dad, I thought, cranky. *I'm the heir.* I hefted the garment bag and the computer from the trunk and carried them into the house. "Porter service."

Jay smiled at me. "Thanks. George looks terrific, doesn't he?"

I had to smile back. "Grand is the local word for terrific."

Dad beamed on both of us like the rising sun. "This calls for a drink. I have a bottle of Jameson's I bought on the plane."

I was scandalized. "Before lunch?"

"With. I made sandwiches."

Jay rubbed the back of his neck. "I suppose a glass of Jameson's won't kill me." He rarely touches hard liquor.

"The tranquilizers!" I was doubly scandalized.

Dad said, "A spot of cheer, Lark. Lighten up."

I stared.

"It's what my students say."

So each of us had a shot of Jameson's, neat. I must say it tasted good all the way down. Lunch was sloppy but generous ham sandwiches.

I took Jay downstairs after that to show him the scene of the crime, but he spotted the futon.

"Sleep." He ripped off his jacket and tie.

"You slept all the way through scenic Wicklow, the Garden of Ireland."

"Too bad." He kicked off his shoes, lay down on top of the duvet, and fell asleep. Like that.

6 ❧

The host is riding from Knocknarea
And over the grave of Clooth-na-Bare;
Caoilte tossing his burning hair,
And Niamh calling Away, come away:
Empty your heart of its mortal dream.

—William Butler Yeats, "The Hosting of the Sidhe"

I STARTED A pot of spaghetti sauce while Jay slept and Dad worked on his notes. The sauce took me about fifteen minutes. When I finished, Jay was still asleep and Dad was still deep in the records of the Dublin Meeting. So I shoved the pot onto the cool side of the Rayburn and went for a walk.

Bright yellow crime-scene tape isolated the potting shed. The Stanyon gardeners were working on the mucked up area of lawn, raking out boot prints and replanting. I said hello and watched the men awhile, but my presence seemed to inhibit them. I climbed back up the flagstone path and decided to see where the road led, other than to the big house.

It tunneled through an arch of rhododendrons. In a week or so, the rhodies would burst into exuberant blossom. Now the span of dark leaves drooped like the gateway to the Underworld. I ducked below it, shivering, and emerged into the open again.

Gravel gave way to packed dirt. The road skirted the pond I had seen from the cottage the first day. The pond might at some time have been an ornamental lake. Close to, I could see that it needed to be cleaned out. Clumps of weed and twists of rusting metal had trapped human and animal litter, but a couple of mallards swam in the turgid water.

I walked past two roofless stone outbuildings. There the lane shrank to the status of a path and dead-ended at a low stone wall. I found a stile, climbed over it, and entered the Stanyon Woods.

It was a plantation, not a natural copse. Stately oaks, lesser trees I didn't recognize, laurels, two giant hollies, male and female, and assorted bushes that looked as if they were about to bloom formed a screen to hide the fiduciary heart of the grove.

Beyond the screen, long before the Steins bought the estate, some tree accountant had set out rows of conifers with spacing appropriate to moderate growth. In the not-distant future, the trees would be harvested like wheat. The current accountant would see to that. Perhaps Slade Wheeler would have seen to it when he tired of his war games.

The trees looked tall and spindly in the gray light and their uniformity depressed me. Someone had mowed the undergrowth that spring. I felt as if I were walking through a field of living telephone poles. In a hundred years the great evergreen forests of the Pacific Northwest were going to resemble Stanyon. Hundreds of square miles of telephone poles.

Some of the conifers, I think they were Scotch pine, sported red blazes as if a displaced timber cruiser had marked them for cutting. It took me a few minutes to realize the marks were left over from Wheeler's war games.

When I stepped onto the mat of fallen needles I made no sound. I walked without haste, trying to imagine what it would be like to stalk and be stalked in this tame wilderness. The land sloped upward, and a few bushes here and there had survived to provide lurking places. Ferns sprouted like feather dusters over the mown areas. Foreign birds sang. I couldn't decipher their song. It sounded like a lament. A light wind brushed my cheek.

81

I was begining to spook myself. In a lifetime of reading I had encountered enough enchanted forests to know that Stanyon Woods was too dull for magic. It wasn't even haunted. Slade Wheeler's ghost, if it lingered at all, hugged the ground like a patch of stale smog.

I made myself look for signs of a police search. The Gardai had to have searched the woods for the site of the murder, if, as Kayla said, they were assuming her brother was killed by one of the game players. Once I put my mind to it, I spotted broken branches, trampled ferns, scuffed needles. The cops had been there all right.

I hiked upward, shoving branches aside when I had to. I wasn't lost because I knew the woods were not a forest. If I walked a quarter mile farther, I'd come to a cow pasture or a potato field plowed and ready for seeding. When I stopped and looked around me, though, I saw only the stiff rows of conifers. Watery gray light sifted through the needles. I might as well have been lost.

As the thought formed, I caught motion at the edge of my visual field. I whirled and stared. Nothing—a trembling of leaves that might have been caused by the wind. I took another few steps and stopped again, the hairs on the nape of my neck prickling. Somebody or something was watching me.

I stood very still, though my berserker impulse was to run, screeching, directly at the spot where I had sensed the intruder. Or perhaps *I* was the intruder.

I breathed in, out. Finally, I started walking toward the trembling bush. Slowly. With dignity. So what if there were game-players hiding in the woods? I thought of Grace Flynn's "protector." He was shorter than I was and no heavier. I could handle Artie.

I parted the offending bush and entered a tiny glade. Nothing. I said, "Okay, who's here?" Nobody answered. Then, on the far side of the clearing, I saw the stone.

It was huge, a boulder of dolmen dimensions scabbed with lichen, and it was splotched with red paint. As I walked over to it, I caught what might have been the blur of someone else's passage in the calf-high ferns. The trail, if it was a trail and not a trick of light, led up the slope and into the trees.

I approached the stone warily. Nothing. A faint sound from the woods halted me in my tracks. I listened until my ears ached but heard nothing more and, indeed, it may have been nothing. The red paint, a blotch at waist height, was dry to my touch. I leaned against the stone and scanned the undergrowth.

The wind was picking up. Clouds scudded overhead. I straightened and started to walk away. As I glanced back over my shoulder at the stone, I saw the design. A huge double spiral in the form of a figure eight lying on its side incised the flat surface. At the heart of each vortex was an eye.

When I examined it, I could see the carving was ancient. Indeed it was so overgrown with lichen it was visible only at an angle, or up close if the observer knew it was there. I traced it with my finger from the unblinking eyes at the center to the outer rim, half-afraid that if I reversed and followed the maze inward I would be sucked into the heart of the stone. My hand shook. I stood still so long the birds started their song again.

Eventually the breeze picked up, the light changed, and I came out of my reverie. It was time to go back to the spaghetti sauce.

My mind had calmed. I reentered the woods without trepidation, though there was no path and one row of trees looked like the next. I had walked steadily up the slope. Now I walked steadily down it. It was not until I reached the stone wall and found the stile again that I realized I had forgotten the mysterious watcher in the woods. He or it was irrelevant to the stone carving.

Dad was pottering around the Rayburn heating water for tea. He gave me a tentative smile. "Been for a walk?"

I nodded, not quite ready for speech. A glance at the kitchen clock told me I'd been gone about an hour. I had the sensation that something had happened in the woods, something important, but the meaning eluded me.

While Dad brewed a pot of Earl Grey, I went downstairs and poked Jay until he woke up. He'd had enough sleep—too much, probably. If I let him sleep until he felt like waking, he'd spend the night reading Anthony Trollope.

Finally, he flopped over onto his back and blinked up at me. I said, "Without prejudice to our quarrel, do you want to make love?"

He blinked, grinned, pulled me down onto the futon.

Afterwards we showered in sequence, dressed, and went upstairs. Dad had gone back to his notes. "Tea's cold," he murmured without looking up. His pen made a squiggle on a photocopied document.

It was ten past six. I set the kettle on the cooker and gave the sauce a stir. It seemed to be stewing nicely. Jay took a drink of water from the tap and made a face. I ought to have warned him to drink the Evian water in the refrigerator. The tap water was potable but it had a chemical odor.

"Do you want tea or a cocktail?"

Jay raised an eyebrow.

"I just remembered that Barbara invited Dad and me to drop in. The Steins hold a happy hour at six-thirty. I should warn them their cottage has another tenant."

"Well . . ."

"I could phone but it's a nice walk, and you might as well take a look at the suspects." I described Kayla Wheeler.

His eyes narrowed. "Okay. Let's go. You can tell me about the rest of the cast on the way."

We didn't leave immediately. I replaced the steaming kettle with a large pot of hot water for the pasta and set the pot on the cooler side of the Rayburn. When we returned I'd have water ready to cook the spaghetti fast.

Dad didn't want to come. In fact, he was so absorbed in his notes I'm not sure he registered where we were going. I made Jay unpack his anorak and I put my own on, too, in case it rained. It was well past the equinox, so the sun hadn't set and wouldn't for a couple of hours. We strolled along side by side. Jay said, "Wanna fight?"

I stopped and blinked at him. His whiskey-brown eyes met mine. Something had happened all right. My anger no longer burned with a hard and gemlike flame. "No. Not now. Maybe not at all, Jay, but we do have a problem and we're going to have to talk about it."

He was wearing his impassive face. "Wonderful what good sex can do."

I drew a breath. "No, my friend. Do not delude yourself. The sex was fine, but the problem exists."

He frowned and started to say something, then shrugged and walked on. "So tell me about the folks at Stonehall Enterprises."

I filled him in, starting with my discovery of the body, and I gave him a sketch of the dinner party, too.

"Kennedy sounds like a clown."

I considered. "Only in the sense that he's funny. He's a shrewd observer. He probably used Maeve Butler's invitation as an opportunity to meet with the Stonehall people when they were off guard. I think his experience with this kind of crime is limited. . . ."

Jay snorted.

"What?"

"I don't know anybody with experience of the setup you described. It's one of a kind."

I had meant that I thought Sgt. Kennedy's experience of the executive-level milieu was limited. Jay was patronizing me. I felt a flare of anger and bit it back. We walked on in silence.

"So Kennedy was scoping out the victim's business associates. That means the chief inspector, what's his name . . ."

"Mahon."

"Whatever Mahon may have told the dead man's sister, he isn't sure Wheeler was wasted by one of the kids."

"Or Sgt. Kennedy isn't sure."

"You think he's running his own investigation?"

"I think he knows the area, and the boys involved in the game, better than Mahon does."

"You may be right."

"I am. Occasionally."

"What do you mean—" We had come to the fork in the road. Jay broke off and stared down at Stanyon Hall. "Where are we, the Magic Kingdom Annex?"

"Stanyon does have a Disneyesque air. Wait till you see the wood carvings inside, and the stained glass in the library."

He shook his head. "It reminds me of Beverly Hills."

"Oh, come on, Jay."

"It's fake, right?"

"True."

"It's pretentious, right?"

"I catch your drift."

"Fun," he said. "But not as much fun as the Arab guy who had all those nude statues around his L.A. estate painted in realistic colors."

I said austerely, "Alex and Barbara are restoring Stanyon as an investment. Alex, at least, regards it with a certain ironic detachment." I told him about the company logo picked out in stained glass.

"Jesus." He shook his head but he was smiling.

We slipped through the huge oak door as a group of women were leaving. The data processors, obviously. They nodded and said good evening. One of the women whipped out a cigarette before she stepped off the veranda and lit it with a flourish. I grinned at her and she grinned back. She was old enough to be Slade Wheeler's mother.

I gave Jay a moment to admire the towering staircase, then I led him to the salon.

Our entrance created a stir. There were six people in the room—the Steins, Liam, Mike, Tracy, and Kayla Wheeler. Kayla sat by herself next to the open window. The rest clustered around the drinks trolley.

Kayla stared and went back to her brooding cigarette, but the others broke off their conversation. Barbara took a step toward us. She looked startled rather than pleased.

I said, "My husband flew over to babysit, so I thought I'd better bring him to meet you."

Barbara's eyes widened and she extended her hand. "I'm Barbara Stein."

"Jay Dodge. Interesting house." He shook hands.

Alex came forward. "It's pretty horrible, really. The loo in the cloakroom backed up this morning and our builder's disappeared. I'm Alex. Welcome to Ireland. Do you want wine or something stronger?"

"I thought this was beer country," Jay said amiably, shaking Alex's hand.

"Guinness?"

"Might as well try it."

"Lark?"

"A glass of red wine," I murmured.

I let the Steins introduce Jay to the other Stonehouse people. With a grimace, Barbara led him over to Kayla. He shook hands with Wheeler's sister and murmured condolences. Kayla leaned forward in her chair, wobbling a little. Though I didn't hear what she said, I could see her eyes gleaming all the way across the room. Barbara drifted back. She looked at me and shrugged. It was clear that Kayla was taken with Jay.

That is not uncommon. He is no more than ordinarily good-looking, he was wearing a mungy Shoalwater College sweatshirt over jeans, and, at forty-four, he was the oldest person in the room, but Jay has never lacked charm. Apparently he turned it on for Kayla.

I asked Tracy how her disk was coming along and she described a programming glitch in gloomy detail. In fact, the general atmosphere was glum. Mike and Barbara were arguing about something without heat, while Alex and Liam worried aloud about the cost of a new electronic scanner. Jay rejoined the group after a decent interval, leaving Kayla to her chilly perch by the open window. She lit a Player's and watched his buns through the smoke.

"How do you like the Guinness?" Alex moved aside to make room for my husband in the cluster by the trolley.

"Heavy but tasty." Jay slid into a discussion of Irish versus American beer with a smooth comment on microbreweries. He was drinking his stout slowly, but he tends to do that.

Kayla stubbed out her cigarette, rose, and wobbled across the room. " 'Night, everbuddy."

No one reminded her that she had not yet eaten dinner. Polite murmurs from the group. She brushed Jay as she wobbled past and he put out a hand to steady her.

" 'Night, big boy."

"Ms. Wheeler."

She made it to the door, clung to the frame a moment, then lurched through.

Alex watched her progress with anxious eyes. "Why doesn't she go back to London?"

Tracy's lip curled. "Free gin?"

We picked up the frayed threads of our conversations and sipped at our drinks. I checked my watch but it wasn't yet seven. I'd told Dad we'd have dinner at eight, so there was lots of time.

Tracy wound down her technical complaints and set her empty wineglass on the trolley. "Well, I'm off, folks. Heavy date with my landlord."

Mike hooted. "That old fraud?"

Tracy grinned. "He may be old and he may be a fraud, but he takes me to dinner at Grayble's at thirty punts a whack. And he dances like Fred Astaire."

"Sure, he's Fred Astaire's illegitimate brother," Liam murmured.

General laughter. Jay and I smiled, though I missed the full flavor of the joke. Tracy left. She was scarcely out the door when Maeve, looking cross, appeared with Sgt. Kennedy *en train.* Kennedy wore tweeds again and a dark bruise showed on his left cheekbone. He was at his blandest and he was holding something in his left hand.

I introduced Jay to Maeve first. Irritation vanished. *Her* eyes gleamed. She shook hands and said something graceful, then slipped past us to the bar where Barbara was already pouring her a glass of wine.

The two men shook hands warily and Kennedy held out a dust-jacketed book.

"I took the chance you'd be here, Mr. Dodge. I've brought the latest edition. Hot off the plane from London. Will you sign it for me? Sure, my copy of the original is all dog-eared and covered with tea-stains."

Jay blushed.

As I watched him take Kennedy's pen and sign the book, I must admit I was amused and surprised. Clearly the Gardai had a direct line to Passport Control, if they knew Jay had come.

It was possible that Kennedy did own a copy of the first British edition of Jay's book. The previous year, Jay had published a slim textbook on modern techniques of gathering and safeguarding evidence in criminal cases. It was published simultaneously in the U.S. and Britain in slightly different versions.

The text must have fulfilled a real need. It went through two printings in six weeks. Of course, the initial run was small. Jay had seen an updated version to the printer in September. Not a best-seller, exactly, but a winner with police departments and training programs.

In my opinion the book was successful because of Jay's style, which is terse and clear without oversimplifying what is becoming a highly technical subject. Nevertheless, he doesn't think of *Modern Evidence Procedures,* a.k.a. *Evidence,* as a real book, like our friend Tom Lindquist's novels or my mother's collection of poetry. It embarrasses him when anyone treats him like an Author.

I thought he ought to get over that. I also wondered what Kennedy was after. I distrusted his innocent country-boy air.

I watched Jay hand the book back and cap the pen, and decided I ought to come to the rescue. "What happened to your face, Sergeant? That's a nasty contusion."

Kennedy heaved a sigh. "Wasn't it just Aidan Flynn defending the family honor when we brought Gracie home for a wee chat with her da?"

Jay looked from Kennedy to me and back.

"Good heavens," I said, "how did you subdue him? With a choke hold?" I'll admit that was malicious.

"Sure, we're not so quick with our hands as the boys in the States. The missus laid him out with a frying pan." Sgt. Kennedy stuffed Jay's book into the patch pocket of his tweed jacket. He smiled at Jay and at Alex Stein who came up with a glass of stout. "Ah, that's the ticket. Thank you, lad."

Alex said, "We owe you a dinner, Joe."

Kennedy touched his cheekbone. "It may be Gracie owes me a dinner, or at least a beefsteak." The bruise was not quite a black eye.

Everyone laughed and the tension eased. At least my tension eased. The others may not have felt any. Jay's ears were no longer scarlet.

Maeve took the book from Kennedy and showed it to Liam and Mike. The sergeant seemed to be in an expansive mood. He evaded Barbara's questions about the investigation with aplomb and gave Jay and me a reassuring account of what I could expect at the inquest.

"... and the coroner won't keep you on the stand very long, Mrs. Dodge," he concluded. "Ten minutes at most. How's the old gentleman?"

"My father? He's well. We left him working on his Quaker research."

"Sure, you're a literary family."

"Scribble, scribble, scribble," I said cheerfully. "I barely write invoices myself."

Kennedy laughed and drew Jay aside.

Barbara said, "Your mother's Mary Wandworth Dailey, isn't she?"

I sighed. "Yes, and she's fussing over Dad like a broody hen. She bullied Jay into flying over." That was probably not the whole truth but it would do for public consumption.

"I was thinking of giving a dinner for her when she comes."

"I'm sure she'd like that, Barbara, but don't go to a great deal of trouble."

"It's no trouble," Barbara said slowly. "The thing is, I wouldn't want her to feel used. The Irish like poets, you know, and her reputation here is substantial. I need to mend a few social fences. We've been busy gearing up and haven't had time yet to return the hospitality we received when we first came."

And a poet might help counter the association of Stanyon with war games. She didn't say that but we both understood the context.

Why not? At least Barbara's chef wouldn't feed Ma rubber chicken. "Do remember Dad's condition and spare him a formal banquet."

She smiled. "I can guarantee that. I'll keep it small." The smile faded and a puzzled frown creased her forehead. "I thought your husband was a policeman."

"He used to be. These days he runs a police training program at Shoalwater College."

"Ah, I see. Another academic."

I said, "Jay is well read and a pretty good seat-of-the-pants scholar, but I think he'd balk at being labeled an academic." That was also true. Strange, but true.

Maeve had joined us, leaving Mike and Liam to thumb through Jay's book. I couldn't imagine why they wanted to.

Maeve had caught my mother's name. "Would your mother be interested in meeting with women poets who live in the Wicklow area, do you think?"

I suppressed a twinge of annoyance. When I was younger I resented my mother's mild fame. "If you have a pen, I'll give you her phone number. I think she knows Eilis Lachlan." Lachlan was an outstanding academic poet. "Call Ma and distract her from worrying about my father. It would be a favor."

Maeve fumbled in her handbag and came up with a slim gold pen and a rather grubby notebook the size of my palm.

I scribbled the number. "It's unlisted—ex-directory, that is."

"I won't give it out. Thanks, Lark." She took the notebook back with an air of reverence and gave me a ravishing smile. "How fortunate your husband was able to come. I'm not clear about the American academic calendar, though I know you finish well before we do."

"That's true." I remembered she was an archaeologist and wondered if she lectured at Trinity or the National University. Perhaps she just worked for the OPW. I wondered if she was into dolmens. I wondered if she knew about the incised stone I had found in the woods.

"Does he have a long Easter holiday or is the term over already?" Maeve persisted.

Jay said, "It's in full swing. I'm a truant." He looked ruffled, as if Kennedy had said something to trouble him. Kennedy regarded me blandly, the blue, blue eyes wide and innocent.

I saw no reason to condone Jay's truancy. "Who's covering for you?"

"The adjuncts and Cason in sociology."

Professor Cason had not been enthusiastic about training police officers when Jay set up the program, but the two men got along well enough. "I'll bet he likes that."

"Probably not," Jay said curtly. "But he owes me."

The impracticality of Jay leaving his students in mid-quarter had been bothering me. Why had he done anything so headlong and unnecessary?

I didn't intend to conduct our quarrel in public, but I couldn't resist asking, "What about the report-writing class?" The report-writing class was the grand finale for degree students. They had to pass it or they didn't graduate. Fortunately there were only eight or ten of them.

By this time the rest of the group was listening, though I couldn't see why. The subject couldn't have been interesting to outsiders.

Jay sighed. "I brought the laptop, Lark. It has a modem. They can submit their assignments via e-mail." He glanced around. "And if I'm going to set that up, we'd better go back to the cottage." He swallowed the last of his Guinness and set the empty schooner beside Tracy's wineglass.

He had said the magic word, however. The idea of conducting a college class by e-mail was meat and drink to the Stonehall crew. They began asking Jay excited and extremely shrewd questions.

At first he responded with terse impatience, but their interest was genuine. What was more, they had useful suggestions. Barbara got out a pad of yellow legal paper and jotted down a crucial Internet address. Mike Novak flipped *Evidence* open to the table of contents and began analyzing the ease with which it could be transformed into an interactive disk. I thought of my spaghetti sauce.

Sgt. Kennedy caught my eye. "They're moon-mad, lass."

I looked at my ruffled husband, caught in a whirlpool of techie enthusiasm, and raised my wineglass. "I'll drink to that."

Maeve laughed and clinked her glass on mine.

7 ～

I'm a rake and a rambling boy.
There's many a city I did enjoy . . .

—American folk song

"Why do I feel older than Methuselah's granddaddy?"

I glanced over at Jay's damp, unrevealing profile. "I thought the Stonewall crew had fine ideas."

"Yes, and it's a good thing Barbara wrote them down. Otherwise I'd forget them."

"Is your short-term memory going?"

"My teeth will be next."

Laughter seemed indicated. I laughed.

The mist thickened.

"Where are we?"

"Just follow the road."

"Geez, Wilma, how long before we get to Bedrock Cottage?"

"I thought it was a silly name, too, but I suppose it was inevitable."

"Stonehall. Bedrock."

"You got it." I wiped mist from my face with a tissue. It wasn't raining. The overcast was just very, very low.

"How about a run?"

"Not tonight." I probably needed a run but I didn't trust the surface of the road, and I didn't want to sweat all over my pullover, either. "What did Joe Kennedy tell you?"

"Eh?"

"Cut it out. After he got your autograph, he took you aside and spoke to you at some length. There's nothing wrong with *my* short-term memory."

"I'm not chummy enough with the sergeant yet to call him Joey . . ."

"Are you jealous?"

"Hell, Lark, he's your age and he looks like a Marine Corps recruiting ad. Of course I'm jealous. Also curious. You didn't phone me. Is it possible you were distracted?"

"It's possible I'm going to swat you upside the head if you blather on like that. I didn't call you because I was embarrassed to tell you I'd found another corpse." That was partly true.

"It is getting to be a habit."

"See? I knew you'd say something snide." I thought of Slade Wheeler's eerily peaceful body and shivered.

"Was it bad?" Jay didn't sound sarcastic.

I stopped and blinked at him through the mist. He was frowning at me, eyes dark and intent, as if I were a difficult puzzle he had to solve.

"It was strange," I said. "Very strange. This is a strange place." I thought of telling him about my incised stone and the watcher in the woods, but the whole experience was so odd I hesitated to expose myself to further satire.

"It's a foreign place, sure enough." Jay walked on and the moment passed.

I caught up with him in a few steps. "Now, about Sgt. Kennedy . . ."

"Lover Boy was very respectful of his seniors."

"I don't know why you're on this age kick, but it's boring. You're a mere six years older than I am . . ."

"They were the wrong six years."

I hewed to the point. "Tell me what Kennedy said."

"He told me the investigation was dead in the water. The

Gardai put out the equivalent of an APB for the two men who are missing—what's the name?"

"Tierney."

"That's it. Kennedy said they waited too long, the trail's cold. No leads. The older man . . ."

"Toss. Short, I think, for Tomas." I pronounced the name Spanish-style since I didn't know what the Irish phonetic system required. "The son is called Tommy."

"Right. Toss is an old-time nationalist with underground connections. Mahon thinks the boy killed Wheeler and the father helped dispose of the body. Toss meant to work on the cottage and had keys to it. They may have left the body in the downstairs hallway overnight, then carried it out to the shed, hoping Toss would have time to move it before you and George arrived. They miscalculated."

"That sounds logical."

"Wheeler was killed Sunday or early Monday morning. Tierney knew you were due to arrive some time Tuesday."

"But not as soon as we did?"

"Right. He also knew the gardeners were set to plant the lawn and would rake over inconvenient footprints. Mahon thinks Tierney intended to move the body again in his van, but you and George arrived before he could get back to the cottage. That's the theory. It's speculation, of course, though there's some evidence to support it. Wheeler wasn't killed at the cottage. He was definitely carried to the shed. There's postmortem bruising, particles of floor wax on Wheeler's fatigues. The brand of floor wax," he added with a clinical air, "is also used at Stanyon Hall."

I digested that. "Alex says Toss is chronically late."

Jay hunched his shoulders in the anorak. The chill mist was penetrating. "Maybe so. Maybe it just took him longer to arrange for his son's disappearance than he thought it would."

"Do they have any idea where the boy could be hiding?"

"In England, probably. The father may have been shipping him out of Dublin Airport as you were coming in."

"A nice thought."

"Isn't it?" We were within hailing distance of the cottage. The kitchen light showed, fuzzy in the fog. Jay stopped again. "Kennedy told me all that. Then he suggested that the Gardai hire me as a consultant. He was only half joking."

"Why would it be a joke?"

Jay grimaced. "I don't know Irish rules of evidence, Lark, and I damned well don't want to hang around here playing the amateur sleuth. I told him that." He cocked his head. "I think he was relieved."

I reflected. "Maybe Mahon was afraid you were going to try to horn in."

"And told Kennedy to butter me up. Hence the charade with the textbook."

"I don't think that was a charade. I think Joe had read the book and wanted you to know he had."

"Did you mention it?" He sounded paranoid.

"No, but the Gardai had two days to check up on me, and checking up on me would lead them to you and the book."

"I suppose you're right." He gave a short laugh. "And now Stonehall Enterprises wants to turn my sorry little volume into a CD-ROM disk. Life is full of weird connections."

"Fractals."

"What?"

"Elementary chaos theory," I said loftily. I owed him.

We ate our spaghetti a little late. Afterward, Dad and Jay coaxed the modem to life. They had read Jay's e-mail and were playing with the Internet, and I was putting around the sink, when Toss Tierney showed up at the kitchen door.

The knocking was so tentative I didn't hear it at first over the swish of sudsy water. When the sound penetrated, I dried my hands on a towel and strode to the door thinking irritable thoughts. I yanked it open.

The solid middle-aged man standing on the front step pulled his tweed cap off and gave me a disarming smile. His eyes were wide and childlike in the dim light. The mist had thickened to fog. "Sure, you must be Mrs. Dodge. Me name's Tierney."

"Toss?"

"The very one."

So nice of you to call. I am rarely nonplussed but I stood gaping at him too long for politeness. The man was a fugitive and very likely an accessory to murder. He had to be aware that the police were looking for him. I didn't know what to do.

He cleared his throat. "Me mates tell me your man's a grand American detective."

I said, "Er."

"I'd like a word with him, missus."

"Good heavens, why?"

He squeezed the cap in one beefy hand. "About my son."

"Tommy."

"Aye, Tommy. The lad's innocent." The guileless eyes pleaded with me. The cap twisted.

I sighed. "You'd better come in, Mr. Tierney. It's a cold night."

"It is." He made to wipe his boots on the nonexistent mat.

I stood back. "Please sit down at the table. I'll get Jay."

He perched on the chair nearest the door.

I, and I suppose he, could hear Jay and Dad talking in the next room. I had once admitted an armed and distraught shootist to our house in Shoalwater. Jay had not been pleased. With a mental shrug, I ducked through the arch into the living room.

Dad was sitting with the laptop on the desk in front of him, peering at the screen, and Jay was leaning over him, showing him something. Jay glanced around as Dad manipulated the "eraser-head" control.

I said, "Toss Tierney's in the kitchen. He would like to talk to you about his son."

Jay straightened, eyes on mine. "Tierney. Is he . . ."

I kept my voice low. "He seems calm and unarmed, but worried about his son."

Dad turned the desk chair around. "What's the matter?"

I explained—softly.

"Good heavens, should I call—?"

I put my finger to my lips. Dad stopped mid-sentence.

Jay murmured, "Slide over, George, and let me back out of the program." With the modem on, we couldn't telephone the Gardai. Dad scooted his chair sideways. Jay bent to the screen and fiddled.

"Is it one of them new laptops?" Tierney was standing in the archway.

Jay said, "Toshiba. Nice machine. Weighs four pounds." He blanked the screen and disconnected the modem cable.

I breathed.

Dad creaked to his feet. "Mr. Tierney? I'm George Dailey. I'm glad of the opportunity of meeting you. You've done very fine work on the cottage." He walked over and shook hands. "Alex sent me photos of the place as it was originally. You've performed a miracle." Beaming, he backed Tierney into the kitchen.

I glanced at Jay. He picked up the receiver, frowned at it a moment, then set it back on its cradle. I could hear Dad offering Tierney a drop of Jameson's.

Jay caught my eye and grinned. "George to the rescue. I guess I'd better hear what Tierney has to say for himself."

I gestured at the phone. "Shall I . . ."

He shook his head. "Not yet. Time to negotiate."

I followed him into the kitchen.

There is a great deal to be said for ceremonies of courtesy. Jay introduced himself. Dad poured generous shots of neat whiskey into four small glasses and we all sat at the table, I with my back to the Rayburn, which was rather warm. Dad raised his glass. "*Sláinte.*"

Tierney ducked his head in acknowledgement and took a substantial gulp. "Ah, that's the stuff on a cold night."

"It is indeed." Dad sipped. His hand was perfectly steady. I admired him.

I raised my own glass and tasted. Jay turned his, tracing a circle on the smooth surface of the table.

Tierney killed his shot and set his glass down. "I've come to ask your help, Mr. Dodge. The guards have a warrant out for my son's arrest in the death of Slade Wheeler, the spalpeen. Tommy never killed him, never touched him. It's true they had words."

"They quarreled?" Jay sounded politely interested.

Tierney nodded. "Easter it was, after Mass, in the car park at Jack White's."

Jay kept his hands on the table and his gaze didn't stray from Tierney's face. "Jack White's?"

"That's a pub a wee bit north of Arklow. There was others heard them, more's the pity, and blabbed to Joe Kennedy. Joe's down on Tommy, you see."

"What did your son and Wheeler quarrel over?"

"Some nonsense about them war games of Wheeler's." Tierney shifted in his chair. "Tommy fancies himself a strategist, but that git Wheeler always had to call the tune. Tommy threatened to take the Killaveen lads out of the club."

"And . . . ?"

Tierney flushed a deeper red. He was sweating a little. "Ah, as I said, there was words. The thing is, Mr. Dodge, Tommy come home. We'd a fine Easter dinner at me sister's, and wasn't all the uncles and aunts and cousins buzzing about like bees in a bottle? Tommy was laughing and joking, showing off his new cycle, and devil a word did he say about Wheeler the whole evening. He come home with his mum, too, afterwards, meek as a lamb."

Jay said mildly, "The Gardai think Wheeler was killed very late on Sunday or early Easter Monday morning."

Tierney said, "You don't take my point, Mr. Dodge."

"Then tell me what you mean."

"Tommy's state of mind." He ran a hand through his thinning hair. "He'd got over his snit, d'ye see? He wasn't angry. I know my son." He shot a defiant glance around the table as if we had contradicted him.

Dad gave him an encouraging smile. "You know his temperament."

Tierney heaved a sigh. "That's it. When Tommy's angry he broods. He was merry as a grig all evening, my oath on it."

Dad said, "Another glass?"

"I won't say no."

Dad poured.

Jay hadn't drunk any of his whiskey. He said, "Where is Tommy, Mr. Tierney?"

Tierney's eyes shifted. "On the run. 'Tis a sad, unsettled kind of life. I'd a taste of it myself in the old days."

Jay raised his glass, sipped, and set it down. "If your son didn't kill Wheeler . . ."

"Whhsht," Tierney interrupted. "You're after saying if Tommy's innocent he should turn himself in. I'll let him do that when I can *prove* he's innocent, Mr. Dodge. I can hold my own with the guards, but they're down on the family itself, d'ye see? And Tommy has a hot temper. He'd a row with Joe Kennedy last summer, and doesn't Joe haul him over the coals whenever there's a rude word scrawled on the pavement?" He shook his head. "Tommy didn't kill Wheeler."

"He told you that." There was no satire in Jay's voice. He was just verifying.

Tierney looked uncomfortable but held his ground. "Aye, he told me. Wheeler didn't turn up when the lads assembled in the woods Monday morning, so they splashed each other with paint, larking about, and when they tired of that they went on to Wexford. I meant to attend the Sinn Fein gathering meself . . ."

"Sinn Fein?"

" 'Twas Easter Monday." He sounded impatient. "The local lads always meet at the cemetery. We've a by-election coming up. I didn't want to miss the speeches, so I drove over to the cottage early. I found Wheeler in the potting shed . . ."

"Not in the cottage?" Jay interjected, sharp.

"Eh? In the cottage?" Tierney blinked at him. I thought the man was genuinely bewildered.

"You have a key."

Tierney rubbed his nose, eyes narrowed. "I do, but I'd no reason to enter the house Monday morning. Alex Stein told me to finish me work on the shed before Mr. Dailey arrived. I was set to install the knob and lock Saturday, but what with one thing and another I didn't get to it. So I came over early on Monday," he repeated, "and found your man Wheeler lying in the shed. I didn't touch him. When I saw the daub of red paint . . ." He touched his forehead.

"You thought of the war-gamers and went looking for your son?"

He nodded. "And a fine time I had of it, with the holiday scattering his mates from Cork to Drogheda. When I finally traced Tommy to Wexford, I borrowed my cousin Seamus's Fiat, seeing my van's a bit conspicuous. I winkled Tommy out of a pub near closing time Monday night and drove him . . . drove him to a safe place. And made arrangements."

Jay said, "You've put yourself in an awkward position."

"Aye, accessory's the word." Tierney didn't seem to find the thought unbearable. "I need your advice, Mr. Dodge. I need to know how you'd go about it to prove it wasn't Tommy did the murder."

Jay said, "Supply Chief Inspector Mahon with an alternative."

"Eh?"

"Find out who killed Slade Wheeler." When Tierney just blinked at him, Jay went on, "Your son was an associate of the dead man. He quarreled with Wheeler. He's gone into hiding. Those things make him the prime suspect. Unless you can prove that Tommy was elsewhere during the crucial hours, or that he's physically incapable of committing the crime . . ."

"How was it done, then? I didn't see a mark on the body, saving the smear of red paint."

"You'll have to ask the Gardai." Jay took a sip of whiskey. "I don't think the method has been made public yet."

"But you know."

"Yes. The coroner's inquest is set for Monday, so you'll know, too, soon enough. Hire a good lawyer," Jay added. "You're not in the clear yourself, Mr. Tierney."

"Of the killing? True for you." He heaved another sigh. "Jaysus, what a coil. I can always confess, come to that, but I'd sooner not. Are yez sure there's no test Tommy could take to prove he's not guilty?"

"Test? Like a lie-detector test?" Jay shook his head. "They're unreliable. If Tommy came forward and volunteered to take a lie detector test, it would be a step in the right direction . . ."

"But not proof."

"Not iron-clad. You know the war-gamers, Mr. Tierney. They're more likely to talk to you than to Chief Inspector Mahon. Ask them what they saw. Tell them if Wheeler was killed as a result of horse-play, they won't face a capital charge. See if you can trace Wheeler's movements, who he was seen with, that sort of thing. Maybe you'll turn something up."

"I won't shop the lads." Tierney's eyes narrowed, suddenly shrewd.

"You're a hard man to advise, Mr. Tierney. You won't bring your son in for questioning, you talk about making a false confession, and you don't want to pressure the other likely suspects. It's a good bet your son or one of your son's friends killed Wheeler. Everything points to it. You say Tommy's not guilty. Find out who is. That's my advice to you."

" 'Tis possible one of the lads killed Wheeler, but there's others might have wanted him dead." He jerked a thumb in the direction of Stanyon.

Jay gave a slight smile. "At least you're thinking. The staff at Stanyon or the sister?" He spoke easily, without emphasis, and Tierney's face muscles eased. Jay slipped his next question in without a pause. "Who did Wheeler cut out with Grace Flynn?"

"Tommy."

In the moment of charged silence, the Rayburn clanked. Dad shifted on his chair.

Tierney rubbed his jaw, rueful. "She's . . ." He shot me a glance. "She's a friendly lass, is our Grace."

"Who else? Artie?"

He snorted. "Him with the ring in his nose? Not likely, but she's took up with half a dozen boyfriends since she left school."

"Then look to the boyfriends. The lady is pregnant with Wheeler's child."

"Do you say?" He scratched his jaw again, ruminating. "That puts a different light on things. Thank you, Mr. Dodge. I'm that grateful . . ."

"I think you should turn yourself in." Jay kept his voice easy.

Tierney stiffened. "Eh? Now?"

"Yes. Call your lawyer first, if you like. The police will arrest you and question you, but the bail will be lower if you come in of your own accord."

Tierney scowled. "Did you ring up the polis?"

"No. However, I'll call for you now, if you like, and put in a good word."

He hesitated.

"Would you prefer to surrender to Mahon or Kennedy?"

Tierney gave a rueful chuckle. "The devil and the deep sea, is it? Ah, Jaysus, lead me to it. I'll phone my solicitor. You can ring up Joe Kennedy for me afterwards. I've never met Mahon."

Better a devil that you know.

To my surprise and intense relief, Tierney was as good as his word, though he wheedled another drink out of my father. The liter bottle was almost empty.

Outside the mist had coagulated in a dense fog. Kennedy and the lawyer arrived simultaneously to escort Tierney to the Killaveen station. Tierney drove his daffodil-yellow van, the lawyer followed, and Kennedy brought up the rear in his white patrol car. All three of us stood on the gravel in front of the door and watched as the procession disappeared, taillights turning the fog as red as venous blood.

Jay and Dad had gone downstairs, *hors de combat*, and I was putting the last of the dishes away when the phone rang. It was Maeve Butler inviting Jay and me to a concert of folk music, a *céilí*, the next evening. It was clear she had no idea of the latest development in the Wheeler case. I didn't enlighten her. I did accept the invitation. Jay hates folk music.

8 ॐ

Hard are the trials of all womankind...

—American folk song

"A WHAT?"

"A *céilí*," I repeated, passing the marmalade. "Folk music."

Jay groaned.

"A hooley."

Both of us stared at my father.

He took another spoonful of virtuous porridge. We were all eating porridge for breakfast. "In the early sixties there was a fashion for folk music." His spoon clacked on the bowl. "My students called their impromptu concerts hooleys. I wonder if that's an Irish word."

"I thought they were called hootenannies." I cut three more slices from a loaf of soda bread and took one. I was not crazy about Irish oatmeal but I did like the bread. I lavished my slice with butter and reached for the bitter-orange marmalade. "It was thoughtful of Maeve to invite us. I said yes."

Jay grimaced. He had lately returned to drinking coffee after a ten year abstinence, but he liked it strong, so I was fairly sure his grimace was not a comment on the brew.

"No doubt the inquest will be a truly Irish experience." I brushed crumbs onto my plate. "But I'd like to witness a more typical happening. And we should do something social. Saturday night is Saturday night."

"How kind of Miss Butler." Dad finished a nibble of bread. "I'll look forward to it."

I was disconcerted. Maeve's invitation had not specifically excluded my father, but I thought she was expecting Jay and me *sans* papa. "She says it's held in a pub in Killaveen," I offered, thinking that might discourage him.

Dad beamed. "All the better."

I looked at Jay.

He shrugged. "I know when I'm outnumbered."

Someone knocked.

Jay was nearest. He rose, coffee cup in hand, and opened the door. "Good morning, sir."

I heard the rumble of a male voice.

"I see," Jay said. "Come in. You're at it early."

Chief Inspector Mahon entered, followed by the sergeant with his tape recorder and the hapless constable. Jay led them into the living room. While he was introducing himself and seating them, I plugged the kettle in. Dad finished his porridge, rose, and went into the living room, too.

I stacked dishes until the kettle hummed. When it shrieked, I unplugged it and stuck my head through the door arch. "Coffee or tea, inspector? I have both."

Mahon said, "Tea, Mrs. Dodge, if it's no trouble."

"None at all." I looked at the other men and they nodded. Tea. Following the leader.

Mahon was taking Jay through the events of the previous evening and sounded rather stiff. I wondered if the inspector's nose was out of joint. Sgt. Kennedy's absence was conspicuous.

When I brought three mugs on a tray with sugar and cream, Mahon gave me a faint, approving smile, but he continued to direct his stiff questions at Jay. I served the three policemen tea and sat on the fireplace ledge to listen. After all, Dad and I were

107

witnesses, too. Dad was playing solitaire with the computer but I thought he was also listening.

"Have you questioned Tierney?" Jay asked when Mahon had finished the second run-through.

"Not yet," Mahon said bleakly. "His solicitor arranged bail last night, after I'd driven back to Dublin."

"Quick work. Then he's free?"

"Yes." Exasperation tightened Mahon's face muscles. "Tierney has political connections, you see."

"I gathered that when he told us he'd arranged his son's disappearance."

"The old network. It's still in place." Mahon took a swallow of strong sweet tea and set his mug on the tray. "If the boy's guilty we've seen the last of him."

Jay was standing by the fireplace. I twisted my neck so I could see his face. He frowned. "Tierney believes his son is innocent, inspector. That was my impression. He was looking for a magic bullet."

"I don't follow you."

"He came to me because he imagined I'd know of some new technology, some 'test' Tommy could take that would exonerate him. I told Toss that was nonsense, of course, that what he needed was another plausible suspect. I suggested the other war-gamers."

"They've been questioned."

"And?"

"Young Tommy is still the likeliest bet. There's one other lad with no alibi for the relevant times, but he also seems to have no motive."

"Whereas Tommy was challenging Wheeler's leadership." Jay nodded. "There's the girl, too."

"Grace Flynn," Mahon said without joy. He rose and his subordinates followed suit, the constable with a mournful look at his half-full mug. "The case against young Tierney seems clear-cut, but I don't like this business about the key to the cottage. You say Toss insists he didn't enter the cottage, yet the body was here, inside, for six or eight hours."

"Have you accounted for all the keys?"

"There's a set at Stanyon on a whacking great board in what used to be the butler's pantry. The keys are in place, labeled Bedrock Cottage for the convenience of passing burglars. Apart from Professor Dailey's keys, which Alex Stein posted to him in Dublin last week, Tierney's are the only other set."

"Besides the Steins, who has access to the pantry?"

"Easy access?" Mahon shrugged. "Murtagh, the chef, and the kitchen staff." He turned to me. "Refresh my memory. You're sure the outside door downstairs was locked?"

"I tested the handle. It was locked."

Mahon sighed. "I'd best tackle Tierney. He has to be lying."

"Does he?" I thought he was telling the truth most of the time. Not that I'm an expert.

Mahon's brows snapped together. After a moment, he said, "It's the daub of red paint on the dead man's forehead, d'ye see, Mrs. Dodge? If it weren't for the paint I'd take a closer look at the Stanyon lot and the sister. Wheeler was a heavy investor in Stonehall Limited, and he liked to throw his weight around. What's more, he was on bad terms with Miss Wheeler. She admits that. But the paint is plainly symbolic. The man was killed because of his game-playing."

It seemed silly to point out that anybody can shoot a squirt gun at an unmoving target, or make a wax copy of an ordinary Yale key, so I didn't say anything. The Gardai were professionals. Whatever Mahon's favored theory, I was sure they were following all leads in the methodical way of police investigators.

Shortly thereafter, Mahon took his leave. He had an appointment to interview Toss Tierney—with the solicitor present. When the police had gone I told Jay and Dad to clean up the kitchen, lest they imagine dishes were women's work. I took a run into Arklow to buy Sunday supplies.

It was still misting out and I drove with paranoid care. I had anticipated that everyone in County Wicklow would be shopping at the same time, so the congestion at the High Street roundabout didn't surprise me.

At Quinnsworth I bumped into Maeve. I told her my father wanted to come to the concert and warned her that he tired easily. She nodded, smiling. Though she was perfectly courteous, she seemed preoccupied, so I disengaged and went on my way. As I was drooping over the cabbages in the produce section, however, she came up to me again.

"Is it true Toss Tierney surrendered to your husband at the cottage last night?" She kept her voice low because we were surrounded by shoppers—male, female, all ages, alone and in family clumps. Every cart in the store was in use, most of them in produce.

I said, "He wanted to talk to Jay. He surrendered to Joe afterwards. Didn't Joe tell you?"

Spots of color burnt on her admirable cheekbones. "He did not. I shall have words with that man."

"I imagine Chief Inspector Mahon is leaning on him. We had a visit from the Dublin contingent this morning."

"Even so . . ." Maeve's eyes flashed.

"Do you mind?" An impatient housewife gestured to the cabbages.

"Sorry," I murmured, moving my cart out of her way.

"I'll come for you at half eight," Maeve hissed.

"We'll be ready to go." I picked one of the leafy green cabbages at random and tossed it into my huge cart.

Maeve darted off, swifter than I because she was unencumbered by a cart. She was carrying a small basket with a loaf of bread in it. I drifted over to the potatoes. They were interesting colors—purple and tan and red, varieties I hadn't seen at home. I took a fancy to the purple kind.

A customer among the oranges pointed out to me that I was supposed to weigh my produce choices at a clever little computer-scale device. When I pressed the right buttons, it

110

emitted a bar code on a sticky label. I fiddled with the machine for a while—a technology that hadn't yet reached the Pacific Northwest. It would save the clerks time and memory when it worked. Sometimes it didn't. Before I took my laden cart through the check-out stand, I found a replacement bottle of Jameson's for my father. It seemed odd to be buying whiskey in a supermarket. The state of Washington confines hard liquor to government stores.

When I got back to the cottage, the kitchen was spic and span and Jay had heated soup. Dad took a long nap after lunch. Jay worked at the computer. I read Trollope until it was time to cook dinner. Life was just one damned meal after another.

When Maeve turned up, on time, in a battered van, she was alone. No sergeant. I wondered if they had had words. She made no reference to Kennedy, inserted Dad in the front passenger seat with considerable charm, and went around to the driver's door. Jay and I climbed in the back.

She slid in, slammed the door, and hooked her seat belt. "The Steins may be coming, too."

"Grand," Dad said.

I scrunched against the far side. There were two rear seats. Jay and I sat in the narrower, middle one. Maeve explained over the thrum of the engine that she used the van to haul her students back and forth to excavations. It looked as if she had been carrying people with large muddy boots.

Maeve's van trundled up the drive and back down to Stanyon. She went inside and returned within ten minutes. "They've decided to take their own car. They're waiting on *la Wheeler*."

"Kayla's coming? Horrors."

Maeve made no comment. She engaged the gear and we chugged off. Dad asked about her current project and she said her digs usually took place in summer. She was surveying a tumulus out of season because it lay in the path of a proposed highway ramp. The EU were funding a motorway project to connect Wexford and the French ferry with Dublin. The dig sounded rather dull. Maeve's voice sounded dull, as if she were tired.

111

I hadn't yet driven through Killaveen so I was curious about Kennedy's turf. It seemed like a pleasant village. One post office, a Protestant church with a tall belltower and an aggressively modern Catholic church, one tiny grocery, one turf accountant. I caught a glimpse of the Garda station on a side lane as we whisked down the steep high street. The station looked like an ordinary two-story house, except for the illuminated sign. A patrol car was parked in front and lights shone upstairs.

Maeve turned into the lot of a large brick pub. When she had parked and set the brake, she loosened her seat belt and turned around. "I brought you early, so we can snaffle a table in the saloon bar. The public's apt to get a bit noisy between sets."

Dad said, "Do they still divide the drinking space into public and private bars? Surely ladies can be seen in the public these days."

Maeve smiled at him. "They can, and upstairs and downstairs and in their nightgowns into the bargain. Shocking, I call it."

Dad laughed and we all got out.

The pub, the Stanyon Arms, had been tarted up, though the gleaming oak bar looked like the real thing. Maeve said there was quite a good restaurant upstairs. She led us around the long bar to the small, dark saloon. We found a table free, though a multi-generational family with at least two underage children were chattering away around another table. They fell silent as we entered. The children stared. Maeve gave them a big smile and went over to greet a woman in the group.

My father held a chair for me. Jay scooted around to the built-in bench where he could sit with his back to the far wall. Typical. Dad sat on the bench beside him and we waited. Eventually Maeve returned.

"The mother of one of my better students." She eyed us. "What's your tipple, Professor Dailey?"

"Whiskey."

She shook her head, sad. "They're not licensed for the water of life, I'm afraid."

Dad's face fell. "Lager, then."

112

"There's quite a good selection of wines."

"White bordeaux?"

"Bordeaux it is. Jay?"

"A pint of Guinness."

"What else? Lark?"

"Smithwick's," I said firmly. Guinness looked as if it would float an egg.

She wheeled and strode to the bar and we could hear her bantering with the bartender.

Jay got up. "I gather there's no table service." He made his way to Maeve's side and the two of them stood with their backs to us. Evidently Maeve was introducing Jay, for the bartender set Dad's glass of wine on a tray and shook hands before he began pulling levers. Beer foamed.

The noise level in the public was rising. I couldn't hear the bar dialogue over that and the chatter of the family party, but I watched Maeve reach for her purse and Jay take out his wallet. A pantomime debate followed and Jay prevailed. He paid while Maeve carried the tray over to us.

"He's a golden-tongued devil," she said gaily. "I'll get the next round."

"Ah, no," Dad said. "Let me."

I didn't offer to buy drinks and I wondered how stiff the drunk-driving laws were in Ireland. Clearly the booze was going to flow free.

I could see Jay and the bartender telling each other their life stories. Maeve seated herself, took a sip of her wine—it looked like sherry—and eyed the table. "Room for the Steins?"

"The Steins, yes," I said. "They're small. Kayla isn't."

"She can sit on the bench by your husband and pat his knee." She winked at me. "Cheers."

"Cheers," I muttered and took a swallow of Smithwick's.

Dad tasted his wine. "Ah, that's grand." He gave the impression of a man determined to enjoy himself. I was glad he had taken a nap.

Eventually the bartender turned back to his clamoring patrons and Jay returned to us. He sat and sipped Guinness and looked smug. The first musicians were tuning up on a tiny platform at the near end of the bar. I was going to be able to hear the concert, but visibility was somewhat impaired by beer glasses dangling from the bar overhang and by a large tweedy man who sat at the end with his nose in a glass of Guinness.

I gave Jay a gentle kick under the table. "You and the bartender must have hit it off."

Jay licked foam from his lip. "He was telling me about the local trout streams. The pub owns fishing rights on that creek that runs behind the place."

Dad sat up. "It's early for flies."

"True. He rents gear, though. And there's coarse fishing in the pond outside of town."

Dad's eyes gleamed. Maeve listened to their fish talk with an indulgent air. I swallowed Smithwick's.

The Steins and Kayla Wheeler did not arrive for the opening set. The musicians, two thirtyish brothers with guitars and a friend who played the pennywhistle, launched into a series of music-hall songs. Their voices were pleasant but ordinary, and the accompaniment more rhythmical than interesting, but they sang with rowdy enthusiasm and the crowd responded.

I knew some of the songs and not others. I was particularly taken with a little number called "The Night Before Larry Was Stretched," stretched being a euphemism for hanged. By the time the singers got to "Finnegan's Wake," my mood had lifted. I applauded enthusiastically as they bowed off the stage.

"Sorry we're late." Barbara Stein had slipped past the tweedy man at the bar during the last song. "Alex is parking the car."

"Where's Miss Wheeler?" Maeve asked.

Barbara rolled her eyes. "She's done a disappearing act. She told us she wanted to come but she vanished after dinner. We hung around waiting for her. I even went up and knocked at her door. No response, so we said the hell with it and came anyway. How are you, George? Smoke getting to you?" Cigarette smoke hung on the air. Irish smokers have no inhibitions.

Dad smiled at her. "I'm enjoying myself. Can I get you a drink?"

"No, thanks. I'll wait for Alex."

Alex arrived as the next act, a fiddler of about ninety, was tuning up. Dad went off to the bar and returned with red wine (Barbara) and a Guinness (Alex). The fiddler swung into an impossibly intricate jig. By the time he wound down, two men were dancing in front of the stage and the audience was thoroughly roused. Even Jay smiled. The old fiddler was a true artist. We listened without trying to talk. I wanted to dance.

At the end of the set, the old man called up his great-granddaughter, a child of ten or eleven with braces and straight brown hair. She was carrying a violin. They played a fiddle duet, the old man leading. The music was clearly below the gaffer's talents and a bit above the child's, but they brought the piece to a spirited end and everyone cheered them off the stage. The little girl blushed and looked up at her mentor with shining eyes.

Barbara said in a softened voice, "My mother is a violinist. She and my Uncle Moishe and two of their friends worked up a string quartet concert in our living room every winter. They weren't professional but they enjoyed themselves."

Dad said, "Perhaps we've lost our tolerance for amateurs in the States. People used to participate in their own entertainment."

Barbara gave him a wry smile. "And now our music is digitally reconstructed."

Alex shifted on the hard seat. "You can't record spontaneity. We've tried."

Jay sipped his Guinness. I wondered what he was thinking. His idea of music is instrumental jazz of the Wynton Marsalis class or down-and-dirty blues. He is more musical than I am. I listen for words.

Maeve said, "This group is popular with my students."

Three young men and a girl in a scarlet mini with blue hair were tuning up. They sang in Irish. The *a capella* songs were traditional, but a couple of the others sounded familiar. We listened politely. I was straining to recall where I'd heard the last song when my father snorted. I stared at him. He appeared to be choking.

Alarmed, I reached toward him but he patted my hand, grabbed a bar napkin and wiped his eyes. The song ended and everyone applauded, including Dad.

I leaned toward him. "What's the matter?"

"The song . . ." He chuckled and wiped his eyes again. "Do you recognize it?"

Jay said, "It sounded familiar."

Dad laughed again. "Oh dear, I don't know why it struck me so funny. It's a pop song from the fifties. You may remember it, Jay, from your childhood." It was Hank Williams's "Jambalaya," so to speak. He chanted the words. Sure enough, the Irish song had the same tune.

The Steins and Maeve stared. Jay grinned. "Authentic Cajun Irish?"

I turned to Maeve. "Is that usual?"

She shrugged and smiled. "Not usual, but it happens. Young people aren't always traditional-minded and they're very fond of American country and western music."

I sighed. "Cultural imperialism?"

"Perhaps."

"Country comes out of the same ballad tradition," Jay offered. "Some Appalachian songs exist in English and Scottish variants."

"I thought you hated folk music," I muttered.

He shrugged. "I don't find the music interesting, as a rule. And the folk milieu didn't appeal to me. I like this stuff, though. Especially the fiddler."

Alex rubbed his shoulder as if it were sore, but his eyes glowed. "We could do an historical disk—alternate versions of the same ballad—and illustrate it with woodcuts."

Barbara groaned. "Geez, Alex, we're taking a break from the business tonight, remember?"

He looked sheepish. By way of apology he bought another round. I thought he moved stiffly when he walked to the bar.

The Cajun choristers were succeeded by a tenor with a formidable vibrato who headlined at a major hotel in Kilkenny during the summer. The tenor did "Kathleen Mavourneen," a song of which I am not fond. It was followed as the day the night by "Danny Boy" and "The Harp that Once Through Tara's Halls." I thought the applause was merely polite.

At eleven-fifteen there was a break. People got up and walked around, visiting. Alex looked at his watch and his wife. "I think we ought to go home, Barb."

She made a face. "I suppose so. Kayla's probably surfaced by now. She'll be mad as a yellowjacket at a barbecue."

My father said, "May I hitch a ride with you?"

I felt a twinge of anxiety. "Are you tired?"

"We can leave any time you like," Maeve offered.

"Don't cut your concert short. I'll ride with Alex and Barbara." He stood up and directed a courtly little bow at Maeve. "I thank you for a most diverting evening. I don't know when I've enjoyed myself more. I'm not tired yet, but I don't want to be, either, so I'll call it a night."

Jay rose, too, and so did Maeve and I. In the flurry of leave-taking Jay touched Dad's arm. "Son of a gun," he said. "Some kind of fun, huh, George?" Dad laughed and went off with the Steins through the blue haze of smoke.

We stayed until midnight. A woman played the small Celtic harp and sang sleepy songs in Irish. When a man brought in what Maeve called *uilleann* pipes, though, Jay started to squirm.

Maeve and I exchanged looks and she said, "Shall we wind down with a nightcap at the Troutdale Hotel? The bar's quiet in winter." It was not winter, of course. She meant before the tourist season started.

"Sounds good," Jay said gratefully.

We slipped out between songs. Pipes are an acquired taste, though these had a mellower tone than bagpipes.

The Troutdale lay on the N11 north of Arklow. Aside from

the morose bartender and a German couple, we were the only patrons. I had drunk three glasses of ale at the Stanyon Arms, so I used the loo. When I returned to our table, Maeve was adjusting her lipstick and Jay stood at the bar. He brought a sherry, a glass of ale, and a cup of coffee. He took the coffee.

I slid onto the red leather banquette. "Is Joe Kennedy on duty tonight?"

"We're not joined at the hip," Maeve snapped. She drew a deep breath. "Sorry. We quarreled. We do that once a fortnight on average."

Jay said mildly, "He can't discuss the details of a case that's under investigation, you know." He must have tuned in on her discontent earlier.

Maeve scowled. "I know it. You may omit the lecture."

"Sorry."

"So how did *you* get to be a policeman?" She said "polis" in palpable imitation of Kennedy's accent.

I squirmed. The sergeant's pronunciation was local though his language was sophisticated. Maeve's accent was pure and very U. I wondered whether a class conflict underlay their sparring.

"I needed a job." Jay tested the coffee and set the cup back on its saucer. "The department was hiring."

"You were at university."

"A senior," Jay agreed. "In history. There wasn't much demand for BAs in history. We were going through one of those mini-recessions. My marriage was foundering in shoals of student loans, and I thought I'd better take what was offered."

At the word "marriage," Maeve's eyes flew to mine.

"Not me," I said ungrammatically. "I'm number two."

"Only in the sequential sense," Jay murmured, bland.

Maeve shook her head, her mouth easing in a smile. "Americans. You do realize we have only just recognized divorce in this country."

Both of us nodded.

Maeve sighed. "So you chucked a history career and took up sleuthing."

Jay winced. "Not exactly. I did my stint on patrol and went into community relations. I speak Spanish."

"Spanish?"

"Los Angeles is one of the larger Spanish-speaking cities in the world."

The LAPD had received several years' worth of bad PR in recent months. I could see Maeve gearing up for questions about race relations.

Possibly Jay could, too. He said, "That was a while back. I was with the department eight years and wound up negotiating with hostage-takers. A big urban department has a lot of divisions. The captains move officers around as a matter of policy."

"Then you weren't a detective?"

"Well, yes, afterwards. Elsewhere. In small departments. When I met Lark, I was head of the Monte County CID." He smiled at her. "That means I was the senior of two detectives."

"Two!"

"It's a big county geographically but the population density is roughly twelve per square mile."

"Good heavens, why did you go there?"

"I was asked," Jay was evading the truth—editing history, so to speak. He retired on a medical disability from the LAPD.

He took a sip of coffee, adding, "I got interested in the problems small departments have dealing with evidence. In a large department officers have time to pick up on the finer points."

"And your book came out of that. I see. Did your first wife follow you to your rural fastness?"

"Linda? Good God, no. We split while I was still driving a patrol car."

"She didn't like being married to a policeman?"

I knew where Maeve was coming from and I suspected Jay did, too.

He shrugged. "Linda got a fellowship at the University of Texas the next winter, when she finished writing her master's thesis. I didn't see myself as a Texas Ranger."

"But . . ." Maeve frowned. "Then you left her?"

"It was a mutual disengagement. No hard feelings. She's now a successful clinical psychologist, married to another successful clinical psychologist. They have two perfectly adjusted teenagers."

Maeve laughed. I did not. Lovely Linda. Lovely fertile Linda.

Jay changed the subject with elephantine deftness. "How did you get to be an archaeologist?" He can read me like a book.

She made a face. "A dull story. When I was ten, the OPW did a dig on my father's land. The students who were working that summer made a pet of me."

"OPW?"

"The Office of Public Works," I said. "They do thoroughly explanatory bilingual signs at public monuments."

That tickled Maeve. "Among other things. What public monuments have you visited?"

I described the dolmens and she told us of several others within driving distance. It was likely, she said, finishing her sherry, that her tumulus contained a similar megalith. As we left to drive back to the cottage, she gave us a rueful picture of the politics of funding digs. She also offered to show us the site she was investigating. I thought Dad would find it as interesting as I did and said so.

The van jounced over a road bump and Maeve slowed to turn off for Stanyon. We were halfway down the lane when a klaxon sounded behind us and a revolving light flashed. Maeve swerved onto the shoulder, swearing, and an ambulance passed us at high speed.

"Dad," I said. "He's had another stroke."

Maeve accelerated. "Surely not. He seemed relaxed and cheerful. . . ."

Jay took my hand in a warm clasp.

At the Y we could see that the ambulance had headed down the hill to Stanyon. A patrol car, its light whirling, stood on the drive in front of the main entrance.

Maeve slowed. "Do you think . . . ?"

I swallowed. Dad might have been stricken in the car on the way home. The Steins would have driven him down to Stanyon Hall and called in the emergency from there.

Jay said, "Drive to the cottage, Maeve, if you will. George is probably snug in bed. If he isn't, we can walk back . . ."

"If he isn't," she said crisply, "I'll drive you to Stanyon." She wrenched the wheel to the right and we headed through the arch of rhododendrons to Bedrock Cottage.

9 ❧

Her skin was as white as leprosy,
The Night-mare LIFE-IN-DEATH was she,
Who thicks man's blood with cold.

—Samuel Taylor Coleridge, "The Rime of the Ancient Mariner"

THE LIGHTS WERE on in the cottage kitchen. We had left them on. Maeve parked the van at the front door and set the brake. I was out, scrambling over Jay and fumbling my key into the lock, before she had killed the engine.

Jay followed right behind me. "Quietly."

I yanked the door open. "Dad?"

No answer. The living room lay in darkness. We had left it dark.

"Wait here. I'll check on him." Jay kicked off his shoes and padded through the living room. I heard the stairs creak as he walked down them.

Maeve sidled in the door and stood watching me.

"Have a chair," I croaked, sinking down onto the nearest myself.

She sat and folded her hands in her lap.

We waited. When, at last, I heard Jay returning, I jumped up and went to the arch that led into the living room. As soon as I could make out his face, I said, "Is he there?"

He nodded. "Sound asleep, snoring a little. He flopped over on his back. It's okay, sweetheart."

I let out my breath in a whoosh. "Thank God. But what . . . ?"

He squeezed my shoulder in passing.

"If Professor Dailey is here and well, then what's going on at Stanyon?" Maeve stood up. "I'll drive over and find out, shall I?"

Jay was shaking his head. "Give them time to get it sorted, whatever it is. Barging in with questions in the middle of a medical emergency is a bad idea."

"But . . ." She sat again. "I daresay you're right."

He went on over to the sink, filled the electric kettle, and plugged it in. He made tea and we sat there drinking it in preoccupied silence. Finally, Maeve shoved her cup away.

"I can't stand it. I'm going to drive to Stanyon."

Jay looked at his watch. "Ten more minutes? The ambulance may be gone by then. I'll telephone."

Reluctant, she nodded. "Very well. I need to use the loo. Is it downstairs?"

I said, "Foot of the stairs. I'm not thinking. I should have offered."

"Aspirins?"

"In the cabinet above the sink."

She gave me a grateful smile. "I'll try not to wake your father."

"He'll just think Jay and I are heading for bed."

"Right." She whisked from the room.

I turned to Jay, who had got up and was peering out the small window. "What in the world do you think is going on?"

"I don't know."

"Don't be so damned literal. Neither do I."

"It could be anything from somebody with a bout of indigestion . . ."

"To another murder?"

He turned back, his eyes still dilated from looking into the night. "You said the word." He blinked and perched on the end of the kitchen table.

The telephone shrilled twice, as Irish phones do.

Since Jay was closer, he answered it. "Speaking. Yes, about half an hour ago. We saw the ambulance."

I leaned against the arch, watching him. The phone quacked. Downstairs the toilet flushed and I heard water running.

"She's still here. Has something happened?" His shoulders stiffened. "I see, yes. Yes, of course. I'm sorry to hear it. We'll wait for you." He hung up slowly.

"What is it?"

We went back to the kitchen.

"What happened?" I repeated. "Tell me."

Jay's face was grave and his eyes dark and watchful. "That was—"

Maeve appeared in the door arch so abruptly both of us jumped. She was carrying her flats. "I heard the telephone. . . ."

Jay said, "It was Sgt. Kennedy. Kayla Wheeler is dead."

I drew a sharp breath. Maeve's eyes widened. "How . . . ?"

"He didn't supply details."

Maeve gave an exasperated cluck.

"He's not supposed to, Maeve."

"Terribly correct of him," Maeve said sweetly. "Terribly correct of *you*." She plunked her shoes on the floor and scuffed into them.

"I don't think Miss Wheeler died of natural causes," Jay said wryly. "Kennedy wants to question you."

"Question me? Whatever for? I barely knew the woman." Spots of indignation burnt on her cheeks.

"You went into Stanyon Hall this evening, remember?"

Her hands flew to her mouth. "Are you saying she was dead then?"

Jay shook his head. "I don't *know* anything, Maeve. I'm guessing he wants you to describe what you saw."

Maeve kept her eyes on his. After a moment, she gulped and nodded. "All right. I'll stay, of course."

124

"He said it won't be long. Chief Inspector Mahon is there already—"

"From Dublin?" I interjected, surprised at the speedy response.

"Mahon and his team stayed in Arklow last night," Jay explained. "Mahon wants Kennedy to take Maeve's statement as soon as possible."

I said softly, "I wonder where Toss Tierney was this evening?"

Maeve looked from me to Jay.

He said, "I don't know about Toss, but if Tommy Tierney was in England and can prove it, he's going to look less like suspect number one in the first murder."

"And Mahon will start investigating the Stonehall people in a serious way," I mused.

"Alex and Barbara?" Maeve sat with a thud. "That's daft! They wouldn't harm anyone, certainly not a guest."

Jay was frowning. He didn't speak. I knew what he was thinking because I had heard the sermon before. Under the right circumstances, anybody can kill. It is a theory I still cannot accept. My father would not kill under any circumstances.

I groped for conversation. "Was there local resistance to Stonehall?"

Maeve frowned. "There was local rejoicing."

"That may be." I remembered Liam's comic turn about smoking. "But foreign companies impose foreign values, even when they don't intend to interfere."

Maeve thought. "There's always talk in the pubs, mostly hot air. The usual bigots made anti-Semitic remarks about the Steins, but most people wanted Stonehall to succeed, even to expand."

"Jobs," Jay said.

Maeve leaned forward, earnest. "To be sure. If the younger people can't find work, they emigrate. The old pattern. We're still losing population. Of course, emigration's not the wrenching experience it once was. Families used to hold wakes for people who were leaving for America."

I cleared my throat. "They can fly home now."

She nodded. "For holidays and funerals and weddings. Still, it's hard on their families. Every sensible person wished Stonehall well. It wasn't until the war games started that there were serious grumblings." She ran a hand through her hair. "At least, that's what my father says. In term time I live in Dublin, so I'm not necessarily up on the local gossip."

The gravel outside crunched and a car door slammed.

I opened the front door. "Come in, Joe."

Kennedy entered. He looked as if he had spent a sleepless night and a long day.

He nodded to me, unsmiling, and shook hands with Jay. The fading bruise stood out on his cheek.

Maeve raised her chin. "I'm given to understand the inspector wants you to interrogate me."

Kennedy's mouth compressed. "Briefly."

"A sorry business," Jay muttered. I stared at him. He didn't indulge in obvious remarks, as a rule.

"It is that."

"I thought Kayla was a sad woman," I ventured. "Has Mahon ruled out suicide?"

"She did not kill herself," Kennedy said with such heavy conviction I felt ice touch my spine. After a moment, he went on, "You said 'sad,' Lark. I would have found other words myself. Why sad?"

The fact of Kayla's death was beginning to sink in. I blinked. "She seemed lonely, isolated. Maybe self-isolated. And she drank in a practiced way, as if she were anesthetizing herself."

Maeve made a face. "The woman was a sot. No doubt she had reasons for being as she was, but, as she was, she was distinctly repellent."

"A born victim?" Kennedy was cutting her no slack. They must have had a royal quarrel.

Maeve's cheeks reddened and she bit her lip.

He set a tape recorder on the table.

Jay said, "Do you want Lark and me to leave?"

Kennedy frowned.

"We can wait in the living room."

He shrugged. "Ah, the devil with it. I'll take Maeve's statement—without interruption, if you please—then I'd like to talk to the three of you about the Stanyon ménage. May I beg a cup of tea, Mrs. Dodge?"

I went to the sink. "You called me Lark a moment ago."

He gave me a rueful smile. "A wee lapse of professionalism. You induce lapses, missus."

"Ma'am," I shot back. "A true cop would say 'ma'am.' And don't tell me 'ma'am' is reserved for addressing royalty. This is a republic."

"God help us, so it is. Ma'am."

Jay took in this badinage without expression, but I could feel him watching me.

I filled the kettle while the sergeant shoved a fresh cassette into the player and adjusted the volume. Neither Jay nor Maeve wanted more tea. I didn't either but I made myself a cup by way of civility.

The kettle shrieked. When the tea had turned peat-black and he had sugared his, Kennedy took a scalding sip. He set his mug down. "Now, then, Miss Butler, if you'll state your full name and direction."

Maeve complied. Her middle name was Margaret and the Dublin address sounded like a flat. She was thirty-four. She indicated that she was a lecturer at Trinity College.

"How long have you known Mr. and Mrs. Stein?"

"A year. I met them last Easter holiday shortly after the company removed to Stanyon Hall."

"And you are friends?" He swallowed tea.

"Yes, we see each other when I'm stopping at my father's house—most holidays and whenever I have a dig nearby."

He took her local address, which sounded like an estate rather than a cottage. "How long have you known Kayla Wheeler?"

"Not long. I first met her evening before last."

"At what time did you enter Stanyon Hall this past evening?" His voice droned. He was going through the motions.

It occurred to me that the Steins had called Joe when they found the body, leaving him to call Mahon. Mahon might have perceived that as interference and directed him to interrogate Maeve as a way of removing him from the crime scene. Mahon didn't seem small-minded, but territoriality is a strange phenomenon. Jay also reacted to Joe territorially.

"Half eight," Maeve was saying. "A bit past that."

"Who answered your ring?"

"I didn't use the doorbell. The Steins leave the front door unlocked whilst they're up and about. I walked into the foyer. I expected Alex and Barbara to be waiting for me, but they weren't, so I nipped along to the drawing room. I found Alex there. He said Miss Wheeler hadn't come down yet."

"He used those words?"

"Approximately. He was impatient. He said Barbara had gone to knock her up."

"His words?"

Not bloody likely, I thought.

"That was the gist," Maeve snapped. "Alex said Miss Wheeler had been drinking and intimated he thought she might have, er, passed out."

"I see. How long did you wait before Mrs. Stein appeared?"

"Not long. She came in almost at once. She told me she and Alex would have to wait for Miss Wheeler and drive to the pub in their own car. She knew I had guests sitting outside in my van."

"The three of you were alone in the drawing room?"

"No. Mr. Novak was reading in a corner. He had greeted me and made a few remarks. He, er, commented on Miss Wheeler's propensity to drink deep. It was well known."

"Novak was there?" Kennedy's voice rang sharp.

Maeve blinked. "Employees are often there in the evening."

"Working?"

"It's not a conventional workplace."

"It was Saturday night."

Maeve said nothing and looked rather alarmed. After a moment, she added, "Mike Novak and Alex had been talking when I entered. Casually, I thought. Alex seemed to take Mike's presence for granted."

"Did you see other members of the Stonehall staff, or of the household staff, when you were in Stanyon Hall?"

"No. I left at once."

"Thank you." He shut off the machine and swore. "Novak. The Steins didn't mention him. We accounted for the chef and the housekeeper. I wonder who locked the front door and when."

"Mike had probably gone home by the time you were called." Maeve sounded worried, as if she had betrayed Novak or the Steins, or both. "I daresay they forgot him."

Kennedy scowled. "Would the Steins have locked the door before they left for the pub?"

"I don't know, Joe. Ask them."

"I shall." He rubbed the back of his neck. "The housekeeper had secured the other doors by half seven, and there's an electronic alarm in place. Why install an elaborate security system if you mean to leave the front door wide to the world?"

I winced. Until that moment I had forgotten the security system at the cottage. We had not rearmed it that evening.

"It's inconvenient to be jumping up and answering the doorbell every ten minutes," Maeve said. "Wicklow's rural. My father has never locked his doors in daytime."

"Your father has a bloody butler."

"My father *is* a bloody Butler," she rejoined. The more irritable the sergeant got, the sweeter Maeve sounded. She turned to me with a confiding air. "Like the Steins, Papa has a resident housekeeper. Barbara told me they locked the place up and activated the alarms twenty-four hours a day when they first came—because of the computers. They had false alerts every half hour."

I sighed. At least I locked the door whenever we left.

Kennedy sighed, too. He reached into his tunic and pulled out a small notebook. Apparently he used the recorder only for official statements. "In a general way, an open door would be understandable. This isn't Dublin. I remember the false alarms, God knows, but you'd think Slade Wheeler's murder would have registered at Stanyon. The *neighbors* are locking their doors."

When no one replied, he went on, "This death puts a different complexion on the first one."

"The war-gamers are out?" I had trouble with that. I remembered the daub of paint on Wheeler's forehead too vividly to discount it.

"Not out." Joe frowned. "But the motive seems less apparent. Also . . ." He hesitated. "The *modus operandi* was different this time." He looked at Jay, still frowning.

Jay didn't react. His impassivity had begun to annoy me.

"How was she killed?" I asked the obvious question. Maeve leaned forward, her eyes on Joe.

He looked at me. "Not with a choke hold. Sure, I can't give you the details, Lark, though the press will be hot on the trail soon enough. The coroner will adjourn the inquest on her brother. I can tell you that much."

"But I'll still have to give evidence?"

"He won't keep you ten minutes."

"Pity there's no other Wheeler heir about." Maeve was fidgeting, buttoning and unbuttoning her short coat as if she meant to leave.

Joe flipped the notebook open. "Why?"

"*Cui bono?* You need a fresh suspect."

"There is another Wheeler heir," I said. "Grace's child."

Maeve drew a sharp breath. Had she forgotten Grace? Perhaps she didn't take Grace's claim seriously. "Caitlin says the child's rights will be disputed even if the DNA establishes paternity. Our laws are no more generous to bastards than they are to women. But Wheeler was an American national. Caitlin wants to make a test case." She glared at Joe.

He was impassive. "We'll have to speak to Gracie. I . . . that is, Mahon thought the killer was out to wreck the war games. It may be he's out to wreck Stonehall."

"Or exterminate Wheelers," Jay said dryly.

"The press will play that up, too."

I groaned. My relations with the fourth estate in an investigative mood have sometimes been less than cheerful. Surely Irish journalists would not be as adhesive as the staff of the *Daily Blatt,* my favorite English tabloid.

I caught Jay suppressing a grin. Remembering my earlier media disasters had cracked his blank facade. He said in a warmer voice, "We'll set the security alarm here . . ."

"If you please." Joe apparently missed the byplay. His tone was heavy. "I've a constable on duty at the station. Better a false alarm than none. This is an isolated house and I don't like its proximity to Stanyon Woods."

Jay's eyes widened, then narrowed. "Do you think there was action in the woods today?"

"Action? I don't know. The estate is an odd place altogether, house and grounds." He hesitated. "It had unsavory associations in the last century."

Maeve made a rude noise. "Sure, it's the Orangemen out to get us."

Joe gave her an unloving glance and turned back to Jay and me. "For a time there was a sort of Hellfire Club convened at a folly in the woods. Scandalized the local gentry. The folly was torn down long ago."

"In the woods?" I asked. I was thinking of the incised stone. "Where?"

He shrugged. "I'm not certain. The place has been planted with conifers since then. An Orange Lodge met on the grounds during the land wars."

Jay frowned. "Orange?"

"Ultra-Unionist, anti-Catholic fanatics."

"Ian Paisley types?"

Joe flipped his notebook shut. "Exactly, except that that lot were in power at the time. The army and the constabulary were riddled with Orangemen, and old Stanyon, the man who built the hall, was a ringleader. His son played a prominent role in the Curragh Mutiny."

Jay said mildly, "You may take my ignorance for granted."

Maeve clucked. "Americans."

"The Strange Death of Liberal England," I murmured, citing a good popular history. "I read it because it dealt with women's suffrage."

"And Home Rule for Ireland." Maeve bestowed an approving nod on me as if I were an apt pupil. "In 1914, the Liberal Parliament passed a bill that would have given Ireland self-government."

"Limited self-government," Joe growled.

Maeve ignored the interruption. "Army officers stationed at the Curragh—that's in Kildare—swore an oath they would refuse to obey orders if Parliament directed the British army to withdraw from Ireland. The officers were Anglo-Irish, of course. Technically, they were in a state of mutiny."

Jay raised an eyebrow. "As if an American officer had refused a presidential order?"

Maeve frowned, considering parallels.

Joe said impatiently, "Close enough. They were traitors, but well-connected Protestant traitors. The English hanged Catholics who defied the law like pictures in a gallery."

"True enough." Maeve spread her hands. "The Great War broke out a few weeks after the Home Rule Bill passed, so Parliament suspended the bill for the duration. They couldn't deal with the Germans if the officer corps was in a state of mutiny. Most of the officers were killed in France."

"And by the end of the war it was too late for a peaceful settlement," Joe said flatly.

I ransacked my memory. "The Easter Rebellion?"

"Sure, it happened in 1916."

" 'A terrible beauty is born,' " Jay quoted.

Maeve looked surprised, as if she thought cops shouldn't read poetry.

Joe rose. "Stanyon's two sons were killed at the Somme. There were grandchildren, but his executors sold the estate after the Civil War. A wonder the house wasn't burnt."

Maeve said, "You know very well it wasn't burnt because the Irregulars were using the woods as a munitions depot."

Joe's lips clamped together.

Jay looked from one to the other. "I deplore ignorance of history including my own, but has it occurred to anyone that Ireland might be better off with a case of collective amnesia?"

The Irish contingent looked at him without expression. After a moment, Maeve gave a short laugh. "Better off, perhaps, but not half as Irish."

They left shortly after that, Joe first. Maeve waited until we could hear the car engine whine and the gravel crunch as he pulled out. I think she was avoiding any possibility of private conversation with him.

She stood up and looked at me. "My mother is English," she announced with an air of detachment. Without further ado, she collected her handbag, buttoned the short coat, and headed for the door.

Jay said, "Thank you for the concert, Maeve. I'm sorry fetching us embroiled you in this."

She cast a brilliant smile over her shoulder. "Ah, I was bound to entangle myself in it one way or another. I like the Steins. If you think of a way I can help them, be sure to let me know. I'm off to Dublin after the inquest. I've lectures Tuesday and Wednesday, but I shall bring the first lot of students down to the site the next day. If you'd like to drive over to see the dig on Friday, ring me up at my father's."

When she had gone it occurred to me that I had no idea what her father's first name was. There was bound to be a surfeit of Butlers in the telephone directory.

Jay was fussing around the kitchen, tidying things.

"So how was Kayla killed?"

He shrugged. "Kennedy didn't say." He sounded irritated.

I yawned and stretched. "Bed?" It was two-thirty, or, in Irish usage, half two. I was pooped or knackered, take your pick; too tired, at any rate, to pursue a quarrel.

"I'll be down later. I want to look at my e-mail."

Pouting? "Suit yourself." I yawned again.

He said, "I had a cup of coffee *and* a cup of tea, Lark. I'm wired."

"Okay. G'night." Trudging downstairs, I told myself that may have been the truth. While not exactly a caffeine virgin, Jay was sparing of the stuff. Maybe he was wired—and maybe he was pouting. I was too tired to sort it out.

I surprised myself by not falling asleep at once. I lay alone on the futon and listened to the *creak-creak* of the floor joists as Jay walked around upstairs. Perhaps I was wired, too.

Kayla was dead. Poor graceless, unhappy Kayla. I would have to think of a way of telling my father what had happened, but I didn't know what had happened.

Eyes closed, I chased the possibilities around until, at last, I drifted into an uneasy sleep. I had a nightmare in which Kayla, dressed in mourning black, fell down the long Stanyon stairway. I tried but was unable to stop her fall. She drifted like a dark leaf on an autumn wind, spiraling down to the heart of the stone.

10 ❧

Come all you fair and tender ladies,
Be careful how you court your men...

—American folk song

I WOKE LATE. I am the sort who annoys everyone else by rising spontaneously at six A.M. Whether it was jet lag or going to bed at half past two I can't say, but I slept until eleven. I gathered from the dent in Jay's pillow that he had tried to sleep at some point, but I had no memory of his presence beside me.

I felt sluggish and stupid, even after a long, hot shower. When I drifted upstairs, my father greeted me mournfully from the computer. He was playing solitaire again.

"Where's Jay?"

Dad placed a red five on a black six. "He went out for a walk."

"A run?" I wanted a run. I needed a run. Resentment stirred. Jay should have waited for me.

"A walk," Dad repeated, swiveling the office chair around to face me. "He told me about Miss Wheeler's death."

Memory rushed back. I felt my stomach knot. "I'm sorry, Dad. It's a shocking thing. Sgt. Kennedy came over last night and took a statement from Maeve before she left. He says they'll adjourn the inquest tomorrow."

He was nodding. "Jay told me. Are you all right?"

"Are you?" We eyed each other warily.

Dad sighed. "As you see, daughter. When I heard of the murder, I didn't fall on the floor in a stroke or foam at the mouth."

"Dad . . ."

"I'm well enough, Lark, though I find the situation depressing, and I can't seem to concentrate on my notes."

"Shall we drive to that Quaker village near Waterford?"

"Portlaw?" His face brightened. "If you feel up to it."

"Of course." After all, I had come to Ireland to drive my father to the historic sites he wanted to see. Besides, it was Sunday. As in Britain, things closed down in Ireland on Sunday. Might as well drive around gawking at half-deserted villages.

"What about Jay?"

"He can come with us or not, his choice."

Dad frowned, watching me. "You sound cold. Have you quarreled with Jay?"

"Not yet." I relented when I saw his anxiety. "I'm feeling a little annoyed with him. He seems to think I can't take care of myself."

Dad's mouth relaxed in a small smile. "Now you sound very like your father. I'm glad Jay is here, and not just because we may find time for a little fishing. He's a good man, Lark, and good company. As far as I can see, he's a good husband, too. Make peace."

"Is that an order?"

"Heavens, no."

He looked so distressed I went over and kissed his cheek. "Have you had breakfast?"

"Bacon," he said. "And two eggs. Jay cooked."

I fixed myself toast and scrambled eggs. I didn't feel sufficiently righteous to eat porridge.

Jay returned around noon with a newspaper and a healthy glow from his long walk. I fixed the men sandwiches while Dad read the news stories aloud. There were two in Friday's *Irish Times,* which did not publish on the weekends. One article was a factual report based on police releases, and one a profile of

136

Stonehall Enterprises with an accompanying photo of Stanyon Hall.

Mahon was playing it close to the chest. Neither the specific cause of death nor the daub of red paint on Wheeler's forehead was mentioned. The news story didn't use my name in connection with the discovery of Slade Wheeler's body, either, but the cottage figured prominently. We were in for a press siege which would intensify after I gave my evidence at the inquest. The thought filled me with gloom.

Jay didn't want to come to Portlaw with us. He claimed he was working on the student reports. He offered to cook dinner. I thought he had probably never dealt with a hunk of authentic Irish ham, *tres saline.* Neither had I. Maeve had said I should boil it mercilessly, so I put it in the spaghetti pot, cranked up the Rayburn, and left Jay to deal with the consequences.

Traffic was light. I drove south on the N11 through mild showers and listened to Dad reflecting on time, chance, mutability, and the fate of Kayla Wheeler. He sounded almost tearful.

The gorse was in full bloom, intense yellow against gray and the multitudinous green. By the time I cut off to the west at Enniscorthy, aiming for Waterford, Dad was cheering up. At New Ross, I sweated through a traffic jam generated by construction on an approach to the bridge over the Barrow, but the congestion was purely local. By then Dad sounded almost jolly. He was telling me all about Quaker grist mills. I kept my eyes on the road and let the details wash over me. My father is a master of details.

Once I deciphered the signage, I nosed across the high bridge over the tidal Suir and down into Waterford. From the looks of it, Waterford was a late Georgian and Victorian port town, though it had to be much older. Dad said it was a Viking foundation, like most of the seaports of Ireland. I knew I'd enjoy a walk through the historic center, but I pushed west, past a large technical college and the ultra-modern glass factory. I thought we'd better save the factory until my mother arrived. She collects Waterford crystal.

Dad liked Portlaw. Though I saw nothing to dislike, my mind was prying at the puzzle of Kayla Wheeler's death. Thinking about it was an exercise in futility because I had so little information, but I knew enough to feel anxious for the Steins. Kayla would have inherited her brother's interest in Stonehall Enterprises. Apart from the universal response to her negative charm, that was the only motive that made sense of her death.

When he had filled his mind and a small notebook with impressions of stolid Portlaw, Dad mentioned a dolmen, the largest in that area. Since the site, Leac an Scail, lay a few short kilometers to the west, I couldn't resist driving to it. Again, I experienced the ambiguous *frisson* that had stirred me at the other monuments.

"Impressive," Dad murmured as we walked back to the car.

My tongue locked. It was in my mind that the dolmen, impressive though it indeed was, had been a tomb, a death symbol. Ireland was rife with monuments to death.

I stuck the key in the passenger door and opened it. "We could drive to Clonmel."

Dad sank by stages onto the low seat. "Another time, Lark. I'm tired. Let's head home."

"Are you all right?"

"Fine. Just tired."

I inserted myself behind the wheel and started the engine. "I hope Jay didn't forget to change the water in that kettle." Maeve had suggested tossing the water from the first boiling.

We reached the cottage before six. Dad dozed most of the way, so I had too much time to think. I didn't know how Kayla had died, and I couldn't shake the feeling that the first death was curiously stylized, almost, you might say, symbolic. That insight led my suspicions to the Stonehall staff: the Steins, Alex especially, who was so focused on his work he couldn't stop thinking about ideas for new projects, and Barbara, with her open hostilities; the ebullient Tracy—like Alex an enthusiast;

138

Liam with his talent, his scruples, and his nightmare memories; volatile Mike Novak who had been on the scene last evening. They were bright people, gifted people, capable of elaborate, symbolic ironies. The more I thought about the Wheelers, the more incongruous their presence at Stanyon seemed. Sludgy, dreary Kayla embodied pointlessness. I had never met Slade alive. Why had the Steins taken on so incompatible a business partner? A genius with software, Barbara had said, and "fiscally responsible," at least in the counting of paperclips, but emotionally immature and invincibly ignorant. An idea man? If the war games typified his ideas, I couldn't help thinking his creativity was a dead end. I meditated about computer nerds.

My brother-in-law, Freddy, Jay's much younger half-brother, had been immersed in virtual experience since childhood. His obsession left him a little backward socially, but Freddy had come over to the human race in recent years, and he had not lost his touch with computers, nor his enthusiasm for them, in the process.

Without humanizing social interaction, though, Freddy might have followed a pattern similar to Slade Wheeler's—technical brilliance allied with arrogant ignorance. Freddy had learned how to love. Had Slade? He hadn't loved his sister. Had he loved Grace Flynn—or just made love to her?

Make love. What a misleading euphemism that is. Any rapist can fuck. Loving is more difficult.

I thought of Jay, about whom there was nothing virtual, except possibly his report-writing class. He loved me. I loved him. So why was I miserable? I parked in front of the cottage and set the brake.

"The windows are steamed up," Dad observed, unhitching his seat belt.

In fact, the ham was boiling away cheerily, but Jay had vanished. His computer was on. I touched the space bar and got a screenful of text. He was not downstairs, Dad reported on his way to a proper nap. I went outside and walked as far as the rhododendrons that hid Stanyon from our view. A patrol car sat in front of the house, but I saw no sign of life and no sign of my husband. He wasn't walking by the pond, either. When I returned to the kitchen, *I* was steamed.

As I searched out a paring knife, I told myself to relax, that Jay wouldn't leave the computer on if he expected to be gone long. I found the purple potatoes and started peeling. I was doing a lot of potato peeling these days. Rice, I thought. Pasta. I would lay in a supply.

I tested the ham and it seemed done. The water level was high enough to convince me Jay had followed instructions. I set the kettle on the cool end of the Rayburn, ladled juice from it into a pot, plunked the potatoes into the liquid, and set the pan, covered, on the hot side. I dissected the oddly green cabbage into three equal chunks, a time-consuming exercise in solid geometry. Still no Jay.

The potatoes boiled. I moved them over by the ham. I sliced fruit and concocted a yogurt dressing. I put out plates and flatware. I found a jar of mustard. I was brooding over the garbage pail and wondering what one did with no compost pile, no disposal unit, and no apparent garbage service, when the telephone rang. I raced to answer it and cracked my crazy bone on the door arch.

"Hi," Jay said. "Been home long?"

I rubbed my elbow. "Almost long enough to finish the cooking of dinner."

He ignored my sarcasm. "Good. I'm bringing Kennedy home for a meal."

I gritted my teeth. "How fortunate I peeled enough potatoes for an army. Where are you?"

"Stanyon."

"How long will you be?"

"Half an hour."

"You left your computer on."

"Oh. Well, I was working."

"I'll shut it down."

"Thanks."

"Don't mention it."

I saved his file, turned the computer off, went back to the kitchen, laid another place setting, and hacked the cabbage into six pieces. The potatoes were almost cooked. I found red wine and twisted the corkscrew so fiercely a bit of cork crumbled into the bottle.

I got out four wineglasses and the tea strainer and poured with exaggerated care. I drained the potatoes and mashed the bejesus out of them. I whipped them with butter and beat in a dollop of yogurt, at which point my sense of humor kicked in. There was nothing left to pummel. I was furious with Jay, I decided, partly because I was relieved. At some level I had been imagining him in the hands of a deranged killer. He wasn't. He might be inconsiderate and complacent, but he was alive. He could bloody well cook dinner tomorrow.

Restored to the semblance of good humor, I went in and beat the computer twelve times at Klondike. When I heard the patrol car crunch to a stop outside, I washed my hands at the kitchen sink and poked the cabbage in with the still-simmering ham.

Jay stuck his head in the door. "Hi. Steamy in here."

"Just like my mood," I said delicately.

He blinked and entered, followed by Joe Kennedy, who looked as if he needed a square meal. And twelve hours of sleep. I greeted Joe with a dazzling smile and directed the gentlemen to wash up and wake my father. They complied.

The meal was a triumph, measured by our appetites. Dad carved. There was enough ham left for sandwiches. We finished off the wine. Joe, who was beginning to look sleepy, begged for tea, so I shooed everyone into the living room and brewed a pot. I brought the tea and a plate of ginger biscuits to the men and told Jay to build a fire. Our first turf fire. It burned brightly enough but induced no visions. It smelled vaguely oily.

We munched and sipped, locked in our own thoughts. At last Joe set his cup down and wiped his mouth.

"More tea?"

"Thank you, no. Time for me to be off." He rose. "A grand meal."

"How did she die?" Dad burst out. When all three of us stared at him, he blushed. "I beg your pardon, but I must know. Speculation is worse than ignorance."

Joe examined the polished oak boards under his feet.

Jay said, "She was garotted, George."

Dad shuddered. So did I.

Joe cleared his throat. "There was a struggle."

"Mahon wanted me to look at the scene," Jay added. "I'm afraid I had nothing to contribute."

Joe frowned at him. "He wanted you to confirm my impression."

"Glad to oblige," Jay murmured. "Without the body, though, I was guessing."

"Sure, the inspector knows it." The frown eased and Joe gave me a small bow. "My thanks for the dinner and the tea, ma'am."

I considered. "I think 'ma'am' is obligatory only during an interrogation. As in 'Just the facts, ma'am.' "

He grinned, shook hands all around, and took his leave. Jay went out to the car with him.

Dad brought the tea tray to the kitchen. He looked gray around the mouth.

I thought about sending him off to bed, though it was only eight. Noon at home. Three in Childers, New York. I took the tray from him. "Why don't you call Mother?"

He gave a heavy sigh. "I suppose I ought to. She'll fuss, though."

Ma might fuss but she would distract him from the image of Kayla purple-faced with her tongue protruding. It was just possible my father had no idea what a strangling victim looked like. I hoped not. I wished *I* didn't.

I said, "It's Sunday. Isn't she expecting you to call?"

He nodded and trailed back into the other room. When I heard him greeting Mother, I started scraping plates into the crammed garbage pail. I had stacked the dishes and run a panful of hot, soapy water before Jay came in. Dad was still on the phone.

Jay stretched and yawned. "Great dinner, Lark."

I handed him a wet sponge. "What impression?"

He blinked at the sponge. "Eh?"

"Joe said Mahon wanted you to confirm his impression. What impression?"

He tossed the sponge into the dishpan and rolled up his sleeves. "I'm not supposed to talk about it. . . ."

"Did Mahon hire you?"

"No."

"Then you are a bystander, my friend. Like Dad. Like me. When you're part of an official investigation, I keep my questions to myself."

"You do?" He scrubbed a plate. "I hadn't noticed."

"Stop patronizing me. You have no standing in this case and you know I won't spill my guts to the *Daily Blatt*. So give." I picked up the dishtowel.

He dunked the clean plate in the steaming rinsewater and handed it to me. "Come on, Lark . . ."

"No, you come on. I will not be treated like the domestic help."

"Look, I'm sorry about dinner. I was getting set to peel potatoes when Mahon called me." He handed me another plate.

I dried it.

"I made the beds."

"Big deal." Making the beds involved straightening two duvets and plumping three pillows.

He handed me the remaining plates.

I wiped them with the soft towel.

"All right, you win. Mahon wanted me to confirm Kennedy's interpretation of certain physical evidence."

I carried the four dried plates to the cupboard. "I'm waiting."

"Joe thought the assailant was probably smaller than the victim. Kayla put up quite a struggle. Things were knocked around. Of course I didn't see the body *in situ,* but Joe described what he saw pretty vividly. There was bruising, too, and it wasn't postmortem."

I closed my eyes, visualizing Kayla. I kept seeing her walking down the Stanyon stairway dressed in black. "Where was she killed?"

He hesitated again, then shrugged. "Her room. It was off by itself in the east wing. They use that room and the connecting bath for guests." He tossed a handful of clean flatware into the rinse water. "Mahon thinks the killer entered through the bath. It has two doors, one to the hall and one to the bedroom."

I fished out a fork and two spoons. "And there were no other guests?"

"No overnight guests. Novak lives in Arklow. He went home."

I laid the dried silverware on a clean cloth. "When?"

"Soon after the Steins left for Killaveen. Or so he says." Jay thrust another fistful of flatware into the water. "He claims he locked the front door but didn't enable the alarm system."

"Alex and Barbara probably told him not to."

"So they say." He didn't sound as if he doubted them. The skepticism was an ingrained reaction.

I dried knives and forks. "Kayla was a big woman."

"Five-ten. About a hundred and ninety pounds. Of flab." He dipped the carving knife in the rinse water and handed it to me.

"Flab or no flab, she would have resisted." I dried the knife and restored it to the big wooden knife holder.

"If she was conscious. The Steins and Novak seemed to think she was pretty drunk when she went up after dinner."

"Is that going to confuse things?"

He began scrubbing the potato pan. "The autopsy will clear up some of the questions."

"Mahon should look for bruises on his suspects."

"I believe the thought has occurred to him."

I stared at him. "No need to be snotty. I was thinking aloud."

He swished the pan. "Alex claims he stumbled yesterday

144

and fell down half a flight of stairs." His tone was dispassionate.

I finished the residual flatware slowly, polishing each piece
and laying it on the soft cloth. "All the Stonehall people are
smaller than Kayla was, shorter and lighter. I don't think Barbara could have tackled her at all. Barbara is barely five feet tall
and a hundred pounds maximum."

"On the other hand, she has studied tae kwon do."

"Wonderful."

"With her bruised husband." He stuck the clean pan in the
tepid water and began sloshing out the big kettle.

"You'll need fresh hot water for the wineglasses."

"Right." He looked at me, one eyebrow raised. "Don't pa-
tronize me."

"Not," I said, "a perfect parallel."

"Few things are perfect." He rinsed the kettle.

I took it, dried it, and slammed it onto the cool end of the
Rayburn.

"Lighten up, Lark."

"Why should I, when you're doing your best to make me feel
incompetent?"

"Lower your voice." He nodded toward the other room.

Both of us listened. Dad was still talking.

I drew a long breath. "Okay, I'm a loudmouthed, interfering broad."

"Not very broad."

"Cut it out."

He poured the water from the dishpan down the drain and
began running a fresh panful. He squirted liquid soap into it and
swore when it sudsed up. So he wasn't as cool as he sounded.
"Supposing you explain what you mean by incompetent. Believe me, the thought has never crossed my mind."

"Not at the conscious level, perhaps."

"Not at any level. You have your quirks, but idiocy isn't one
of them and neither is helplessness." He stuck his right hand in
the rinse water, decided it was too cold, and tipped it out, too.

He turned on the hot water tap with a gush of steam. "It makes me uncomfortable to talk about a case that's under investigation. The response is automatic. I'm sorry if it annoys you."

"I don't like being shut out." I squinted at him through the steam.

He turned the tap off and added a judicious squirt of cold water to the rinsing pan. "Neither do I."

"What's that supposed to mean?"

He washed a wineglass and rolled it in rinse water. "This wordplay between you and Joe Kennedy. What's the deal?"

"The sergeant and I enjoy verbal oddities." I dried the first wineglass as he set two others in the rinse water.

"And that's it?"

"That's it."

He rinsed the last wineglass, dampened the sponge, and began wiping down the exposed surfaces. "All right. He's a nice enough guy, I guess."

"It's not his fault that he looks like a god," I said with great earnestness.

Jay paused, sponge raised, gave me suspicious stare, then started to laugh. "Okay, okay. No more scenes from *Othello.*"

We tidied the kitchen in fair accord and went into the living room as Dad was hanging up. Ma's workshop was going well. Dad had revived. He challenged us to a round of Scrabble and the rest of the evening passed peacefully.

I got up at six Monday morning, the day of the inquest. Jay was sound asleep, face half-buried in the pillow. I got out an exercise suit and my running shoes, dressed, and tiptoed upstairs. I started a pot of coffee, unlatched the front door, and slipped outside. Sunlight filtered through thinning mist.

I did my stretches and set out at a gentle jog. A hard run would have been unwise on the graveled surface. I jogged to the Y and headed toward Stanyon Hall. The drive curved down and looped back with a turnoff to the front door of the house.

I could see a uniformed Garda peering at me from the stone porch. I flipped my hand in a wave and followed the loop back to the Y and on up to the paved road. I didn't have the courage to run on Suicide Lane even at that hour, so I wheeled around and jogged back to the cottage. Not much of a workout. However, when I had showered and drunk a couple of mugs of coffee I did feel better. It was possible that my ill-temper the day before had been the result of a week of sitting. At home I ran on the beach almost every morning.

Jay wandered up at eight and Dad half an hour later. They went for a walk together and returned as I finished toasting the remains of the cottage loaf. I also sliced soda bread.

"There's juice and dry cereal," I announced. "I don't feel like cooking breakfast."

Neither of them complained. They didn't cook anything, though. I don't think my father can. Ma's housekeeper had made splendid breakfasts for us of all the forbidden foods. My brother, Tod, blames his hypertension squarely on Mrs. Schultz's cooking. Me, I think his problem is lack of exercise, a messy divorce, and making too much money as a stockbrocker. Not to mention the Republican Party. I'm fond of Tod, but he's a fussbudget.

I fussed that morning over what to wear. There was an ironing board, thank God. I dragged out my travel iron, hoping the lever was turned to the right voltage. It must have been. By nine-thirty I was dressed in a heather gray suit with a boring silk blouse and a pair of conservative earrings. I even wore pumps. Jay said I looked like a lawyer.

"I see by your outfit that you are a cowboy," I muttered, too dispirited for originality. In fact, Jay looked like an unemployed college professor, which was what he was going to be if he didn't fly home soon. Dad looked like a retired college professor.

"Come and show me the security alarm," Jay said.

"On the wall beside the front door. It's not very far from here to the meeting hall," I added. "Shall we walk?"

Jay shook his head. "Press."

I groaned. "I hate this."

147

The worry lines deepened around Dad's mouth. "Sgt. Kennedy assured us the coroner won't keep you on the stand very long, my dear. I'm sure you'll do splendidly."

I forced a smile. "That part will be fine. I was moaning about the reporters."

"We shall give them the slip," Dad said magnificently.

"They'll photograph me with my mouth open and my eyes crossed."

"Then we won't buy newspapers." Jay took my arm. "The alarm system?"

I showed him where it was and wrote out the code for him that would disable it when we returned. I don't know why I did that. Perhaps, at some level, I was expecting to be arrested.

Jay packed his computer into its case and put it in the hatchback of the car with his anorak draped over it for camouflage. He was taking no chances. "Ready to go?"

"When you are." I took the car keys from Jay and stuck my head back in the kitchen. "Dad?"

My father had gone downstairs for a precautionary pitstop. By the time he finally came outside and Jay had set the alarm, it was ten minutes of ten. I made a jackrabbit start and the engine died.

"Take it easy," Jay murmured from the back seat.

I clutched the wheel and tried again, pulling out with careful smoothness.

We ought to have started earlier. Cars filled the tiny parking lot and spilled out along both sides of the narrow road. I finally nosed as far onto the verge as I could go without trapping my father on the passenger side, and got out. Jay extricated himself from the back seat, took the keys, and locked up for me.

We almost made it into the hall undetected because a clump of reporters and photographers had backed Alex and Barbara Stein against a tombstone—the "yard" of the hall bled directly into the Protestant burial ground. Then Maeve spotted me from the entrance.

"Hullo, Lark!" she called in a lecture hall voice and the game was up. Two reporters and a camcorder leapt for us.

"Mrs. Dodge," one of them shouted, shoving a microphone at me, "what was your sensation when . . ."

My father drew himself up to his full height. "Good morning. We shall have no comment until after the coroner has adjourned the inquest." He, too, can produce a lecture hall boom.

Beside me, Jay chuckled. He took my arm and shoved me toward Maeve. She had saved seats for us, she murmured, leading us rapidly down a short hallway decorated with ancient bulletins and Sunday school art so old it was curling at the edges.

The coroner sat at an ordinary folding table at the front of the small auditorium. He was thumbing through a thick printout, and the green, white, and orange flag of the republic drooped at his elbow. A box had been improvised for the jury. I saw a blur of tweedy suits.

Maeve led us to seats on the far aisle, two rows from the front. The hall was packed and everyone watched us. Much whispering. I felt my ears burn and I kept my eyes on the floor. We sat without major upheavals, I on the aisle because I would have to get out to testify.

The coroner whisked through the opening ceremonies and called Joe Kennedy. Joe was in uniform. Most of his testimony eluded me. It sounded dull and official. I was trying to remember what I had seen and done in what order.

The coroner called the police doctor. More officialese, this time confounded with doctor talk. There were no surprises. Slade Wheeler had suffered from fatty degeneration of the arteries. He died as a result of manual compression of the carotid arteries in the neck. The compression had cut off the supply of blood to the brain. What the medical examiner actually said was "vagal inhibition." He meant a choke hold.

The time of death lay between 2200 hours Easter night and six the next morning. The doctor was apologetic about his vagueness, but it had been cold. He believed that the body had been moved at least twice after death, once to the downstairs hall of the cottage and, some hours later, to the potting shed.

Slade Wheeler had been killed outdoors, very probably in Stanyon Woods, and conveyed to the cottage on a cart of some kind. The cart had not been found but garden loam and wood fibres caught in the fabric of his fatigues suggested a gardener's large wheelbarrow. The Stanyon gardeners had left their equipment by the cottage over Easter weekend. The crime laboratory was studying the possibility that one of their barrows had been used.

Postmortem bruising suggested manhandling consistent with Wheeler being carried downstairs and, later, to the shed. The medical examiner could not say how many people had been involved in transporting the corpse. Wheeler had been a large man.

The coroner was not happy with the examiner's vagueness as to the time of death and there was a fairly sharp interchange between them, but the doctor held firm. He would not narrow the time frame. When the coroner dismissed him, he rose and made his way past me to the back of the hall. He was composed but a bit flushed.

"Call Thomas Tierney!"

I jumped. Beside me, Jay sat up straight. The hall buzzed. Everybody craned as Toss made his way from the back of the room to be sworn in.

Swearing in. Oh, God. I stole a sideways look at my father, who sat on Jay's left. Quakers do not swear. They affirm. Should I refuse to take an oath?

I listened through a haze of pointless anxiety as Toss swore to tell the truth. I was not, after all, a Quaker. I had no reason to avoid taking an oath, and no desire to create an unnecessary sidebar for the press, either. My mind had engaged in irrelevance in order to avoid focusing on the here and now.

Why had they called Toss?

"Mr. Tierney, I believe you were the first to discover the body of the deceased Slade Wheeler," the coroner said, as if on

150

cue. "Will you tell us why you came to the house known as Bedrock Cottage?"

Toss was red in the face. He mumbled and had to be prompted to speak louder. *Don't mumble*, I reminded myself. He was explaining about the unfinished shed and our imminent arrival. When he described the body, it sounded as if it was exactly as I had found it. The red paint on Wheeler's forehead caused a burst of whispering. The coroner scowled at the crowd and resumed his questioning.

"He was stiff, your worship," Toss was saying. "Still and cold as a dead flounder. And he looked as if somebody laid him out. His eyes was closed, and the paint had run down over the eyelids. I thought 'twas fresh blood. 'Twas tacky, like blood. It give me a turn, your worship."

"I am not a judge," said the coroner. "It's not necessary to address me in that manner."

"Aye, sorry, your . . . sir."

"Did you report the presence of Mr. Wheeler's corpse to the Gardai, Mr. Tierney?"

"No, sir." Toss's eyes shifted but he spoke in a voice loud enough to be heard over the murmurs of the audience.

"Did you notify your employers at Stanyon Hall?"

"No, sir. 'Tis this way, your worship, there's me son, Tommy . . ." And he went on to outline his reasons for fearing Tommy would be suspected of the killing.

The coroner, who was in his sixties and looked as if he suffered from low blood sugar, listened to Toss's chronicle impassively, though the audience was leaning forward with avid interest. He rebuked Toss—Toss looked as repentant as a sanctified and pious bawd—and let him go. Then he called me.

I gulped and stood up. Somehow I made it to the witness chair, which looked as if it had been borrowed from a very old office. I placed my hand on the Bible and mumbled the oath. Then I sat. The chair creaked.

The coroner seemed inordinately interested in how I came to be at the cottage. He took me, stage by stage, from the airport in Portland to Dublin Airport, to the car-rental desk, and down the Eastlink. I tried to keep my answers brief and clear. No, I had not hired the cottage, my father had. I identified Dad by name and the coroner made a note.

"And how did you come to enter the potting shed, Mrs. Dodge?"

Why had I looked into the shed? My mind went blank. My throat was dry. I cleared it. "I . . . er, it was ordinary curiosity. The door was ajar. When I tried to push it open, it, er, struck the body. I peered around to see what was blocking the entrance and I found, er, the deceased."

"Did you disturb the body in any way, Mrs. Dodge?"

"I, er, I touched the neck to see if there was a pulse."

"Did you, indeed. Why?"

"I thought perhaps he had fainted or suffered a heart attack. I thought I might have to give CPR."

"I beg your pardon?"

"Er, cardiopulmonary resuscitation."

He stared at me and a rumble in the hall underlined his apparent surprise. "Are you medically trained, then?"

"I've taken CPR courses three times over the years." I was not going to explain that when I coached women's basketball at Monte Junior College the school required all the coaches to have CPR training.

"And have you used this emergency procedure?"

"Yes, but I didn't use it on Slade Wheeler," I said bluntly. "He was quite dead, as Mr. Tierney said. Cold and still stiff, as far as I could tell. I didn't try to move him but I did touch his forehead." I raised my right hand and touched the center of my brow. "The mark looked too red and shiny to be blood, and it was definitely dry when I touched it."

The coroner's eyebrows shot up. Murmurs from the audience. The seats nearest the exit had been reserved for the press and I could see reporters scribbling away. The camcorder had not been allowed into the auditorium.

"Dry," the coroner repeated. "Thank you. That is a useful

observation, taken with Mr. Tierney's testimony. You were remarkably cool and collected, Mrs. Dodge."

I said, "I was horrified. Still, I had to be sure he couldn't be revived. And the paint puzzled me. It looked . . . theatrical."

Several gasps from the crowd.

"Ah." The coroner was regarding me thoughtfully. "You're a woman, Mrs. Dodge. Did you feel no inclination to scream or faint?"

I saw the drift of his questions but remembered in time that I was in a different culture. The coroner didn't intend to be insulting. I said carefully, "I was upset, of course, but my father was resting within earshot. He suffered a stroke last summer." I glanced at Dad and he gave me a small smile. "He has made an excellent recovery. Still, I didn't want to startle him. And I, er, don't make a habit of screaming. When I was sure Mr. Wheeler was dead, I reentered the house, went upstairs, and called the Killaveen Garda station at once."

"You didn't dial 999?"

I drew a breath. "The number of the Garda station was on a list beside the telephone because of the cottage's security alarm system. People are always setting off their own alarms by accident. If they call the station immediately they can save the police an unnecessary trip."

"You seem very knowledgeable."

"The alarm system was explained in the detailed printout my father received from Mr. and Mrs. Stein when he hired the cottage from them. He had just read me the printout, so I knew about the Killaveen station. Sgt. Kennedy responded and I told him what I had found in the shed. I then called Mrs. Stein who very kindly came to the cottage at once. Sgt. Kennedy arrived shortly afterwards and I showed him the body."

"That's very clear. Did you know the deceased, Slade Wheeler?" He shot the question at me out of a clear blue sky.

"No." I clamped my mouth shut. I was explaining too much.

The coroner stared at me over the top of his glasses, then nodded. "Very well. You are to be commended for your coolness

153

in an emergency, Mrs. Dodge." He made a point of thanking me for public-spirited behavior, glared at Toss to drive the point home, and let me go.

Relief left me a little dizzy but I found my way back to my seat. Jay took my hand and gave it a squeeze. The coroner was calling Chief Detective Inspector Mahon.

Like Joe, Mahon spoke officialese. He explained briefly that Kayla Wheeler's murder had complicated the questions raised by her brother's death, that Kayla's death removed any thought that the first death might have been an accident followed by a coverup attempt. He announced that the Gardai were pursuing the investigation as a case of murder against person or persons unknown.

"Then you request that I adjourn this inquest?"

"I do, sir." Mahon's eyes were shadowed with sleeplessness and he looked edgy, but his voice was calm.

The coroner scrutinized the jury. The mostly male faces seemed mildly disappointed. He dismissed them, adjourned the session, and stood to go, clutching the printout. Mahon stood and stretched, wriggling his shoulders. The crowd rose, milling. Maeve reached over to me and patted my hand. "Bravo!"

"Thanks," I muttered. "I suppose there's no way out the back."

She leaned across Dad and Jay. "I've parked my van on the far side of the old church. Wait a few minutes until the door over there is clear and I'll drive the three of you home."

She was as good as her word. She whisked us out past the ruined church to the van. Toss Tierney's daffodil-yellow vehicle was parked beside hers. As we approached, a faded woman in a good wool coat got out and greeted Maeve.

Maeve said, "Is he home yet, Teresa?"

"Tonight, God willing." She turned to us. "You'll be the Dodges, then, and Professor Dailey. I'm Teresa Tierney, Toss's wife. I must thank you for talking sense into Toss." She blinked and gave a watery smile. "And now my Tommy's coming home, too."

We shook hands and Dad murmured something sympathetic.

"Ah, you're that kind," she said in her soft, lilting voice, "and your poor daughter, having to speak out like that in front of all them reporters." She turned to Jay. "Mr. Dodge, thank you. 'Twas grand advice. Toss swears by you. And Mrs. Dodge." She shook my hand and gave me a look that was warm with compassion. "Ah, the creature."

We escaped with Teresa Tierney's blessings raining down on us. Maeve jolted the van through the departing crowd rather like a tank driver edging through a friendly infantry column. I spotted Alex and Barbara in a clot of reporters.

Maeve zipped down Suicide Lane and took the Stanyon turnoff.

"Hell, I forgot my computer," Jay muttered. "It's in the Toyota."

"Never mind. Walk up to the church in an hour and it'll be there waiting for you. That lot won't hang about long." She steered through the rhododendron arch and the cottage came into view. "Bloody hell."

A patrol car sat on the gravel by the front door. As we neared, we could hear the alarm sounding.

11 ～

What's the news, what's the news, O me bold chevalier . . .
—Irish folk song

MAEVE ROLLED DOWN her window. The uniformed Garda, a fresh-faced kid who looked sixteen and was probably twenty-five, walked over to the van. She raised her voice over the raucous alarm bell. "Hullo, Declan. What's the trouble?"

He bent down, the better to be heard, and gave her a two-fingered salute. "I don't know yet, Miss Butler. I just got here. The front door was ajar. When the alarm lit up at the station, I hopped in the car and called for the lads at Stanyon. They'll be here in a pig's wink."

Jay got out and I followed. Dad stayed in the van. The bell continued to clang. Jay introduced himself to the constable, whose surname was Byrne, and they shook hands.

The Garda touched his visor when Jay said my name. He turned back to Jay. "D'ye see, sir, the burglar may still be inside."

"And you want backup? I don't blame you." Jay approached the front door from the side, walking with care along the grassy edge of the gravel. He didn't step up onto the small stone porch or touch the door handle, but he did peer through the window. "No sign of movement. Have you gone down to the back door?"

"No, then. Was it locked?"

"We locked both outside doors, checked the windows, and set the alarm before we left for the inquest."

The constable nodded. "Right, sir. I'll just go in . . . Ah, that'll be the boys from the Hall."

A marked car approached rather too rapidly, slewing on the gravel, and pulled off onto the turf on the far side of the van. The light was revolving. It stopped, the door opened, and Joe Kennedy emerged. He was still in uniform.

Byrne stiffened to attention. I thought he looked dismayed.

Joe gave Jay and me a nod and took Constable Byrne aside for a low-voiced consultation.

The alarm bell was driving me nuts. I tugged Jay's arm. "Have you got the code?"

He drew the slip of paper from the breast pocket of his jacket. "Yes, but I can't—"

Joe came over to us. "It's a fine day for the guards. The lad took off in such a flurry he forgot to bring the keys and the code."

Jay's mouth eased in a smile. He flapped the paper. "Lark wrote it down for me."

"What it is to have foresight." Joe didn't return the smile. I suppose he was embarrassed for his subordinate whose ears were bright red.

Jay said, "I think there's a shoe print on the porch."

"Let's hope it's not Declan's. He churned the gravel in front of the door with his great heavy boots. At least he didn't dash in over the evidence and thrust himself into the villain's arms."

I forebore to mention that Byrne had been ready to dash into the cottage when we arrived. It seemed unkind. "The alarm."

"In a minute, missus. I think our bird has flown, but I'd feel easier if you got into the van."

I opened my mouth to protest, closed it, and crawled back inside the van. To my surprise, Jay followed me.

Joe was giving Maeve directions. I could tell from the set of her jaw that she was not happy. She revved the engine and Joe stepped away.

Dad said, "What's going on?"

I patted his hand.

"They think the burglar may still be in the cottage," Jay said.

I kept my tone light. "Maybe it's not a burglar at all. Maybe it's an overzealous reporter looking for color."

"Lovely thought." Maeve shifted gears and began to back the van along the lane. When she had cleared Joe's car, she pulled around onto the turf behind it and set the brake.

The alarm bell continued its maddening clangor. It was so loud I didn't notice the other patrol car approaching from Stanyon until it passed us. It drew up in front of Joe's car. Two uniformed Gardai jumped out, and Joe went to meet them.

Dad was grumbling under his breath. Maeve turned around. "I daresay they'll take hours sorting this." Her observation was directed at Jay.

"Could be."

"It's noon. I've a tutoring session in Dublin at half three." Jay meditated.

I dug in my purse and found my keys. "Why don't I walk back to the road and get the car? Then we can sit in it, or drive to Arklow for lunch, and let Maeve go about her business."

I expected Jay to offer to go for the car himself, but he just nodded, "One of us should retrieve the Toyota. I'm worried about my computer."

One of us. I reached past him and turned the handle. The door slid back. I crawled over his knees and got out, bumping my handbag across his lap. "See you in ten minutes."

Dad said, "I'll come with you, Lark."

"Thanks . . ." I started to say it wasn't necessary, then bit the words back. Why shouldn't my father come with me? As I waited for him, I glanced at the Gardai. They were still conferring and had apparently not noticed my emergence. I gave Dad my hand as he stepped down. He straightened, grimacing slightly.

"Okay?"

He nodded. "I need to stretch my legs."

Jay stuck his head out. "Wait a minute, Lark. Do you have the key to the downstairs door on that keychain?"

"Yes."

"Leave it with me. Kennedy may decide to enter the house there."

I found the right key, removed it and handed it to him.

"Take care," he said, his eyes on the cluster of uniformed men.

I turned to Maeve who was craning around, watching us. "I'll be back in ten minutes. Don't let Jay do anything foolish."

She looked startled. He ignored the comment. I don't think he heard it.

I hate hiking in pumps. The gravel felt rough through my thin soles and I kept thinking I was going to twist an ankle. Dad gave me his arm. Pumps were probably invented by a man who wanted women to cling. We walked slowly. The policemen must have seen us by then but they didn't call us back. The alarm continued to shrill.

Before we reached the rhododendron arch I turned around and looked at the cottage. Jay had got out of the van and was huddling with the uniforms.

Dad said, "I hope we won't have to leave the cottage."

That was a gruesome thought. "We could move to Ballymann House."

"True, or to a hotel."

"Do you want to?"

"No."

I didn't either, though I didn't like the feeling of vulnerability the burglary inspired. And Joe's comments about the sinister associations with the woods echoed in my memory.

We had gained the road. There was no traffic, though a couple of cars remained in the church lot. I could see two little girls in school uniforms peering through the back window of the Toyota.

They fell into giggles as we approached.

"Good morning, ladies," said my father.

The giggles intensified.

"Eh, missus, there's a wee corpus in the boot." The speaker, a pink-faced dumpling with a tangle of orange curls, held her hands out, measuring the dimensions of the supposed body.

I unlocked the hatchback and removed the anorak. Jay's computer lay there in its soft-sided nylon case. "It's only a suitcase," I announced in tones of disappointment.

The girls seemed disappointed, too, but Dad gave each of them a pound coin for guarding the car, and they bounced off looking pleased with themselves.

"Playing hooky," I murmured.

Dad had squeezed in the passenger side. He fastened his seat belt. "A natural curiosity. Still, one could wish their fantasies were less ghoulish."

I started the engine and, when no cars materialized in either direction, made a reverse turn. A lorry roared past in the direction of Killaveen. I swear it scraped the side mirror.

When we reached the Y, I looked down at Stanyon. The Steins' Mercedes stood in front of the house, and a knot of women on the veranda suggested the data processors were taking a smoke break. A regular working day.

I rolled down the window as we approached the rhododendron arch. "They've shut off the alarm." The silence reverberated. Maeve's van was still parked behind Joe's car. A police van, doors open, nosed onto the turf.

"Looks like a convention of cops," I muttered. "That must be the evidence team from Stanyon." As I spoke, one of the men approached the tiny front porch and began taking photographs. He was wearing paper booties over his shoes. Evidence crews wear the shoe protectors to avoid introducing foreign material to the scene of a crime.

I didn't want to box everyone in so I pulled onto the turf on the other side of the lane. Joe stood by the police van, conferring with the other plainclothes technician. He flipped his hand our direction and went on talking. I saw no sign of Jay or the other Gardai. As I unhooked the seat belt and opened the door to get out, though, Constable Byrne trudged up the slope from the potting shed. The discouraged set of his shoulders suggested he was thinking of his sins.

Dad said, "I'll wait here."

"Okay." I walked over to Maeve and tapped on the glass. She rolled her window down.

"What's happening?"

"Damnall. Your husband's in the house. There was no sign of entry downstairs, so Joe sent Jay and Declan in down there." She grinned. "The others headed off to the woods. Noses to the ground like a pair of beagles."

"When did the alarm stop?"

"Thirty seconds ago. My ears are still ringing." She brooded, eyes straight ahead. "Time for me to head north."

"Uh, before you go, Maeve, I have a couple of questions."

She blinked at me as if I had startled her. Perhaps her mind had strayed to the upcoming tutorial—or to Joe Kennedy.

"What do I do with the garbage?"

She blinked again.

I sifted through my vocabulary. "The trash. Rubbish. Litter. It's mounting up." My voice trailed. "I suppose I ought to ask Barbara Stein."

"I daresay." She sounded mildly indignant, as if mentioning garbage was in poor taste.

I felt my cheeks flush. Perhaps I had violated a taboo. "Sorry," I muttered.

"You said you had several questions."

I cleared my throat. "Uh, yes. The woods. Has anyone done an archaeological survey of Stanyon Woods?"

She stared, then began to laugh.

I felt my temper rise and straightened to walk away, but she reached out the window to touch my shoulder.

"Free association, right?"

"I beg your pardon," I said stiffly.

"It's okay. Most archaeological digs involve sifting through ancient middens."

"Rubbish is rubbish," I muttered.

"Why do you ask?"

"I saw what I thought was an incised or inscribed stone in the woods." I wasn't sure of the correct term.

The laughter died from her face. "Do you say?"

I described the double spiral design.

She gave a low whistle. "I've never heard of megalithic remains on the estate, but that doesn't mean anything. If the OPW did an early survey there will be records. Where did you see the stone?"

I confessed my disorientation.

"Pity. Roughly in the middle of the woods?"

"That's my guess. There's a hill or mound. I walked upwards. The stone lay in a small glade."

"Sounds promising. I'll look it up, shall I?"

"If it's not too much trouble. It's nothing to do with this business." I waved a vague arm in the direction of the Gardai, who were now doing things in the porch area. "I'm just curious."

"So am I." She started her engine. "I'll get onto it straightaway, and I'll ring you in a day or so to report."

"Thanks." I stepped away from the van as she backed up. She made a neat reverse and chugged off along the lane.

I returned to the Toyota and slipped into the driver's seat.

Dad said, "Where's Jay?"

"In the cottage, according to Maeve. Shall we drive to Arklow for lunch?"

"Without Jay?" He sounded reproachful.

I drew a breath to point out that my spouse could take care of himself, and that he'd probably be playing games with the evidence crew for several hours, when Jay walked up the flagstone steps beside the cottage. He was carrying a crumpled pair of paper booties in one hand and light polythene gloves in the other—very professional. I had the feeling Constable Byrne had been left outside on sentry duty while Jay went in alone to silence the alarm and survey the damage. What if the burglar had still been inside? I felt my temper heat up. The damn fool.

Jay came over to the car and bent down to me.

I said, through my teeth, "Your computer's safe. How's the house?"

He shrugged. "There's a mess in the living room. I think the alarm rattled the burglar."

I pointed forward across the steering wheel. "That lot will be at it for a while. Shall I drive Dad to Arklow for lunch?"

"Hang on a minute and I'll come with you. I need to say a word to Kennedy."

Jay went over and handed one of the technicians the gloves and the crumpled booties. By the time I had got out and flipped the seat forward so he could climb in, he was coming back to the car. I noticed that he walked on the gravel this time instead of the turf. The evidence crew must have worked fast. Joe Kennedy gave a casual wave and ducked in through the front door.

The drive to Arklow took fifteen mostly silent minutes. I was letting my temper cool. I don't know why the men didn't talk.

I had had my eye on a riverside pub for several days. The car park, a municipal lot on two levels, required a turn across traffic in the High Street, but I negotiated it, parked, and led the two men down to the river. It was too damp and chilly to sit outside.

Our entry caused a momentary lull in the lunch-hour roar but we found a table free in one corner of the saloon bar. Dad and I occupied it and Jay went off for beer. He returned with two pints, a glass of Bordeaux, and a menu card. By that time the other customers had turned back to their own pints and their conversations.

Dad lifted the glass of wine and sipped. "Not bad."

"Cheers." Jay sat and took a large swallow. "Ah, Murphy's. Good stuff."

I sipped and read the carte. Lots of chips. "I'll have the ploughman's lunch."

"Is that cheese?" Jay licked foam from his upper lip.

"Cheese, bread, pickled onion, and chutney, usually. And they throw in a leaf of lettuce for decoration."

"I'll stick to hamburger."

"Better you than me." Foreign hamburgers incline toward eccentricity. I once ate one in England that I swear was ground ham. Whereas local cheese is almost always trustworthy and sometimes interesting.

"Fish and chips," Dad said.

I stood up. "I'll get it."

The bartender took my order on a lined pad. "Where are yez? Ah, over there. I'll bring it when the chips is done." He rang up the order.

I thanked him and paid.

He handed me my heavy change. "You're visitors then?"

"From the States."

"Are you enjoying your holiday?"

"It's grand," I said politely. Clearly he hadn't recognized me, which meant he hadn't attended the inquest. I was glad I'd decided to brave the Arklow traffic instead of driving to Killaveen. Blessed anonymity. When the evening news rolled around we would be the cynosure of Arklow eyes, too. I decided I'd better cook dinner at the cottage.

Dad had vanished by the time I returned from the bar.

"He went to find the gents," Jay explained. "There's a problem, Lark. The burglar trashed his notes."

"Dad's?" My voice squeaked with dismay. I took a gulp of beer. "Have you told him?"

"No. There's paper all over the living room and some of the photocopies were ripped up."

"Vandalism?"

"No."

"Poor Dad . . ." I broke off as my father drifted back from the loo. He paused to peer at a photograph on the wall near the bar, said a word to the bartender, then looked at us and smiled.

Jay said, "I'll break the news."

Dad took it quietly. "I see," he murmured, downcast.

I said, "There's bound to be a stationer's somewhere in Arklow. I'll buy a bunch of Scotch tape and we can all work on reconstructing the torn bits."

He sighed and sipped his Bordeaux. "The photocopies contain records of the Dublin Meeting. I was working on 1845."

"Better get folders, too," Jay said.

I dug in my handbag for a pen and pad. "And scissors. I haven't seen scissors in the cottage, have either of you?"

They shook their heads.

When the bartender arrived with our food, Jay asked him whether there was a photocopying facility nearby. After some virtuoso paraphrasing on my part, the man's face brightened and he directed us to an establishment in the High Street.

There we laid in enough folders, labels, and tape dispensers to start a small business, and Dad cheered up. When we got back to the cottage, the evidence van had left. Joe Kennedy was conferring with the three uniforms. The two men from Stanyon had searched the woods without result, he told us, after he had sent them and Constable Byrne off in their respective patrol cars. Joe led us into the cottage.

"I'd like the three of you to take another look at what's missing."

"Maybe nothing's missing." Jay laid his computer on the kitchen table and gave it a pat. "I think that was the target."

Joe raised his eyebrows.

"They usually aim for electronics, don't they?" Jay said mildly.

"Ordinary B and E, yes. If this was ordinary."

Jay said, "The time of the inquest was well-known and a watcher could have spotted the Toyota leaving."

My anxiety level went down a couple of notches. "Like funerals?"

Jay nodded. Canny burglars have been known to read the obits and time their break-ins by scheduled funerals. The thought reassured me, oddly enough. They—he, whatever—had waited until we left together. That made him sound less like a maddened killer on the loose and more like a dispassionate professional. However, the dispassionate professional had not expected the burglar alarm to be set. Otherwise, when he didn't spot the computer or find a television or a boombox, he would have gone downstairs, rifled our bedrooms, and made a swift exit through the downstairs door.

Dad listened to our chatter, then slipped out to the living room. I heard him draw a sharp breath, and went in to him. My complacence evaporated. The conversation corner near the fireplace was strewn with loose papers, but the desk area looked as if it had been touched by a tornado of pure spite.

Dad knelt and started gathering the torn photocopies.

I had the paraphernalia from the stationer's under my arm. I knelt beside him and pulled out the packet of folders. "Shall we do this methodically?"

He shot me a grateful look and handed me a sheaf of papers. They had been ripped in half. "That's the one I was working on."

"Your man was wearing gloves," Kennedy observed from the door arch.

"Good thing, too," Jay added. "Otherwise everything would be dusted with fingerprint powder." He slid past the sergeant and joined us on the floor. "Any shoe prints in here?"

Kennedy said, "He was wearing trainers."

"Sneakers," I translated.

"Sneakers and gloves," Jay mused, sorting a ripped article.

"And carrying a key to the cottage," Joe said drily.

Dad stared up at him. "A key?"

"There's no sign of forced entry. . . ."

"And we definitely locked up," Jay said. He sounded as if he were repeating an assertion. Well, we had locked the doors.

I squirmed to a more comfortable position on the floorboards. The idea of that loose key wandering around raised my level of discomfort again. I wondered whether we ought to call in a locksmith.

Kennedy said abruptly, "I shall have a word with Tommy

Tierney when he flits home tonight, like a wee pigeon to the coop. His da had a key. Toss swears the lad never touched it, but Toss lies to us as a matter of habit. Tommy could have made a wax impression and had Toss's key duplicated."

"The same might be said of the key at Stanyon," I murmured.

"True for you."

Silence weighted the air.

Joe heaved a sigh. "May I ask you to leave the papers for a minute or two, Mrs. Dodge? Look about you and see if anything's been taken from this room."

I creaked to my feet. Joints seizing up. I was definitely going to have to return to my daily run.

My survey of the room revealed nothing obvious missing. To tell the truth, I hadn't paid much attention to the decor of the living room. We had been living in the bedrooms and kitchen. The burglar could well have made off with a doodad or two without my knowing it.

When I had reassured Joe that I'd found nothing missing, he left. Dad and Jay and I worked in companionable silence for the next hour, and we made progress. I sat my father down at the kitchen table with a cup of hot tea and one of the tape dispensers, and set him to putting the photocopies back together. Jay and I gathered loose papers.

I was puzzling over a set of notes in Dad's crabbed hand when the phone rang. It was Barbara Stein. She sounded distraught and she didn't dally for small talk. She wanted to speak to my father.

I carried the phone in to Dad, kicking the long cord aside. "For you. It's Barbara."

He nodded and murmured hello into the receiver. I went back to helping Jay. We were trying to flatten the papers that had been wadded and sort them by subject.

Dad brought the phone back and laid it carefully on the desk. "Barbara wants us to come for cocktails."

I stared at him. "They're having a happy hour?"

167

He gave me a wan smile. "Not exactly—more like an emergency meeting. Barbara thinks Mahon will arrest Alex tomorrow and she wants my advice." Perhaps he sensed that I was about to protest because he said wearily, "I told her I'd come."

"We'll come with you." Jay didn't pause to consult me. "Mahon may know something that Kennedy doesn't, and they'll want to interrogate Alex again, in any case, but I don't think an arrest is likely at this point."

Dad ran a hand over his face. "Then reassure them, by all means. I believe I'd better take a nap before we go."

He took the words right out of my mouth.

12 ༀ

A man of words and not of deeds
Is like a garden full of weeds

—Children's song

STANYON HALL WAS a compound of memory and current horror. My mental picture of Kayla descending the long stairway was so vivid I half expected her to appear above us as we entered the foyer.

Barbara had met us on the porch. When Dad gave her a hug, she began crying. He soothed and patted, which he does very well, and she recovered her composure almost at once. Even so, her dread shook the air.

She led us again to the sitting room. Tracy Aspin and Liam McDiarmuid stood off in one corner, talking low-voiced, and Mike Novak hovered next to Alex at the drinks trolley. Their greetings were subdued, and, having poured for us, Alex took my father aside for a mournful conference. Barbara deserted us without apology to join Dad and her husband.

Jay and Mike sipped beer and watched each other.

I checked an impulse to walk over and throw the window open. Without Kayla's cigarettes, there was no reason to open it, nor was the room warm, but the atmosphere was thick with anxiety.

"You did a star turn at the inquest." Mike took a morose gulp of beer.

My wine tasted sour. "Glad you enjoyed it."

"Rumor, dear lady. I didn't attend. After three hours of interrogation at the crack of dawn, I was too squeamish to face the details of an autopsy, even Slade Wheeler's." He knocked back the rest of his beer and poured himself another from a tall brown bottle. "Besides, somebody had to hold down the fort with cops crawling all over the second floor. The data processors were set to mutiny, and that baroque disk has to go to the distributor next week."

Tracy drifted over, Liam at her elbow. "Are you still griping about missing the inquest, Mike? I volunteered to stay here and supervise, remember?"

"*I* didn't," Liam said with relish. "I wanted to see Toss Tierney with the egg fresh on his beaming face."

Jay chuckled. "Toss was a pillar of rectitude."

Liam's mouth twisted. " 'Yes, your worship, thank you, your worship.' Jaysus, the shuffler."

"My money's still on Toss," Mike said.

"And wee Tommy, the darling twister." Liam was drinking Perrier. He raised the green bottle in mock salute.

"According to my landlord, Toss has connections." Tracy sounded tipsy.

Silence thickened. No one was going to comment on Toss's republican associations. That was the second spring of the IRA's eighteen-month truce, when there was still hope for peace in the north. Everyone seemed to be tiptoeing around republican sensibilities. Except clumsy Americans like Tracy.

Like me. I decided to bumble, too. "Maeve Butler said the Irregulars used Stanyon Woods as an ammo dump during the Civil War. I'm not sure who the Irregulars . . ."

"A Free State term for de Valera's boys," Liam interrupted. "That's nonsense, though. Stanyon was an Orange stronghold."

"I took a walk in the woods," I ventured.

Liam stiffened. So did Jay.

"I found blotches of red paint here and there, but I didn't see anything that looked like a storage facility." I decided not to mention the incised stone.

"You went into the woods?" Mike gave an elaborate shiver. "You are one ballsy woman. I'd sooner jump into the Avoca at high tide with bricks in my britches. Slade's playmates bragged about setting traps for each other in the woods."

"Lark is a little impulsive," said my loyal spouse. The mildness of his voice warned me he was going to rake me over the coals at the first opportunity. I hadn't got around to mentioning my adventure in the woods to him.

I shut up, though I was still curious. Jay asked Mike a question about the baroque disk, and general conversation flowed.

I turned Liam's remark over in my mind. So the Irregulars were die-hard republicans, ancestors of the present IRA. But I had thought the Orange faction was out of the picture by the time of the Civil War, at least in the south. What better place for a cache of arms than an abandoned enemy stronghold? Liam's grandfather was a staunch republican, though, so he ought to know.

"How can the two of you be so damn passive?" Barbara's voice rang sharp. She stomped to the drinks trolley and refilled her wineglass. My father and Alex, glum-faced, trailed after her.

Tracy wound down a technical comment on the disk. Mike and Liam moved aside to make room for Alex. I gave him a tentative smile which he apparently didn't see. His eyes were dark with worry.

Dad held out his glass and Barbara poured. "About half, thanks. You did ask my advice, Barbara, and you know I'm the last man on earth to advise anyone to fight."

Barbara was not about to be jollied. "I seem to remember a lecture on the perils of passivity. It had to do with the Holocaust."

Dad said gently, "It had to do with the uprising in the Warsaw Ghetto—with the dignity of resistance."

Tears glinted in Barbara's eyes. "And when those Nazis come

171

for Alex, I suppose you want him to go with them like a meek sheep."

"The Gardai are not Nazis," Alex said. "You're hysterical."

She turned on him. "Thanks a lot. I'm not hysterical, Alex, but you damn betcha I'm emotional. We can't afford to have you hauled off on a false charge. The company needs you. I need you." Her mouth quivered. "Mahon has stopped looking. He's found his scapegoat. You have to do something. Hire a detective."

As with one mind everyone, including Dad, looked at Jay. His ears turned red. After a moment, he said, "What makes you think Mahon has it in for your husband, Barbara?"

"We have a trade show in Brussels Saturday. He told Alex not to leave the country. And he made Alex strip naked and they photographed his bruises. Is that good enough?"

Jay said mildly, "It's a little extreme, though I imagine Mahon had a warrant."

"So?"

"Does it occur to you that the photos may eliminate Alex as a suspect? He fell downstairs. It may be that Mahon's looking for a different pattern of bruising."

"A bruise is a bruise," Barbara muttered but she calmed down a little.

Jay said, "What did Mahon say about the burglary?"

"What burglary?"

Jay looked at Dad. "You didn't mention it?"

Dad shook his head. "I didn't talk to Barbara very long this afternoon—"

"And couldn't get a word in edgewise when you did," Alex interposed, acid. "Was there a break-in at the cottage?"

I said, "During the inquest. Or just as it was ending."

The Stonehall people stared. Mike said, "No shit."

I went on, "We hung around at the church hall for a while after the inquest, trying to evade the press and talking to Teresa Tierney. By the time Maeve drove us to the cottage, the alarm was ringing and a constable had driven over from Killaveen."

172

Jay gazed deep into his glass of dark ale. "It would be interesting to know exactly when the call came in. If it was before the inquest adjourned, then anyone who attended would be eliminated from the list of possible burglars."

Mike groaned and Tracy punched his arm, grinning.

"You said it was a professional," I protested.

"Maybe it was. Probably it was, but it can't hurt to check the timing."

I began calculating. "It's ten minutes, tops, from Killaveen to the cottage, and Byrne was driving a patrol car."

Jay looked at the Steins. "How long did the reporters keep you after the inquest?"

Alex stared.

Barbara's eyes gleamed with sudden hope. "Hours. Most of the crowd was gone by the time we escaped. Alex, go call that bastard. . . ."

Jay said, "I imagine Mahon will ask all of you where you were. Novak, you were here. Did you notice when the two uniformed men left?"

Mike shook his head. "I was working right up to the time Alex and Barbara came back. In my office." He sounded irritable.

"The crime-scene technicians from Stanyon also got the call. They came along maybe half an hour later and brought their gear. There must have been a lot of commotion when they left the house."

"I didn't notice." Mike's jaw set. The wispy beard quivered.

Jay sighed.

Tracy wriggled. "I wish I'd come here directly. I didn't, though. I could see those reporters had Alex and Barbara trapped. It was obvious our staff meeting would be delayed, so I drove to my flat for a sandwich. It was almost lunchtime."

Liam said, "I cut out whilst Mahon was on the stand. Went for a walk."

"Guilty!" Tracy grinned at him.

He cocked his hand like a pistol and cracked his thumb joint.

"Ew," Tracy said. "That's gross."

Everyone laughed and the tension eased. Barbara was eyeing Jay with unabashed admiration. She was going to try to hire him. I sought to distract her. "Barbara, I have a small domestic question. I hate to raise it under the present melancholy circumstances, but what do I do with the garbage from my kitchen? It's rapidly approaching critical mass."

Barbara blinked. "Uh, there's a Dumpster behind the house, Stanyon, I mean. You can use that. They collect on Wednesdays."

"Wonderful." It was nice to have one clear answer in a sea of questions.

"If the cops haven't cordoned it off. They're still searching for the garotte, whatever it was." Gloom darkened her intense features once more. "They've put crime-scene tape across the corridor Kayla's room is in and stationed a uniformed guard outside her door. My housekeeper's having kittens."

"Has the chef quit?"

Her mouth relaxed in a genuine smile. "No, he thrives on the drama, says it inspires him."

"He must be a character."

Alex said, "Murtagh's at least as flamboyant as Paul Prudhomme. We're doing a cooking disk with him."

What else? I was willing to lay odds the disk had been Alex's idea. He was a regular fountain of creative thought. *Why* had they needed Slade Wheeler? I opened my mouth to ask, but Barbara beat me to the punch.

"I wish to hell we'd never met Slade."

"Better for him if you hadn't," Jay observed.

Barbara reddened. Dad made a clucking sound.

"Why did you hire him?" I watched Barbara over the rim of my glass.

"We didn't hire him, exactly," Alex said. "He was looking for an investment. Slade designed a game, Battlecock, that earned him a nice chunk of cash. He was interested in developing CDs."

"And in hunting around for a floundering company he could take over," Mike said sourly. When the Steins protested, he went on, with some heat, "All right, so he didn't have a controlling interest. Still, he invested a bunch and you agreed to let him handle the fiscal management. To bully the staff."

"That's not fair!" Alex protested. "We were losing money. We needed cost controls."

"I thought Wheeler was supposed to be an idea man," I said. Barbara made a face and Tracy groaned.

Mike said, "The only idea that crossed that sucker's mind was the bottom line."

"That's not fair," Alex repeated. It seemed to be his tune. "He did a couple of games for us."

"Bo-oring," Tracy drawled.

Alex said, with great earnestness, "Slade wasn't creative. He did have an MBA, though, he kept up on the latest software, and he did know computer people. When Barbara and Mike and I started the company, we followed our own tastes and lost money. Slade understood what people would buy."

A commercial counterweight. That made a certain kind of sense.

"Why are we blathering about Slade?" Barbara asked impatiently.

"Because I'm curious," I shot back. "Because he was murdered. Because I tweedled out the back door of your cute cottage and found his body. Slade Wheeler is a big fat puzzle."

"Big and fat," Mike snickered. "You got it. Fat in the head, too."

"Be that as it may," my father pronounced, "Lark's right. When you solve the puzzle of Slade Wheeler you'll be able to put a name to his killer and Alex will be off the hook. Innocence is Alex's best defense."

It was a sweetly naive remark. Barbara snorted and I didn't blame her. "Not with Mahon in charge."

Jay said, "Mahon is a competent professional and his methods are up-to-date."

Barbara growled.

He took a sip of Guinness. "You don't have to like him, but you do have an obligation to cooperate with him. He has good local information through Joe Kennedy. . . ."

"Kennedy," Barbara snarled.

"I wonder why you're so negative about Joe," I mused. "You were down on him from the moment he walked through the cottage door. Yet you like Maeve."

"Maeve has rotten taste in men," Barbara said darkly. "I know that kind of cop."

"What kind?"

"A big, dumb, good-looking Irish flatfoot."

I drew a breath. "Can it be that you're indulging in a stereotype?"

She flushed. "He's no Sherlock Holmes."

Jay toyed with his glass. "Kennedy's not a detective."

"I think I said that." Barbara's moment of embarrassment faded. She raised her chin.

"He has some investigative experience," Jay went on, as if she hadn't spoken. "But he's not focused that way. It isn't his job. The media have done a lot to glamorize detection, but it's tedious work and getting more and more technical."

Dad said, "I'm sure there are other interesting police tasks."

"Such as?" Barbara tapped her finger on her wineglass.

"Keeping the peace?"

Jay smiled at him. "That's a more challenging problem than picking up the pieces after the fact of a crime. If I understand Gardai structure, Kennedy chose to specialize in community relations rather than detection. My guess is that he does a good job."

Barbara looked skeptical.

Jay went on, dogged, "He knows his turf. He was on top of the war-gamers from the word go. What possessed you to let Wheeler set up a quasi-military training camp in Ireland, of all places?"

"Slade was just playing games."

"So you say, but try looking at those games from Kennedy's angle. You came in here on a burst of favorable publicity, all set to offer new opportunities to local workers."

"We have. We've hired a lot of people from the community."

"Middle-aged women," Liam murmured. He was watching Jay with apparent fascination.

Jay nodded. "And that's good. They need jobs. From the point of view of law enforcement, though, the population at risk is young and male. Their parents thought Stonehall would offer those kids jobs. Instead, you offered them Wheeler's games. The Provisional IRA draws recruits from the same population and uses the same skills."

"And *they're* not pretending," I blurted.

Jay said softly, "Wheeler was playing games. Was Tommy Tierney?"

Alex looked sick. "We should have stopped Slade."

Liam said, "The concept of war games is mad. I never could find out what war Slade thought he was simulating. I asked him was it Vietnam, but he just laughed and said I didn't understand."

"He was probably too ignorant to simulate anything specific. Americans aren't very good at history." Jay sounded tired. Vietnam was his war. He glanced at Dad, who was contemplating his empty wineglass.

Barbara said, "It wasn't *a* war, Lee, it was war in general. Slade created games. He thought that way."

"Ah, I see." Liam set the Perrier bottle on the trolley. He ran a hand over his hair, smoothing it. "Supposing someone, myself maybe, was to organize a group of game-players for the simulation of rape. Would the company give me the loan of the woods for that purpose?"

He had gone beyond joking. Alex made a strangled noise. Barbara opened her mouth to protest and closed it. Dad pursed his lips.

"According to Sgt. Kennedy, there was an offshoot of the Hellfire Club frolicking in the woods in the nineteenth century." I dropped the observation into the rather fraught silence. An amiable practice of the Hellfire Club was mass seduction of housemaids.

"Sure, there's nothing new under the sun," Liam mourned.

Alex was studying him as if he were a stranger. "I didn't know you felt so strongly about the games, Lee."

Mike leapt to his defense. "Lee told you they were trouble. I told you. Joe Kennedy came over in his bloody patrol car to tell you. You didn't hear us. You were too busy appeasing Wheeler."

"He was hard to deal with," Alex muttered.

"Hard to say no to," Mike paraphrased, bitter.

Barbara said, "This has got to stop, Mike."

Mike looked sullen, but he said nothing further. Barbara touched the sleeve of Liam's jacket. "I'm sorry, Lee. I didn't like the games, either. I thought they were childish. Thinking they were harmless as well was my mistake as much as Alex's. And Slade was . . . difficult."

"Somebody simplified him," Mike said.

I considered Mike Novak. I had thought he was a Stonehall employee, but he was apparently a founding partner. If he had seen Slade as a serious threat to the company, his motive for murder was as strong as the Steins'. For Slade Wheeler's murder. But why Kayla? My head ached.

In my brief lapse of attention, Barbara had turned to Jay. "I want to hire you," she was saying, "to clear Alex and to find out who killed Slade and Kayla—"

"No." Jay didn't hesitate. In fact he spoke before she had finished her sentence.

"But why?" The question was a long wail.

"I'm here as a visitor," Jay said patiently. "I don't know Irish law, and I don't have an investigator's license."

"But informally."

"No. Not formally, not informally." He didn't elaborate.

She tried once more, and Alex and Mike seconded the notion, but Jay just shook his head.

I caught Dad's eye. "We really should walk back to the cottage, Barbara, if only to check out the alarm system. Thanks for offering your Dumpster—an act of true charity."

"Don't mention it." She sounded defeated and indifferent. Alex saw us to the door. The others showed no sign of leaving, but Liam shook hands with Dad and Jay and gave me a small bow. Tracy favored us with an unhappy smile. Mike poured himself another beer.

On the porch, which was littered with the data processors' cigarette butts, Alex said, "George, I'm sorry. You know Barbara. Once she gets an idea into her head she digs in."

Dad cocked his head sideways. "It's her great strength. Don't worry too much. Things will sort themselves out. Do you have a lawyer?"

Alex sighed. "The company has a whole firm of civil lawyers on retainer, solicitors they're called here. I'm sure none of them has touched a criminal case. They're far too respectable."

Jay said, "They can recommend a criminal lawyer, Alex. Get some professional advice. It can't hurt."

"Okay. I understand why you don't want to work for us, Jay, though I wish you'd change your mind. I think you're right about Mahon and Kennedy. They're competent police officers." Alex shoved at a cigarette butt with the toe of his shoe. "But they're not Americans."

Jay frowned. "Do you think Wheeler was killed by an American?"

"Christ, I don't know. But both victims were Americans. That has to mean something."

We said goodbye and headed up the shallow slope to the arch of rhododendrons. They were fully budded out, ready to blossom. The long twilight cast a pale enchantment over the whole scene. We walked in a silence I finally broke.

"So why didn't you take an informal watching brief, Jay? Protecting the Steins' interests, translating their viewpoint for Mahon. You wouldn't have to interfere with the actual investigation."

He didn't answer me immediately. Dad said, "It would be awkward. Sgt. Kennedy is almost a friend."

Jay gave a short laugh. I felt my face go hot. Joe was *my* friend. That was what Jay was thinking, and he wasn't entirely wrong. Taking even a watching brief in the case would be a criticism of Irish police work that was bound to chill the relationship.

After half a dozen paces, Jay said, "I was concerned about a more mundane problem, as it happens. I came here to look after *your* interests, George, and Lark's."

"To protect us." I bristled. I couldn't help it.

"I was trying to avoid that word," Jay said wryly.

"I appreciate the kindness." My father eased his long stride and turned toward Jay. "But I don't see a conflict . . . oh."

"Yes. What if protecting the Steins put the two of you in danger?"

Dad's face reflected horror. "Do you think one of them is guilty? Both of them?"

"Not necessarily, though they had reason to resent Wheeler, and Alex, at least, could have done either of the murders. He spent two years in the Israeli army."

That was news Jay had to have got from the police—or from his own network. I thought of the computer. He believed the burglar had been aiming for his computer. If Jay was using it to access police files on the Internet—or if the "burglar" thought he was using the computer for that purpose—that made sense.

". . . and I have to leave Sunday at the latest. I don't suppose either of you wants to move to a hotel," Jay was saying. "Still, it's obvious the cottage is vulnerable. So I called in a locksmith. He's coming in the morning."

"You're going to change the locks without telling the Steins?" Dad sounded distressed.

"It is their property," Jay agreed. "If you insist, I'll tell Alex about the change privately. I'd rather not."

"They're bound to find out," I grumbled. We were approaching the cottage, which looked cozy and undisturbed with the light shining out from the kitchen.

"I'm concerned about the next couple of days," Jay explained. "Things should sort themselves out by Sunday. Kennedy will send a patrol car by several times tonight but he can't keep that up. We may have to hire a security firm."

"We could move to Ballymann House," Dad said unhappily.

"Let's see how it goes, George. I may be overreacting. And my public refusal to take on the Steins' case may do some good. I hope so. I'm glad Barbara asked me in front of witnesses."

"You think the killer was there at Stanyon?" Dad stopped dead on the gravel drive. "No, I refuse to believe it of those young people. And never of Alex and Barbara. I know them too well."

"You're probably right," Jay murmured. It's possible that Dad was reassured. I wasn't.

I unlocked the door. Jay disabled the alarm system.

13 ❧

Shillelagh law was all the rage
And a row and a ruction soon began

—Irish music hall song

JAY FIXED DENVER omelets for dinner. Afterward, Dad took
one of his books downstairs to read in bed. Jay and I stayed in
the kitchen. It was my turn to wash dishes. I soaked the flatware first. I wash the flatware, then the plates. Jay does the opposite. Go figure.

As we cleared the table, and scraped and stacked the dinner-
ware, I could feel tension rising like the steam from the dish-
washer. I suppose there were too many unspoken reproaches
between us.

"So you're flying home this weekend." I cleaned egg from
the tines of a fork.

Jay gave an assenting grunt.

"Nice of you to let me know."

"Wasn't it?" He doled dried spoons onto a cloth.

"I guess you like surprises." *Plop* went the spatula into the
rinse water.

"Love 'em." He dried the forks.

I lowered the three plates we had used into the dishpan. "I
was surprised, speaking of surprises, that Joe Kennedy let you

enter the cottage all by yourself with a putative burglar on the premises. That must have been a kick."

"Pure adrenaline."

"I'm beginning to see how your mind works. You object to it when I take risks. When you do, it's okay."

"If you're referring to the risk you took when you went for a walk in Stanyon Woods, you're right. I do object. It was a stupid thing to do. Also inconsiderate. I know you don't give a rat's ass about scaring me, but you might stop to consider what your father would have felt if something had happened to you."

"Let me deal with Dad in my own inadequate way." I dumped a plate in the water. "The Gardai had searched the woods thoroughly, it was broad daylight, and I am not incapable of defending myself. I also run very fast. As you know. I can outrun you."

"That's childish."

I scoured the omelet pan with vicious energy.

He went on in a quieter voice, "Why did you do it?"

I took a breath. "That was the day you came. I went for a walk because I wanted to be alone. I came to Ireland because I wanted to be alone."

"You told me that in Shoalwater. I was trying to accommodate you . . ."

"When I landed myself in another mess. So you mounted up on your white horse and charged to the rescue. Thanks. I needed your vote of confidence."

Jay dried the three plates without speaking.

I squeezed the sponge and began wiping the nearest counter.

"I wish you'd consider my viewpoint." He set the skillet on the Rayburn. His voice was so quiet I barely heard him.

I turned. "I do consider it. Whatever you may think, I don't go out of my way to worry you. I didn't choose to find a corpse in the potting shed. I understand your viewpoint," I repeated, louder, as if he were going deaf. "It's my own viewpoint I'm having trouble with."

"That doesn't make sense."

"You're a strong personality, Jay. You're older than I am, more experienced. I respect that, but I won't let you blot me out."

"Christ!"

"I have to figure out who I am." He was going to hear that as the cliché it was. Unfortunately, the cliché was also true.

"I don't think we're talking about Stanyon Woods."

"In a sense we are. I entered the woods because I had to enter the woods."

He shoved the dried plates into the cupboard with unnecessary force. "I said I thought you'd fight fair. Is it fair to accuse me of trying to blot you out? Is it, Lark?"

"I didn't mean . . ."

"You're not accusing me of trying to off you." He leaned his hands on the counter, head down. "I can grasp that. So what the hell do you mean, blot you out? I've never forced you to do anything."

I was making pointless circles on the surface of the table with my damp sponge. "It's hard to put into words. And I don't think you're *trying* to erase me, even metaphorically. It's not what you're doing or not doing. It's who you are."

"Can I help who I am? You don't leave me much room to maneuver."

"When I came to Ireland, I was trying to give us both some room."

He whirled. "Don't lay that on me, lady. That was not my choice." He was really angry, eyes a darker brown than usual, mouth set.

I held his gaze. "I feel useless. Your coming over here made me feel more useless."

"Useless! For God's sake, Lark . . ."

"Useless," I repeated. My voice was starting to shake. "And incompetent."

He pulled a chair and sat slowly. "So tell me what you want me to do."

184

"I don't know." I threw the sponge at the sink. "If you'd asked me that when you first came I would have said go home. Now I don't know. You're here. I guess we'll have to work it out."

"Do you want to work it out?" He sounded tired, his anger seeping away.

"Of course I do."

"Well, that's something."

I had a very strong urge to throw my arms around Jay and hang on for dear life. But that was part of the problem. After a moment, I said carefully, "I'm going to turn in early. It was a tiring day. When does the locksmith arrive?"

"Around ten."

"Are you coming down?"

"Not yet."

"Shall I reset the burglar alarm?"

He stood up. "I'll do it. I'm going to work on George's papers for awhile. Good night."

I was too tense to fall asleep at once. I tried reading *Phineas Finn*. It is a very masculine novel. I was having viewpoint problems. A lot of them. I shut the light off and stared at the darkened ceiling for a long time.

I heard my father turning pages in his room and hoped our quarrel hadn't carried downstairs. Dad's light clicked off and the darkness deepened. I heard Jay walking around. Dad snored a little. After a while everything went quiet. Outside, the trees and bushes whispered in the light wind. Rain brushed the window. I didn't try to think because I wasn't ready to. If I tried to think, my mind would move in circles. Spirals. Long elegant double spirals.

When I woke, it was barely dawn and Jay was not beside me. I froze in panic for a moment, then forced myself to relax. When I had dressed in my exercise suit and thick socks, I carried my shoes upstairs. Jay was asleep on the couch with the light on and the computer plugged in. He didn't stir as I tiptoed through the room. Dad's notes lay in neatly labeled folders on the kitchen table.

I stood in my stocking feet for a long time, staring at the folders. Then I sat down and put on my shoes. I even remembered to disable the alarm before I opened the door.

I ran on Suicide Lane all the way to Killaveen. Nobody was awake, not even the dogs that make a runner's life hazardous. I ran past the pub and along the road by the fishing stream. I looped up and around the village and down past the Garda station. A light shone but the place looked empty.

On the way back to Stanyon, I saw a patrol car headed the other way. It was Joe Kennedy. He waved and I waved. Then I ran down the curving drive to the rhododendrons. I didn't stop to look at the Steins' fake castle.

As I approached the cottage, I slowed to a jog and then a walk. In the slanting eastern light the woods looked inviting. Sunlight sparkled on the pond. I walked along the grassy rim, watching the ducks, until my breathing slowed. Then I went into the cottage and made a pot of coffee.

Jay was still asleep, but frowning, restless. I showered and changed into jeans and a T-shirt. On impulse, I carried the duvet upstairs and covered Jay. He had fallen asleep in his shirtsleeves and must have been cold. He made a vague interrogatory noise and burrowed into the cover.

Dad came upstairs as I was stirring a pot of oatmeal. "Jay's asleep on the sofa. Is something wrong?"

"He worked on your notes for a while after I went to bed. He probably didn't want to wake me. Coffee?"

"Mmm." Dad touched the stack of folders. "He shouldn't have done all that. It must have taken hours."

"It's okay, Dad."

He didn't look convinced, but he drank a cup of coffee and ate porridge without complaint. We went for a short walk together, came back, and drank another cup of coffee while Dad riffled through the folders. At that point, Jay woke. He walked into the kitchen unshaven, crumpled, and yawning. I poured coffee and handed it to him.

When he had drunk half a cup, Dad said, "I'm in your debt,

Jay. These are in better order than before the break-in. Thank you very much indeed."

Jay blinked at the folder. "S'okay. They were more interesting than my students' reports." He took another swallow. "What time is it?"

"Nine."

"Hell, the locksmith will be here in an hour." He set the cup on the table half-finished. "Anybody need the shower?" He headed downstairs. Presently I heard water running.

My father said, "You quarreled, didn't you?"

"Yes, but not to the death. We're speaking."

"That's good." He looked unhappy.

I sighed. "Don't worry about it, Dad. Tell Jay you want to go fishing this afternoon. I'll drive you to Killaveen."

He brightened. "We could do that." His face fell. "But it's too sunny out for decent fishing."

"You don't really have to catch anything, do you? Go sit on a rock and think, or whatever it is the two of you do when you fish."

"Maybe it will cloud over." Dad has a hopeful disposition.

Jay agreed to carry the garbage sack to the Dumpster if I double-bagged it. He returned sooner than I expected and said there was a camera crew at Stanyon. He had responded to their questions in Spanish, an old trick. It worked. They got a good shot of the garbage sack.

The locksmith turned out to be as taciturn as Toss Tierney was loquacious. He finished installing new locks on both doors in less than an hour. The alarm system interested him, but he declined a cup of tea and drove off in short order, a model of efficiency. All the same, I would have laid odds that Toss did better business.

Jay called in to the Garda station and reported the changed locks. He said he talked to Constable Byrne. Joe was off interviewing Tommy Tierney. I felt sorry for Tommy's mother.

After lunch I drove the two men to Killaveen. The pub was just closing but they caught the publican in time to rent gear. I left them deep in fish talk and went shopping in Arklow.

I strolled around for a while, admiring the town. I bought a guide to the area in the lone bookstore. There was an Indian take-out and a full-blown Chinese restaurant. The shops in the High Street looked reasonably prosperous. When I retrieved the car, I headed up to the roundabout and spotted a sign for Avoca. So I followed the winding street down to a secondary highway, reached Woodenbridge by the back way, and crossed the river twice. In Avoca, I bought a smashing hand-knit tunic at the famous handweaving establishment—pale turquoise it was, and rather expensive. I ate a scone in the tea shop.

I can't say all that solitary to-ing and fro-ing stabilized my identity, but it didn't hurt. I waited for Jay and Dad in the pub. This was not a brilliant idea. Three men tried to buy me beer, two of them reporters and one a lonesome farmer. I declined all three offers and sipped Perrier. Eventually Dad and Jay showed up with two fat brown trout which they had already cleaned. Jay drank a celebratory beer and Dad drank a whiskey. I drove.

I was meditating over the trout when I heard the phone ring in the living room. Jay brought it to the kitchen. "It's Maeve, for you."

I tucked the phone under my chin. "Hi, Maeve. How's Dublin?"

"Dear and dirty. Fancy what I uncovered in the library!"

I had no idea what she had found and said so.

"There's no evidence of a survey of Stanyon in the OPW files and no site on the register. On a hunch, I browsed through a collection of early nineteenth-century works on County Wicklow—travel journals, diaries, published letters. One English travel diary gave a detailed account of a visit to the Stanyon estate before the present house was built."

"Before the woods were planted with conifers?"

"Right. The diary's awful, full of nonsense about prospects of the river and picturesque natives, but there is a story about an antiquarian Stanyon, someone's loopy uncle, who did extensive digging in a mound behind the estate at the end of the eighteenth century. He found something, a structure, and decided to turn it into a folly."

"The one Joe said was torn down?" I asked, doubtful.

She *tsked.* "Joe thinks it was torn down. Who's to know? The Stanyons have been gone more than fifty years."

"True."

"The book's grand, full of gossip. There a bad sketch of the folly and a view of the estate. Everything's distorted, out of proportion, but the artifacts the loopy uncle uncovered sound as if they might have come from a neolithic grave site!"

"That's uncanny." I was impressed and said so.

She burbled on a bit about the artifacts, all of which had apparently disappeared long ago. "I've taken the book out and I'll bring it to the cottage Thursday around teatime. Shall you be there?"

"Yes, and I'll tell Dad." And Jay. I would enjoy telling Jay. I thanked Maeve again and she hung up.

The Rayburn had no broiler, so I poached the trout with wine and lemon. Nobody complained. Dad was impressed by Maeve's find, Jay silent. I considered describing my megalith for them by way of corroboration, but I didn't. Some things are private.

After dinner, I let Jay give my father a lesson in dishwashing while I lay on the sofa and read the regional guide. Water sloshed, their voices rumbled. I heard words like "bream" and "tench" that led me to believe they were talking fish. Fine with me. Jay and I were speaking to each other, but with a degree of ceremony that made conversation uncomfortable.

I looked up Stanyon Hall in the guide, without result, and paged through *Sights of Scenic Wicklow.* Glendalough sounded worth a daytrip, though the founder of the monastery appeared to have been sainted for misogyny. Liam had mentioned the gardens at Powerscourt. Another pleasant excursion. Dad was bound to run out of Quaker sites fairly soon, and my mother wouldn't arrive for ten days. I began planning an itinerary.

"Tea?" Dad beamed at me. He was carrying the tray.

I sat up. "Heavens, such domesticity. No sugar, thanks."

Jay went to the computer and plugged it in. It made its dialing sound, so he was going on the Internet again. At home it was almost time for his one o'clock seminar. He sat and sipped from a mug and made an occasional entry, while I told Dad about my adventures of the afternoon.

Around half past nine a car drove up. Jay answered the door and ushered in Joe Kennedy. That provoked another round of tea. Joe had come to give us an update, he said.

Results of a preliminary postmortem on the body of Kayla Wheeler had revealed no surprises. She had eaten dinner, she was drunk, and she had been strangled with a cord. There were no skin fragments under her nails, so she probably hadn't scratched her killer. It was early days for an opinion on whether Alex Stein's bruises could have been inflicted in a struggle with the taller, heavier Kayla. The inquest was set for Friday and we wouldn't have to attend. That was a relief.

Dad listened to the concise, edited account of the medical consequences of violent death with such obvious discomfort that I was doubly relieved when Joe finished. He was franker with us than the police generally are after such a crime. It may have been that Mahon was deferring to Jay's status as an expert and had told Joe to be open—or just that Joe trusted us not to talk. He clearly needed to.

"You interviewed young Tierney?" Jay poured him a fresh cup of tea.

Joe nodded. "This morning. Declan said you called the station." He took a test swallow of the tea and added a lump of sugar, stirring. "I didn't have much joy of Tommy. Obstruction runs in the family. However, he says he was with friends of a cousin in Leeds the evening Miss Wheeler was killed. The friends will back him, so Mahon is inclined to rule him out in the first murder, too."

"Do you agree?"

He sighed. "We had only two murders in the county last year. Whatever the Yank media may suggest, killing is a rare thing here."

"Then you think two murderers are unlikely."

"I think Mahon was right to leave Tommy at liberty." He took another swallow and set his mug down. "Not but what it goes against the grain. I told the little perisher Mahon had a full team watching his every move, God forgive me for a liar. We haven't the manpower. And speaking of that, I'm relieved to hear you called the locksmith in." He dug in his tunic and produced a business card. "That's the security firm I mentioned, the one out of Wexford. The local boys say they'd rather not take the job on. They don't like the woods. The place is airy."

It was a moment before I realized he meant "eerie."

Dad had been very silent, sipping his tea and brooding. At the mention of the woods, however, he brightened and told Joe of Maeve's discovery.

Joe listened with an air of polite skepticism. The possibility of finding a neolithic site in Stanyon Woods had no interest for him. Either that or he was still so angry with Maeve he wouldn't entertain any idea that originated with her.

"So her ladyship's gone up to Dublin, has she?" He rose. "Did she mention when she'll grace us with her presence again?"

I decided to put him out of his transparent misery. "She's bringing a crew of student archaeologists down Thursday, and she's having tea with us. Around five, if you'd like to join us."

He forced a smile. "I don't want to curdle the cream. We had words last week and she's still on her high horse."

I said, "I'm sorry," and avoided looking at Jay.

Joe sighed. "Women are the devil. Saving your presence, Lark."

"You sound like St. Kevin." Kevin was the holy founder of the Glendalough monastery.

His eyes widened and he began to laugh. "Sure, if I shoved

Maeve Butler into the lake wouldn't she bob up again and scold me like a fishwife? Good night, sir. I hear you're a dab hand with a fly rod."

Dad smiled. "It's grand country for trout fishing." They shook hands. Jay went out to the car with him and they must have conferred because Jay was gone a good ten minutes.

When Joe had driven off, Jay said, "What was the business about saints?"

I rinsed the teapot. "St. Kevin had a hermitage at Glendalough where he went off by himself and thought holy thoughts. A beautiful woman kept intruding on him, so he pushed her into the lake."

"I may make a pilgrimage."

"According to some accounts," Dad said, "she drowned."

I murmured, "We do but jest, murder in jest."

Dad stared. "What's that, *Hamlet*?"

"I think so."

"It might almost be the war-gamers' motto."

Jay said, "I wonder . . ."

"What?"

He shook his head. "A fugitive thought." He went over to his computer. "I'd better close this down. With the modem running, no one can get through on the telephone."

14 ⁊

Boil the Breakfast Early
—Irish air

"STUFF TASTES LIKE glue." Jay stirred his porridge. "And what's that?" He pointed with the handle of his spoon.

"Smoked haddock," I said with dignity. "A local delicacy." The delicacy had a strong fish odor. It was also a sulphurous shade of yellow. I had found it at the fishmonger's in the High Street.

Dad was delighted. "Haddock! What a treat. I haven't tasted it in years." He transferred a generous portion to his plate and ate it with evident enjoyment. I tried a morsel and returned to my soda bread.

"What's on the agenda for you two?" Dad asked in the hearty tones of one who has no intention of stirring from the house. He had already announced he meant to spend the day with his freshly organized notes.

I dolloped marmalade on the soda bread. "I may go for a walk in the woods."

Jay gave me a sharp frown.

"Just pushing your buttons."

Under ordinary circumstances that would have rated a smile. He shoved his porridge away and rose. "I have to call the security people and the airline."

"A bit early for business, isn't it?"

"Maybe *I'll* walk in the woods."

"If you're bored, you could hold a press conference."

His mouth eased marginally. "I wouldn't have far to look for reporters." He paused at the door arch. "Do you want me to clear up?"

"We haven't finished yet. Relax."

He slid around the corner and I heard the computer hum to life.

Dad took a last bite of haddock.

"More coffee?"

"No, thanks. Why don't you give yourself a respite, Lark? Drive to Dublin."

"Eek."

"Well, drive to Dun Laoghaire or Bray, and take the DART train in to Pearse Station. It's near Trinity and the big museums. The National Museum has a fabulous collection of gold artifacts of the pre-Christian era." He smiled. "Of the Christian era, too."

"I'm tempted." I started to say, "but I already have that on next week's itinerary," when the phone rang. So Jay wasn't using the modem.

He brought me the instrument. "Barbara Stein. For you."

"Hello," I said with caution.

Barbara asked about the garbage and I reported Jay's encounter with the TV crew.

"He answered them in Spanish?" She gave a short laugh like a bark. "Brilliant. Uh, will you do me a favor?"

I went on full alert. "I'll try." No rash promises.

"I want to visit Grace Flynn this morning, see if she needs anything, but if I take the Mercedes the press will trail after me like a funeral parade."

"Do you want me to drive you in the Toyota?"

"Will you?"

"Okay. What time?"

"Ten, I thought. Drive around behind the house to the

kitchen. It's in the stubby wing on the river side. I'll slip out the kitchen door—"

"And hide under the seat. Sounds good. See you then."

"Thanks." She sounded genuinely grateful.

"That takes care of the morning," I announced as I took the phone back to the desk. I explained Barbara's mission.

"Grace Flynn." Jay cocked his head. "Wheeler's girlfriend?"

"No, you cannot come. It's girl stuff."

He started to say something, changed his mind, and turned back to the computer. "Will you get me some cash? I'm short."

"How much?"

"I dunno. Fifty pounds?"

"Punts. I'll use an ATM machine," I assured him, lest he imagine I was going to cash my own traveler's checks for his purposes. I hadn't planned on paying for Jay when I budgeted for the trip.

"Mmm." He was unimpressed. He did something with the mouse and the computer dialed.

I went back to the kitchen. Dad poured himself an illicit third cup of coffee and drifted off with no sign of a bad conscience, leaving the kitchen in a mess. Jay was better trained.

Though there were no reporters or television crews visible when I approached Stanyon, I drove behind the house anyway, found what I thought was the right place, and tooted the horn. Barbara dashed out and ducked into the car with no wasted motion.

"I could hardly wait to escape. It's awful." She hooked the seat belt. "I really appreciate this, Lark."

"No problem." I eased around and headed back the way I had come.

As I drove past the house and up the long driveway, Barbara slid lower in the seat. She was wearing a pair of California sunglasses that would make her the magnet of all eyes, though her jeans and pullover were anonymous enough.

"I didn't see any sign of reporters," I ventured.

"They're here. One of them walked in with the data proces-

sors this morning and strolled around taking notes for a good
half hour before Mike discovered him and threw him out."

"Where was he found?"

"On his way to Kayla's room," Barbara said grimly.

"Is the Garda still in residence?"

"No. The crime scene people finished their work last night.
It's pretty horrible."

"The bedroom?"

"Yes. I told my housekeeper to burn the bedding and scrub
everything down with Lysol, but her . . . Kayla's stuff is still
there. I don't know what to do with it."

"Box it up and ship it to her next of kin."

"There doesn't seem to be anybody."

"Give it to Oxfam. Yeow." That in response to a very large
lorry that careened past me going fifty. I scraped the stone wall,
I was so far onto the shoulder of the road.

"Where does Grace live?" I asked when my breathing went
back to normal.

"She has a bedsit in Arklow."

I negotiated the turn onto the highway and drove south
through the sparse traffic to the bridge over the Avoca. "It's nice
of you to concern yourself for her."

"Somebody has to," Barbara said absently. "It's off the High
Street. Turn left."

I complied.

Grace's nest looked unappealing from the outside. The
walkup entry squeezed between a betting shop and a green-
grocer. I parked in a vacant spot on the street and Barbara led
me up the stairs.

There was no sign of security, no buzzer. The stairway was
narrow and badly lit, but a long skylight brightened the drab
hall and it didn't smell of urine, just of ancient dust. Barbara
looked at the slip of paper with Grace's address and knocked
on the third door.

No response.

When she knocked again, we heard a groan and the creak of

springs. The door opened. Grace, tousled and heavy-eyed in a bright pink nylon negligee, blinked at us. For a hideous moment I wondered whether we were interrupting a Moment of Passion, but Grace was just having a lie-in. A Murphy bed thrust rumpled bedclothes into the living area.

She blushed and said, "Oh, Mrs. Stein. Is it ten? I'll just put the kettle on." She stepped aside and we entered.

There were two upholstered chairs vintage 1955. Barbara perched on one and began talking lawyer. Grace wandered from the Pullman kitchen to the bed, eyes blurry. I wondered how much she was taking in. She folded the duvet and stuffed the pillow into a cupboard. Barbara was making negative comments about Irish inheritance rights.

I stood by the window and saw that the flat had a million-punt vista of the Avoca and the boat harbor. I heard the word amniocentesis. The Murphy bed slid up the wall.

Grace ducked into the bathroom and performed various liquid chores. The toilet flushed.

Barbara said, "This place is a pit. They should have found something better."

"They?"

"The women's aid group."

"I like the view."

She got up, craned around me, and sniffed. "Nice."

Grace reappeared, brushing her curly blond hair, in jeans and a sweatshirt that claimed allegiance to Louisiana State University. She wasn't showing yet, at least not in the sweatshirt.

I smiled at her and she gave me a shy grin. "Me stomach's upset."

I felt a pang, remembering my too brief experience of morning sickness. "Eat a saltine . . . a biscuit."

"Ta." The kettle was shrieking and she went to silence it. All three of us sipped tea and Grace nibbled a biscuit while Barbara mapped out the rest of Grace's life. I thought that Grace would do exactly what Grace wanted to do.

Midway through the education of Junior Wheeler I got up

and strolled around the room. With the Murphy bed back in the wall, the flat was surprisingly spacious. Someone had repapered it and painted the woodwork, though the carpet was icky gray. The place had to have come furnished, but there were some signs that Grace had tried to make it hers. Stuffed toys of the kind people win at fairs peeked from an otherwise empty bookcase. There was an old telly with rabbit ears. A tiny figure of the Infant of Prague stood on the mantle above the gaslog fireplace. The tea table displayed a bunch of daffodils in a fruit jar.

On one wall, Grace had hung a framed photograph. It was the only wild card in the decor: the black and white scene of a bridge—Renaissance or earlier I thought—with a town rising behind it. If Grace had hung a picture of the Sacred Heart, or a photo of one of her boyfriends, or a rock poster, I would scarcely have noticed it. This scene, however, baffled me. I thought Grace was not a great traveler, yet there was something vaguely Mediterranean about the bridge and the town. The photograph itself was handsome and handsomely mounted.

At the first long pause in Barbara's monologue, I said, "I like the photo, Grace."

She beamed. "It's me cousin Liam's work. He gave it me when I left school."

"Our Liam?" Barbara asked. She got up and came over for a closer look. "Yes, I've seen a copy of that one. It's in his portfolio. *The Bridge on the Drina.*" She turned back and went on with a discussion of Irish versus American higher education. Grace nibbled another biscuit.

I turned the implications of Grace's kinship to Liam McDiarmuid over in my mind. I had thought he might have been drooping after her romantically. Mere cousinhood was less interesting. I didn't think an Irish man would feel obliged to defend his cousin's honor by killing her seducer. Italian or Spanish, maybe, not Irish. Besides, I recalled Liam's look of surprise when Grace proclaimed her pregnancy. He hadn't known she was bearing Wheeler's child at that point—and Slade was already dead.

But Liam might have known of the relationship and disapproved of it, I considered. Disapproval was inadequate fuel for murder, surely, yet Grace's father had responded to the news with violence. A cousin is not a father. . . .

"Time for us to go," Barbara announced. "And be sure to eat plenty of leafy green vegetables, Grace. You're eating for two."

Grace looked mutinous but she was too polite to snap at the hand that was, I supposed, feeding her. Perhaps the women's aid group had arranged for the equivalent of welfare, but I thought Barbara had probably paid the rental deposit at the very least.

I said, "Cheer up, Grace. You have a lovely place of your own. Do you like it?"

"Sure, it's grand." Her face clouded. "But I miss jarring with me sisters."

We took our leave and went back to the street. It was a nice day, so I told Barbara we could walk up the street to the bank. We could look at the shops.

She made a face. "They're poky. And I don't want to cause a sensation. I'll sit in the car."

Please yourself, I reflected, and unlocked the door for her. I had spotted a bank with an ATM machine, so I walked to it and had fun watching it spew out punts instead of dollars. Traveler's checks would soon be outmoded.

I didn't dally long. When I returned and settled behind the wheel, I looked over at Barbara. Her nose was pink. I thought she had been crying.

I fastened my seat belt and started the engine. "Are you all right?"

She blew her nose on a tissue. "Yes, sorry. I just get depressed, thinking about Grace. Alex and I talked of offering to adopt the baby that night she came to the house. We talked for hours."

I eased out into the traffic and headed for the harbor. I could turn around there. "Did you suggest the possibility to Grace?"

Barbara gave a watery giggle. "She told me to feck off."

After a pause for translation, I laughed. "Cheer up. The kid might turn out to be a big, flat-footed, Irish cop."

"Better that than Tay-Sachs." She blew her nose again.

After a constrained moment, I said, "Are you a carrier?"

She gulped. "The gene's present in Alex's family, too. We decided not to have children after my little cousin died."

I eased the car right at the nonfunctional stop light. "I'm sorry, Barbara. I lost a baby last spring. We've been trying for years."

"George told us the baby miscarried."

I drove with fierce concentration. The baby miscarried. I had said that myself a number of times, but my thought was always that I had lost her. And yet I had done nothing the doctors disapproved of. Language can tell the truth or lie. Something in my mind shifted.

I deposited Barbara at Stanyon before noon without incident, though several suspicious-looking cars were parked near the house. She thanked me briefly and went in the back way.

"Can you drive me to Dublin?" Jay asked without preliminaries as soon as I entered the door of the cottage.

"What's wrong?"

"The burglar stole his passport and airline ticket," Dad said. Both men were hovering in the kitchen, obviously waiting for me.

"I should have checked more thoroughly yesterday," Jay growled. He looked embarrassed. The great detective.

I didn't say anything, but he went on, defensive, "The downstairs *looked* undisturbed and I was in a hurry to shut the damned alarm off. When I decided to phone Aer Lingus today I couldn't find the ticket. Or the passport."

"What about my stuff?"

"It seems to be in order. He went for mine."

It was possible the thief hadn't been able to find my ticket and passport. I had zipped them into a pocket of my suitcase and left the case in the room's tiny closet, whereas Jay's had reposed at the back of the top drawer of the dresser. The burglar must have gone straight to the dresser when he found the computer missing—with the alarm sounding in his ears. If he'd had that much presence of mind, why the melodrama with Dad's notes?

I looked at my father. "Is your passport missing?"

"I don't think he entered my room at all."

"What about traveler's checks?" I asked Jay.

"Mine are gone. Yours are still in your suitcase. I'm glad I kept my Visa card and driver's license in my wallet. This is going to be enough of a nuisance without having to cancel credit cards."

"Did you call the embassy?"

"Yes. If I come in this afternoon with four passport photos, they may be able to issue a temporary passport by Friday. They said George could vouch for me. There's a fee, of course. Did you get money?"

I described the ATM machine and handed over the cash. "Dublin traffic. Aargh."

"My sympathies," Jay said with only mild sarcasm. "I'm not allowed to drive the Toyota, remember?"

"I want lunch."

"We can grab a sandwich in Dublin."

"Well, hang on while I change." Like Barbara I was wearing jeans and a grubby pullover. That might do for Arklow but it didn't suit my idea of what was appropriate for Dublin. I took the tags off the turquoise tunic and wore it with the skirt of the gray suit. It looked classy.

On the way up the N11 we debated the merits of taking the DART train, as Dad had suggested, but I wound up driving in. The traffic was horrendous. We found a sandwich shop somewhere near Merrion Square and a place that took passport photos. While Jay was saying "cheese" for the camera, I bought a science-fiction paperback at a newsagent. I like SF and the book weighed less than *Phineas Finn*. Dad bought a newspaper.

Fortunately, my father had had occasion to visit the embassy, so he was able to navigate for me. Inside the cylindrical building, a monument to Federal taste of the early sixties, the process was slow. It was also complicated by the fact that, when the clerk found out the passport had been stolen, she demanded to know the incident number of the police report. That meant I had to call Joe in Killaveen on a balky pay phone. It accepted my AT&T credit number eventually. Joe was in.

When we drove south at last, all three of us were cranky and the rush hour was well under way. I got lost because I couldn't change lanes in time for a crucial turn. I finally decided the hell with it and headed south by east. Sooner or later I'd hit either the N11 or the Irish Sea.

I'm sure some of the southern suburbs of Dublin are interesting places, but I was greatly relieved when I finally stumbled on the N11 near the Bray roundabout. At six-thirty, as we were coming up on Arklow, I spotted Jack White's, the pub in which Tommy Tierney had had words with Slade Wheeler on Easter. I pulled into the car park.

Dad jerked awake in the front passenger seat. "What?"

"A beer," Jay said. "Sounds good."

"A beer and a sandwich," I said firmly. "I refuse to cook."

In fact, the roomy and pleasant pub served dinners, so we ate a real meal early. Afterward, in the car park, a reporter came up and asked us for a reaction to the murder of Kayla Wheeler. I unlocked the car doors as fast as possible while Jay and my father dealt with the man, who was polite but persistent. He asked Jay about an article in the *Times*.

When we got home, I brewed a pot of tea and brought it into the living room. Jay had gone onto the Internet straight from the car. I brought him a mug and leaned over his shoulder.

He was loading the *Irish Times*.

"I didn't know that was online."

"I stumbled across it last night. Oh, shit. Look at that."

He had clicked on the Home section. The headline read GAR-

DAI CONSULT U.S. EXPERT IN WHEELER CASE. Though the article was brief and uninformative, it identified Jay clearly. The source was Inspector Mahon.

Dad peered over our shoulders. "I ought to check the *Independent*. I haven't really looked at it. I get sick if I read much in a car. Maybe they covered the story, too."

Jay groaned.

"Yes, here it is. There's a photo."

Jay backed out of the system and disconnected. Then he picked up the phone and called Joe.

Dad handed him the *Independent* article and Jay read it over the phone. I took a peek. The photo must have been taken as the three of us were entering the church hall for the inquest. Dad looked magisterial, Jay looked worried, and I had my mouth open.

15 ❧

We may have good men, but we never had better.
Glory-oh, glory-oh, to the bold Fenian men.

—Peadar Kearney, "The Bold Fenian Men"

MAEVE WAS COMING.

I decided to bake oatmeal cookies. Right after lunch on Thursday I went into Arklow and bought the basics. I hadn't brought a recipe from home, but I remembered the ingredients and thought I could reconstruct the proportions.

At Quinnsworth I also bought a copy of the *Times* for Jay, in case he wanted to collect clippings for his scrapbook.

He scowled when I told him that.

"Just kidding." I handed him the paper and started putting the groceries away.

"You're a great kidder." He was drinking tea. He flipped through the paper one-handed. "No more Yank Expert garbage, thank God, though there's a short article about the inquest tomorrow. The coroner's expected to adjourn that one, too."

I got out the solitary mixing bowl and a tea cup. There were no measuring cups—or measuring spoons, for that matter. When I cranked up the oven temperature, the Rayburn coughed. "Where's Dad?"

"Taking a nap. That trip to Dublin tired him."

"Do you think he's okay?"

He responded to my tone with a searching frown. "George will be all right, Lark. Don't worry about him so much. When you worry, he worries."

I thought about that. "What time will they have the new passport ready for you tomorrow?"

"After two."

I visualized the rush-hour traffic and sighed.

"Why don't we try the transit system? You could drop me at the station in Bray and come back for me."

"I'd like to walk around Dublin myself."

"Okay, and George can have a peaceful day with his notes. Lark . . ."

"Mmm." I began mashing brown sugar into softened butter. "I hope this is the right kind of sugar. It's awfully lumpy."

He got up. "I'm going for a walk. Are there hordes of reporters in the bushes?"

"I didn't see any. You should be safe."

He retrieved his anorak from the other room. It was misting out. "I can always dive into the bushes if I see a journalistic face."

"Shall I make these with raisins?"

He pondered, one arm in the jacket sleeve. "Half with and half without. No nuts." He slipped out the door.

Maeve drove up in the van as I was removing the second batch of perfect cookies from the oven. I stuck my hands under the tap, wiped them on a dishtowel, and met her at the door.

She was laughing. "I didn't even have time to knock."

"I was expecting you."

"Something smells heavenly."

"You did say tea time." I waved my spatula. She took her coat off and hung it on the back of a chair. When I had removed the cookies to a rack, I gave her one piping-hot from oven. Cookies may be an American phenomenon but I've never met a foreigner who rejected them.

"Mmmm. I brought the book."

"So I should hope." I filled the kettle and set it on the Rayburn.

"Where's your father?"

"He took a nap but I heard signs of life a while ago. He'll be up soon."

"And Jay?"

I looked at my watch. "Taking a long walk. You didn't see a beleagured Yank Expert in the bushes as you drove up, did you?"

She hadn't read the article or heard of our Dublin excursion, so I filled her in. The kettle screamed and I made a pot of tea. Dad came in as I was pouring the first mug.

"Just in time. Do I smell cookies?"

"Oatmeal," I said. "I wanted to use it up." Both men had balked at porridge for breakfast that morning.

Dad greeted Maeve. We sat around the table, nibbling cookies and admiring the book. The heavy rag paper with gilt edges was going to preserve an undistinguished travel diary longer than the greatest modern novel. I thought nostalgic thoughts about nineteenth-century bookbinders. The cover was tooled calf.

Maeve had done her homework. Slips of paper marked the references to Stanyon and the folly. She read a description of the artifacts to us, turning pink with indignation as she commented on the looting of ancient sites in that era. I was more interested in the two relevant illustrations.

They were etchings, protected by delicate translucent paper. One showed a foreshortened view of a low mound with a handsome Georgian house below it and to the left. I screwed up my face, trying to superimpose Stanyon-now on Stanyon-then. Where in the woods would the mound be, if the present house had been built on the site of the first? The slope I had walked up seemed steeper than the slope of the mound in the drawing.

"I don't know that the house was built on the original site." Maeve read my mind. "In any case, the artist's sense of proportion is off. Look at the size of that donkey cart in relation to the house."

"Then all this does is verify the existence of a mound."

"And that it was an earthwork, not a natural formation. That's useful. What do you think of the folly?"

"Not much. It looks like a cave. Hey, is that my stone?" I squinted. "No, just a boulder. So the loopy uncle left most of the mound intact and excavated the tomb opening."

"Apparently. He must have had prodigious luck to find it. I wonder how the tomb was oriented."

"Oriented?"

"At the Brugh na Boinne, in the valley of the River Boyne, the monuments have a seasonal orientation, south toward the midwinter sun or east toward the sun at spring equinox."

"Like Stonehenge?"

"Stonehenge is oriented to the summer solstice. It is," she said loftily, "later, smaller, and less important than Newgrange."

Dad chuckled. "And entirely different."

Maeve flushed and gave him a rueful answering smile. "Allow me a little chauvinism. Newgrange and Knowth are spectacular passage graves, Lark, among the most important in Europe. They date to the third millenium B.C. However, your father's wrong. There are some minor similarities between the Newgrange site and Stonehenge. The ring of pillar stones and the heel stone, for instance. When you said you'd found an incised stone, I thought immediately of the spirals on the threshold stone at Newgrange. Double spirals?"

Dad had heard nothing of my stone and I hadn't really described it to Maeve either. Under her expert questioning I managed to give some sense of the design and the sheer bulk of the stone. She got rather excited and talked in technical detail about similar markings elsewhere.

I made another pot of tea.

Dad munched a cookie. "Where's Jay?"

I looked at my watch. He had been gone more than an hour.

A chill ran up my spine. "Out for a walk." My voice was commendably calm. "I'm a little surprised he hasn't come back yet. I know he wanted to see Maeve's book."

Maeve looked at me, eyes narrowed. "Shall we go look for him?"

I said, "Give him fifteen minutes. I'm sure he'll turn up soon."

But he didn't.

I ate another cookie and drank a cup of tea. Maeve read us a couple of passages that dealt with quaint local characters in a patronizing, upper-class way. The cookie sat in my stomach like a lump of concrete.

When Jay had been gone two hours I called Joe Kennedy. He said he'd be right over.

By that time we had moved to the living room and I was frankly pacing. I refused to allow my imagination to paint a picture of what might have happened to Jay. He was a grown man and trained in who knows how many kinds of self-defense. No mad strangler was going to lay hands on my husband.

It took Joe half an hour to get to the cottage. Maeve had made more tea. She poured him a cup while he questioned me about Jay's disappearance.

"Which way did he go?"

"I was baking cookies. I didn't see." I tried to sound reasonable. I should have gone with Jay. No, that was foolish. I'd had my hands in the cookie dough, and Maeve was coming. "He made a joke about avoiding reporters by diving into the bushes."

"In the woods?"

I cleared my throat. It felt awful, as if it might close and choke me. "I don't think he'd go there. He bawled me out for walking in the woods." Jay was neither inconsistent nor hypocritical. "I think he usually walks up to the road and over to the convenience market."

"Findley's? East, then." He was taking notes, neglecting his tea. "Did you . . . er, what was his state of mind?"

"We didn't quarrel."

Dad's turn to clear his throat. I looked at him, pleading, and he said nothing.

I drew a breath. "Jay was worried about the impact of that article in the *Times.*"

"Sure, he didn't like it." Joe's irony was mild. Jay had made his displeasure extremely plain on the phone.

"The story worried him," I repeated. "It made him sound as if he were taking an important role in the investigation." My voice trembled in spite of me. "All he wanted to do was make sure we were safe and then go home."

"But the plane ticket was stolen, and the passport."

"Aer Lingus agreed to replace the ticket and we were . . . we are going to the embassy tomorrow to pick up a new passport. That can't have anything to do with . . ."

Joe said, "I'm sorry, Lark. I was thinking aloud." He fiddled with the notebook. "I reported your husband's disappearance as a suspicious circumstance. When an adult vanishes, Gardai policy is to wait twenty-four hours."

"I won't wait. I want to do something, find him. You should be searching the woods."

"Why the woods? I thought you said he wouldn't go there."

"Where else can he be?" I looked at Dad. He was frowning and rather gray. I stood up. "I haven't called Stanyon. Maybe he's . . ." I broke off. Joe was shaking his head.

"I rang up the Steins from the station directly you notified me. Liam McDiarmuid answered. He asked the others and called me back. They've not seen Jay at all, nor did Declan Byrne when he drove through the estate an hour ago. The area hospitals and the traffic control officers saw nothing of your husband either. However, I must ring up Findley's. May I use your telephone?"

"Please."

We waited, silent, while Joe spoke into the phone. He hung up slowly. "No, he's not stopped in there today. Moira Findley would have recognized him. She said they chatted each time he bought a paper, and she attended the inquest, so she knows who he is. She's a keen observer, Moira, and she watches the road. She says she'd have seen him if he'd walked past the shop, too." He picked up the receiver again and tapped out a number.

"He's bound to be all right, Lark," Dad said for the third time, adding, "Jay can take care of himself. Perhaps he went for a walk in the woods and got lost."

"Then they should search the woods." My voice sounded harsher than I intended. I bit my lip. "I'm sorry. Is it time for your pills? I don't want to have to worry about you collapsing." That was tactless of me, but I was beyond tact.

He got up. "I'll go take them, and I won't collapse, my dear. I promise."

"I'll hold you to it."

I watched him walk downstairs, shoulders hunched.

Joe was saying, "Yes, sir, I know. Call Mahon if you like. He can bloody authorize it. Wasn't Mahon the one gave out the information to that journalist? I want a team in the woods and another at Stanyon. Ah, bollocks. Call in the volunteers, then. I'll stay at the cottage for the time being." He read off the telephone number.

Maeve said, "Are you going to do a search?"

"In the morning." Joe avoided my eyes.

I strode to the wall near the kitchen and yanked my anorak off its peg. "I'm going out now, before dark."

Maeve said, "I'll come with you."

Joe hesitated as if he meant to object, but changed his mind. "All right, but stay together and don't go deep into the trees. Call his name. If he's there and has stumbled into a trap . . ."

"A trap?" I envisaged booby traps, mines, explosions. No. My brain stopped whirling. "Like a pit with sharpened stakes?"

"More likely just a pit, though we found nothing like that earlier. If he's injured he'll hear you and may be able to respond."

I struggled into the jacket. I was having trouble with simple things, like putting my arm in the right hole.

"I'll sit here by the telephone," Joe went on. "I'm expecting Mahon to ring up. There's a fog forming, so be careful. I don't need three missing persons on my plate."

Maeve had retrieved her duffle coat. She followed me to the door.

"Tell my father where I've gone," I called, and went out into the late afternoon drizzle. "Soft" weather, but not yet a fog. The air was motionless.

Maeve and I entered the woods by climbing the stile I had used before. I stood still, orienting myself, then I called Jay's name. My voice echoed. So did the silence.

"No response," Maeve said. "Show me your stone."

"It's fairly deep in the trees, up that way." I pointed. "At least, I think it's there. I'm not sure I can find it again."

"Give it a try."

So I led her into the darkening woods. Every ten yards or so I called for Jay. We heard rustlings and birdcalls. The rows of identical trees told me nothing. The occasional blot of red paint, fainter than before, led nowhere. After ten minutes, I was lost.

I stopped in my tracks and looked around me. "I'm sorry. I have no idea where the stone is, or where we are." Mist curled around the middle branches above our head and left my face wet. It was getting darker.

Maeve turned slowly around, lips pursed in a silent whistle. "I do see the problem. Airy, isn't it?"

It was eerier than a Halloween spook house. I felt my throat closing again so I yelled Jay's name. No response. The needle-thick ground beneath our feet was slippery.

"Pity the light's so poor." Maeve was staring to the right. North, I thought. That's north. I hoped it was north.

"Ja-a-ay!" I called again. No answer.

Something hooted close by and a bush rustled. I whirled but saw nothing.

211

Maeve touched my arm. "Let's go back. I want to look at the book again. I need to check one of the descriptions."

I took a few paces up the slope and called once more without result. I drew calming breaths. "Okay. This is doing no good. We need light and more searchers."

"In the morning," she said gently.

"Which way did we come?" I should have known but the fog and my anxiety left me clueless.

She pointed to the left, downhill. "That way."

"Are you sure?"

"No."

We walked perhaps ten yards through twining mist. I called again.

Maeve took my arm. "Is that it?" She pointed.

My heartbeat quickened but the stone she indicated was much too small. "It's a megalith," I snapped.

"I wasn't sure you'd recognize one."

"I saw the dolmens." I coughed. My throat felt rough with all that yelling. "Tell me about dolmens." Not that I cared, at that point. I just wanted her to talk.

She led me down through the trees. "They're among the oldest monuments in Ireland. Pre-Celtic, of course."

"Really?"

"Really. The Celts didn't invade Ireland—or more likely, filter in—until the Romans and the Germanic tribes began pushing them west. These people, the ones who erected the dolmens, were much older. Formorians, in Celtic myth. The Celts weren't great builders in stone until the Christian era. Of course they invented legends about the stoneworks they found in Ireland, which were obviously the work of giants."

"Obviously." My teeth had begun to chatter. The mist clung in beads to Maeve's hair and, I suppose, mine. It swirled round our knees.

Maeve went slowly, her eyes on the ground. "Dolmens figure in the legends associated with Finn MacCoul. He was a great hero who founded and led a band of warriors called the Fianna."

I swallowed my panic. "Feena? Oh, Fianna—as in Fianna Fail." I named the major nationalist political party. They were out of power just then, but I'd been in the country long enough to hear the name and see it in print.

"That's right," Maeve said easily. We avoided a mist-heavy bush. She knew and I knew she was telling me stories to keep me from panicking. "Fianna Fail nowadays and the Fenians in the nineteenth century."

"So tell me about Finn. Did his warriors use the dolmens as fortifications?"

"No, it's stranger than that. In his old age, Finn took a beautiful young bride named Grainne."

"Did you see something move?"

We stood and stared into the murk. Maeve took my arm. "No, I did not, and the fog's settling. I was telling you about Diarmuid and Grainne."

I stumbled on the slippery surface and Maeve's grip tightened. "Go on. You were talking about Finn's Abishag."

"Like King David's concubine?" She gave an easy laugh, lighthearted. "Grainne wasn't exactly a bed warmer. She was the daughter of the high king, so marrying her enhanced Finn's prestige and brought him wealth and power, not that he needed them. Still, he liked to show her off."

"And one of the warriors fell in love with her." My sleeve caught on a bush and water sprayed us both. "Sorry."

"In love? No. He was true Irishman, cold as a clam." A note of bitterness rang in her voice and I remembered her quarrel with Joe. " 'Twas the other way round. Grainne fell in love with the warrior. His name was Diarmuid and he was more thoughtful than most of the Fianna, a brooder. The goddess of youth had marked him on the forehead with a love-mark guaranteed to make any young woman wild for him. . . ." Her voice trailed.

"What is it?" She had stopped on the spongy surface which was flatter now. "Did you see something?"

She gave herself a small shake. "No. Well, Grainne fell in love with her brooding warrior. He was too honorable to shame the

213

king by seducing her—or too cold-blooded, take your pick."

We trudged on. "What happened?"

"In the end, she put a hex on him that bound him to do her will." Maeve sounded preoccupied. She went on more briskly, as if she meant to be done with the story, "When they eloped, the king set the Fianna and their hounds on the lovers and chased them the length and breadth of Ireland for a year and a day without respite." She walked forward, suddenly confident. "In the legend, the dolmens are the beds Diarmuid made for Grainne in the wilderness. Isn't that the wall?"

I peered ahead. "Yes, thank God."

We had come out at the wall but not within sight of the stile. "Which way?" Maeve asked.

I had no idea. "I think I went left last time."

"We'll try it."

We walked along, silent now, both of us stumbling from time to time on the uneven ground. The fog was so thick I bumped the stile before I saw it. We climbed over and stood for a moment on the turf.

I turned back and called Jay's name one more time. My voice rang on the cold air and echoed eerily, but there was no reply.

Finding the cottage was easy after that, though the fog made everything look distorted. The light from the kitchen window showed yellow. Joe's patrol car and the Toyota hunched in front of the door like monsters of legend, one red and one white.

My father greeted us at the door and I knew at once that something else was seriously wrong.

"What is it?"

Dad took my arm. "Sit down, Lark. They've had a call . . ."

"They? Who?"

"The Gardai. Someone called Mahon and said he was speaking for a republican splinter group. He claims they've kidnapped Jay and are holding him as a hostage."

"Ah, Jaysus," said Maeve behind me. "The gobshite."

16 ॐ

We had fed the heart on fantasies,
The heart's grown brutal from the fare;
More substance in our enmities
Than in our love . . .

—William Butler Yeats, "Meditations in Time of Civil War: The
Stare's Nest by My Window"

IN RETROSPECT, I suppose it was then that Maeve took over. At
the time, I was too stunned to notice. She charged past me into
the living room, and I heard her speak sharply to Joe.

Dad said, "Lark, my dear, do you want a little whiskey?"

"I'd barf."

"It's an old-fashioned remedy, I know, but your hands are
like ice. You need something. Perhaps a cup of hot tea."

Hostage. Jay was a hostage. Every atrocity story I'd ever
heard, every tale of political hostages imprisoned and tortured
for years, whirled in my head. I wobbled over to the door arch
and leaned against it. "I want to know what's going on."

". . . and I can put a name to the man, Joseph." Maeve reached
for the telephone. "That's more than Mahon can do at this
hour."

Joe laid a large hand on the receiver. "You're mad!"

"Give me the telephone. I'll keep it short."

Joe's back was to me, so I couldn't see his expression, but his
shoulders were stiff with disapproval. After a moment, though,

he handed Maeve the phone. She tapped out a number from memory.

Dad said, "Lark . . ."

I flapped my hand, hushing him.

"Mike? Maeve Butler here. Where's Liam? Did he indeed? Let me speak to Barbara, if you please. It's urgent." She waited, tapping her foot. "Ah, Barbara. When did Liam leave the estate? I see. And where has he gone? No, Jay's still missing. He's been abducted."

Joe growled and reached for her.

She backed away. "Does it matter what terrorist group? Sure, they're all alike." She covered the receiver. "Did the kidnappers demand a ransom?"

Joe shook his head. "Not yet. The call was a preliminary contact. And do not tell Barbara anything more, Maeve, or I'll take the phone from you by force. I mean it."

She nodded and spoke into the receiver. "No, I can't. Now tell me about Liam McDiarmuid."

When she said the surname, a chill touched my spine. I went on into the room and sat on the couch. Dad followed like a hen with one chick.

Maeve was listening. I could hear Barbara's voice, though not her words. "Yes, a grand idea. Thanks." She hung up.

Joe grabbed Maeve by the shoulder, marched her over to the vacant armchair, and thrust her into it. "What name, Maeve? If you're withholding . . ."

"Withholding evidence?" She gave a sharp laugh. "Save your threats. Liam's your man." She looked at her watch. "And he has more than two hours' head start of you."

I said, "No!"

She turned to me. "One translation of the Irish name 'Grainne' is 'Grace.' "

"Diarmuid and Grainne," I echoed, still stupid with shock.

My father drew a sharp breath.

Joe kept his eyes on Maeve. "You're daft, woman. McDiarmuid has no ties at all to extremist groups. When he first came back from Bosnia, he used to bait the lads in the pub whenever they got to singing the old songs."

"Liam despised Slade Wheeler."

They stared at each other. That at least was true, I thought numbly. Liam had made no bones about his loathing of Slade and Slade's war games.

"The kidnappers, what are they calling themselves?"

Joe's eyes shifted. "Sons of Glory."

"Never heard of them." After a moment, Maeve added, "Your terrorist group doesn't exist. I'll lay odds Mahon thought he'd got a crank call."

"Then you'd lose. The speaker used an identifying code." Joe rubbed the back of his neck, frowning at her as if she were an indecipherable rune. " 'Twas outdated, to be sure, but that's common enough if a man's been out of touch. We're hunting Tommy Tierney. He's done a bolt."

Maeve hooted. "That yobbo hasn't the poetry."

"Poetry? Don't spin me one of your fairy tales, Maeve."

"I won't spin you anything, Sgt. Kennedy. Get yourself onto headquarters and tell the Gardai to pluck Liam off the Rosslare ferry."

"Only an idjit would try to escape on the bloody French ferry."

"If he thought he was being pursued. As far as Liam's concerned, he's off scot-free. Barbara said he left for the trade show in Brussels directly you rang Stanyon with the news of Jay's disappearance. The show doesn't start until Saturday, but the Stonehall concession has to be set up. It's a convenient cover. Barbara didn't question it. Tracy's flying to Brussels tomorrow."

Joe pulled at his lower lip, still frowning. "Poetry."

"There was," she said carefully, "a mark on Slade Wheeler's brow, and no one denies he was Grace Flynn's lover."

"In the legend, 'twas Diarmuid had the mark. . . ."

"Liam saw Slade as Diarmuid—the warrior, the seducer—and himself as Finn MacCoul."

"Shite." He turned away, disgusted.

"Or as the high king, or as one of the druids, more like, a wise man and a protector. Liam is Grace's cousin. It fits, Joe." She stood up and gave him a shove in the direction of the telephone. "Call it in."

"And tell the despatcher I'm after looking for Finn Mac-Coul?" Joe's voice was thick with sarcasm.

Maeve raised her chin. Her eyes were bright and her color high. When she spoke, though, her voice softened, "You're a good man, Joe, and what's more you're a man of learning, try as you may to disguise it. You said it yourself. Slade's body was laid out like a hero waiting for a requiem mass—on Easter Monday with a mark on his forehead, his fatigues brushed, and his toes cocked at a military angle. Tommy Tierney hasn't the wits or the patience."

Joe's shoulders sagged.

"Tell the despatcher you're looking for a suspect trying to leave the country without Garda permission."

My father said, "That's a sensible precaution, surely."

Joe turned to us. "You agree, sir?"

Dad nodded. "He should be questioned."

"Lark?"

I was too confused to say anything but I nodded, too.

Joe turned without a word and picked up the receiver.

While he dialed and identified himself, Maeve went into the kitchen and brought back the travel diary. I remembered her saying in the woods that she wanted to check a description. Ages had passed since then. She sat in the armchair and pored over the book, riffling the pages. Finally, she leaned back with her eyes shut. Dad and I watched her.

Joe made three calls, speaking with crisp efficiency. He telephoned the ferry terminal first. Then he put out a general call, an APB, for Liam and Liam's car. Through my numbness, I remember being surprised that Joe had the make and license number of Liam's Saab in his notebook. The third call, to Chief Inspector Mahon, reassured me that Joe had not lost his sense of policely propriety, and that the Gardai had not given up the search for Tommy Tierney.

My initial shock was beginning to give way to ordinary terror, and my mind was throwing out serious questions about Maeve's theory. It seemed to me that she was ignoring the whole problem of Kayla Wheeler's death. I could imagine Liam killing Slade—just. But Kayla's murder was gratuitous. It didn't fit the mythical pattern. It was straightforward, brutal slaughter.

When Joe hung up and came over to us, I finally found my voice. "I know Mahon's technicians photographed Alex Stein's bruises. Did they examine the other suspects?"

Joe gave a sharp approving nod. "You're thinking."

"I don't see Liam killing Kayla."

"He's unmarked," Joe said bleakly. "No bruises. A wee mote in her ladyship's grand vision."

Maeve opened one eye. "I don't pretend to know all the answers, Joe. . . ."

There was a knock at the door.

Joe ushered Barbara in. She was carrying a carton and her eyes were swollen from crying. Joe took the box from her and set it on the kitchen table.

I had risen, hoping the knock would bring news of Jay, but residual manners kicked in and I greeted Barbara.

Her lip trembled. "I'm so sorry, Lark. Alex and I feel responsible."

My mouth opened and shut. The truth was that part of me agreed with her. If Dad and I hadn't come to the Steins' cottage, Jay would have been safe at home in Shoalwater.

But guilt is a sticky game. If I blamed Jay's abduction on Stonehall Enterprises, then I was going to have to take some of the blame myself. I had behaved badly to Jay. *Oh God, just let him be safe and I'll never do anything unkind again ever to anybody in my whole life please.* A sample of my mental processes. The sight of Barbara's tears opened the fountains and I wept all over her.

Somehow we wound up sitting on the couch with my father

patting Barbara's shoulders and Maeve patting mine. How long that went on I don't know.

Meanwhile, Joe was on the phone again. In fact, the phone was his duty station. He told us Mahon had directed him to stay with the family and to field all incoming calls. Whatever the reason, I was glad Joe stayed with us.

I remember that night as a series of telephone calls punctuated by bowls of Murtagh's soup. Barbara's chef had risen to the occasion. He had sent a beef and barley potage so potent it could have cured shingles, along with a loaf of fresh soda bread. I wasn't up to more than a few spoonfuls of soup myself but it kept Dad going—and Maeve and Joe, after Barbara left, carrying the empty carton with her.

Around midnight Mahon himself showed up with his sergeant and a medic in tow, in case we needed tranquilizing. I needed something. I needed Jay. I refused medication. The medic listened to Dad's heart. Mahon took a statement from me and a brief corroboration from my father. Then he left, with the sergeant and medic *en train.* Joe went back to the telephone.

After he sent his constable off to Liam's flat, Joe called the American embassy, which would no doubt notify the FBI. When he had explained to me the extraordinary measures the Gardai were taking to find my husband, Joe made it clear the abductors could have taken Jay anywhere in the country. Though he thought it unlikely they had left the island with him, they might have spirited him across the border into Ulster. That possibility shook me to the core.

Later, a messenger from Mahon came to the door with a tape of the abductor's call and a cassette player. Joe played the tape for me in the hope that I could identify the voice. All I knew was it wasn't Liam's voice. Dad didn't recognize it either.

The caller sounded young and muffled. When he had identified his group, a name that clearly meant no more to the police than to anyone else, he announced that Jay was being held hostage. He called Jay "your grand Yank detective," and spoke in vague but menacing terms of justice and retribution. The call nauseated me in its very banality. Up to that point I had hoped I was caught in a nightmare. The tape made it all too real.

Mahon had set up an incident room at the church hall and was mounting a world-class search for evidence of the abduction. He had, Joe reported without a gleam of satire, called out the army and set up a machine-gun nest at the Killaveen crossroads. A roadblock had been established at the other end of Suicide Lane, where it joined the N11. There would be no more reporters in the bushes at Stanyon—and no shortage of experienced searchers. They were going to search the entire estate at first light.

"I assume they know what to look for." Maeve's lip curled. She had made another pot of tea and brought it to the living room. She sipped her own, delicately.

Joe's fists clenched. "If you know something else, out with it."

"Are they looking for signs of the abduction, or are they looking for Jay Dodge?"

He glowered. "Both."

"There's a hideaway somewhere in the woods."

"The folly? 'Twas torn down in the last century, and Mahon's men have been all through the area twice. I've had enough of your fantasies, Maeve. Give over."

I said, hesitant, "There is the mound." My own tea sat untouched on the tray, cream scumming the surface.

Joe's frown shifted from Maeve to me.

I told him about my incised stone, gathering confidence as I spoke. Maeve trotted out the etching that showed the mound.

Joe flicked his fingers over the drawing. "Faugh, we know there's a hill. I don't see your point."

She gave him a sweet smile. "That's because you don't understand the nature of follies."

"A serious flaw in my otherwise sterling character."

She ignored his sarcasm. "Face it, you're thinking of a gazebo, a nice little circle of columns with a roof. A folly was a fake ruin."

He made a sound expressive of extreme skepticism.

"A folly could take any shape, and the diary says, explicitly, that the Stanyon folly was an extension of the tomb—the dolmen that's buried beneath all that dirt and all those rows of trees. It's a cave, Joe, an underground bunker."

He drew noisily on his fifth cup of tea and set his mug back on the tray. "If it is, it's a cave without an entrance."

"The devil. Your men didn't *find* the entrance. It's concealed. But Orangemen met there in the last century and de Valera's boys stored ammunition in it in the twenties. We know that much. I'll lay any odds you like there are a dozen old-line republicans in the county who could walk right into the shelter. Notably Toss Tierney."

"We've a warrant out for Tommy Tierney's hide. How much cooperation do you think we'll get from Toss?"

"He's a twister," Maeve said coolly. "Teresa is another story, though, and Toss listens to her. Let me call her."

"No!" Joe thrust his fingers through his thick black hair.

Maeve took another tack. "The tomb faces north. I'm sure of that from the description in the diary. Whssht, man, I could draw you a picture. I *shall* draw you a picture. I've an ordnance map in the boot." She stood up, tea forgotten on the arm of the chair. "Let me bring my excavation team to the woods in the morning. They're idle tomorrow, settling into their quarters. We'll find the folly."

"Ha! If you fancy Mahon will put up with a crew of university students mucking about his crime scene, you're daft." Joe paced to the desk, wheeled, and paced back.

My father, dozing on a corner of the couch, snorted and sat up.

"If it's just Mahon . . ." Maeve began, as if persuading the chief inspector were the easiest thing in the world.

Joe stopped dead on the gray and white rug. "No, it's not just Mahon. It's the whole mad notion. What makes you think they're holding Jay anywhere near here?"

Maeve made a wide gesture. " 'They.' There is no 'they.' We

are speaking of Liam McDiarmuid. I'll wager he sneaked out of Stanyon the back way, overpowered Jay, and took him into the woods in the space of half an hour or less. He was back at his desk at Stanyon by the time you called. He could have done that easily, without his absence causing comment, but he couldn't have spirited Jay off to Dublin or Cork."

"Not without accomplices," Joe agreed.

I shivered, wondering who the accomplices might be.

The telephone rang. All of us jumped. Joe answered. From the scraps I heard of his side of the conversation, I gathered he was speaking to Mahon and that something had happened. My stomach roiled.

Dad took my hand.

Joe hung up. "Neither Liam nor his Saab is on the ferry."

Maeve took a step toward him. "That means nothing." I could see she was shaken.

"Nor in the car park at the terminal. Nor do the customs men at Rosslare remember seeing anyone of his description."

"Even so."

"It's no good, Maeve," he said softly. "I was mad to listen to you."

I said, "Wherever he may be, Liam is missing."

I knew that because, at some earlier point in the surreal evening, Declan Byrne had called in. He had sweet-talked the landlady into a search of Liam's flat. Liam wasn't there or at the neighborhood pub or at any of his known hangouts. And, as we now knew, not on the Rosslare ferry. "He disappeared. The timing can't be a coincidence," I added after an exhausted pause. I was tired to the bone and wide-awake. It was past three in the morning. "Maybe Liam's a victim, too."

That got their attention, if only because it was a fresh thought. Dad put in a half-hearted vote for the idea. He sounded as tired as I felt, and I was abruptly reminded of the state of his health. I persuaded him to go to bed on the premise that one of us would have to be functional the next day. I went downstairs myself, took a hot shower, and changed into sweats.

As I was brushing my hair dry I heard the phone ring again. The bedsprings creaked in Dad's room.

"It's okay," I hissed. "Just the phone." I tiptoed upstairs.

Joe was listening and rubbing his eyes with his free hand. Maeve had gone into the kitchen. I joined her. She looked fresh as a jonquil and had spread her ordnance map out on the table. She was working on a bird's eye sketch of the folly entrance, to scale.

She gave me a smile. "He's in the folly. I'll lay odds."

"Alive?" I let the question hang between us.

She laid down her pencil. "You're imagining horrors, Lark. Liam had no reason to kill Jay."

I said flatly, "He had no reason to kill Kayla either."

"No reason we know of. Look at this." She tapped the map at a spot where isometric lines indicated a small hillock. "That's the mound. The entrance to the tomb ran along here." Her finger traced a short line. "It's my guess the Stanyon uncle extended the opening northward and roofed over the original earthwork. See? The mound is asymmetical in that direction. A long, north-south passage with the dolmen at the southern end."

"I'm convinced, but wouldn't later users—the Orangemen and so on—have altered things?"

She tapped the pencil again. "No doubt they did—and concealed the entry. That's why we need Toss Tierney." She flashed me another smile. "Toss and a pair of thumbscrews." She cocked her head.

Joe had hung up. He came into the kitchen and looked me in the eye. "They've taken Tommy Tierney into custody at a motel outside Limerick. He was making for Shannon Airport. He's not talking."

Then make him talk. I felt like screaming that. Instead I cleared my throat. "If he won't talk, how do you know he was involved in the kidnapping?"

"We don't." Joe pulled a chair and sat. "However, he did have your husband's passport and the Aer Lingus ticket in the pocket of his jacket. Both were crudely altered." He hesitated. "He'd been in a barny."

"What do you mean?"

"In a brawl," Maeve translated.

Joe knuckled his eyes. "The police surgeon thinks one of the cuts on his body is a knife wound. It's a new wound."

My blood ran cold.

17 ❧

When shaws been sheen and shrads full fair
And leaves both large and long
'Tis merry in the fair forest
To hear the small bird's song

—Medieval ballad

AT EIGHT IN the morning, my mother called from New York. She had watched the eleven o'clock news. There was a story. . . .

"Jay's been abducted." I winced at the sound of my own voice, as if saying the hard fact made it truer.

"Oh, my dear!" Ma said good things. She has an instinct for that. Through her verbal facility, I caught the undertone of genuine concern. Both of my parents loved Jay. As I answered—or tried to answer—my mother's questions, I thought how strange it was that my parents had come around so thoroughly. Both had had reservations about my marriage. As far as I knew, Jay had made no extraordinary effort to win their affection, yet he had it.

I answered the telephone myself, because Joe had gone, and took it into the kitchen, because Maeve was napping on the couch in the living room.

At first light, when the police ground-search began, Joe had joined it. In spite of his reservations about Maeve's theory, he wanted to make sure the searchers looked for the remains of the Stanyon folly. He had been gone nearly two hours.

I listened as Ma worked her way around to asking about my father's health and state of mind. I wished she would hang up. I didn't want to talk, yet I kept making noises.

"May I speak to George?"

"He's asleep. He was up until three and I hate to wake him so soon."

I could hear in her hesitation that she approved of my solicitude, though she wanted to talk things over with Dad. "Ah. Well, when he wakes, tell him to call me and never mind what time it is here."

"All right, Ma."

"I love you, darling."

"Thanks," I said with stiff lips. "I love you, too."

"I'm sorry, Lark."

"I know."

When she hung up I felt wrung dry. I went into the kitchen, but the thought of another cup of coffee revolted me. I ate a piece of bread. It seemed to calm my stomach. After a while, I went out on the tiny stone porch to see what I could see.

The sun was bright and the sky an innocent, smogless blue with fat white clouds out of a children's-book illustration. A light breeze off the Irish Sea lifted the leaves of the shrubs across the graveled drive. At the far end, where the drive turned down to Stanyon Hall, I could see that the rhododendrons had bloomed at last, blood-red.

The search had taken its way well into the woods and surrounding fields. I saw files of dim figures in the sheep pasture that rose up to the northeast, and, farther to the west, from among the trees, I heard an occasional cry as if someone found something. I could see movement in the woods, but nothing specific, no one identifiable.

A helicopter rose like a horsefly in the direction of Arklow. It hovered a long minute over Stanyon Hall, the *whop-whop* of the rotors steady. The noise intensified as the chopper moved toward the cottage and the woods. It was a sound out of Jay's worst nightmares, but I hoped he was where he could hear it, because at least then he would know someone was doing something.

I ached to do something myself, though I wasn't sure what. My teeth clenched with the effort to keep still, not to run to the stile, leap over it, dash through the trees calling Jay's name. Maeve and I were not allowed to enter the woods until the official search for evidence associated with the kidnapping was over. If the searchers found the entrance to the folly, well and good. If not, Maeve could supervise a limited excavation after they left. The site was not registered and she had permission from the owners to dig, so the only red tape would be yellow—crime-scene tape.

As soon as Joe left, Maeve rousted her assistant, a doctoral candidate, and warned the sleepy student what would be needed and why. At the very least, she wanted her theodolite and the chest of excavation tools. It goes without saying that I eavesdropped on Maeve's conversation. She spoke longingly of sensors that could detect variations in density and magnetism beneath the mound's surface. However, such devices were costly. Locating them and getting permission to use them would have taken too long.

Too long for what? I wondered, chilled. Jay had been gone more than twelve hours. If the kidnapper had in fact imprisoned him in the folly, did he have water? Air? Was he warm enough? Hypothermia was a frightening possibility. The night had been cold.

When Maeve finally hung up, she yawned, stretched, and announced she was going to take a "kip" on the sofa. Fine with me. I was deadly tired but could not close my eyes.

I sat in the kitchen and tried to read the SF novel I'd bought in Dublin. My mind wouldn't focus on the page. I kept thinking about Jay. I tried to call up the many good times we had shared, but my mind returned, over and over, to the image of a man tied to a chair in a cold dark cave: a man, it might be, with an untreated knife wound.

When the helicopter swung back on its return flight, it flew so low I thought I could feel the prop-wash on my face. I waited outside until it disappeared and the noise dwindled to a distant throbbing. Then I went back into the cottage.

Maeve slept, curled on the couch like a cat. She didn't move. I retrieved the telephone directory and the printout of useful phone numbers from the desk. If I couldn't do anything to assist in the search, at least I could take care of niggling details. I called Aer Lingus.

It was the time of morning for business flights out of Dublin. The first clerk heard my woeful story with impatience, but she transferred me to a man who was willing to listen. He had heard of Jay's abduction on the radio, and he sounded both sympathetic and excited. People can't help it. A disaster, especially someone else's disaster, stirs the blood. He agreed to cancel Jay's reservation for the Sunday flight to Seattle—there was no direct flight to Portland—and to place him on standby. Jay would have to pay a fee, of course, but not a large one. I thanked the man, accepted his sympathies, and hung up.

When I called the embassy, the clerk sounded as if she hadn't had her morning tea fix. Yes, we could pick up the replacement passport Monday. After ten. In view of her evident grogginess, I decided not to tell her the Gardai had retrieved the original passport along with the thief. I assumed Tommy Tierney had been our burglar. At some level, a message to that effect had probably already got through to the embassy, though I supposed it would take days to percolate down to the people who dealt with distressed citizens face-to-face.

I decided my third call would have to wait. I ought to notify the Dean of Instruction that Jay was missing. It was not yet two in the morning at home, however. No point trying to get through much before four in the afternoon, Greenwich Time. If I woke him, the dean would just dither. He had an ulcer.

Almost as soon as I replaced the receiver after my call to the

229

embassy, the phone rang. Maeve stirred. I said hello, low-voiced.

It was Alex Stein. He sounded as tired as I felt. He expressed his sympathies and made the vague offer of assistance people make when they don't know what else to say by way of comfort. I thanked him.

"Barbara and Mike and I have to attend Kayla's inquest this morning."

"They haven't postponed it?"

He gave a short laugh. "That would probably disrupt too many official schedules. However, the coroner did move the hearing to Arklow, to accommodate the press."

I wished him luck.

"How is George holding up?"

"Pretty well."

"That's a relief. We'll come over to the cottage as soon as we can. Barbara says the Gardai suspect Liam. That's insane. He's an artist."

I didn't comment. So Liam was an artist. Van Gogh had cut off his own ear. Byron had fomented a revolution. Allen Ginsberg had dropped his pants at a peace rally.

"He's a gentle man," Alex insisted, more to the point.

I cleared my throat. "That's my impression." It was what prevented me from believing Liam had killed Kayla.

Reassured that I wasn't baying like a hound for Liam's blood, Alex disengaged.

Our conversation roused Maeve. She trooped down to the loo and returned for a cup of the very old coffee in the electric pot. "Your father's stirring."

"Is he? Alex phoned. The inquest on Kayla Wheeler has been moved to Arklow. Were you called, Maeve?"

She moaned and checked her watch. "It's set for ten o'clock. I'd best get things rolling. But first . . ." She closed her eyes and swallowed coffee. "Ah, that's more like it."

My stomach gurgled. I cut a slice of Murtagh's soda bread. "What do I do if they finish the search before you return?"

"Wait for me." She looked at my face and said, "I'm sorry. The waiting has to be the hardest part."

"The hardest part," I said grimly, "is imagining my husband weltering in his own blood. Waiting comes after that."

Rather to my surprise, Maeve's first action was not to contact her excavation team. She called Teresa Tierney and I was treated to an exhibition of the purest Butler blarney.

Maeve flattered and soothed the poor woman, sympathized with her over her obnoxious son's plight, and presented her own attempt to find the folly as something of a patriotic duty. She said nothing negative about Teresa's menfolk but didn't hesitate to vilify Liam. If Tommy had been involved in the abduction at any level, it was as the mere dupe of a diabolical and cunning intelligence who had led the innocent lad astray. Finding Jay in the folly, alive, would somehow exonerate Tommy.

I wondered how Teresa could swallow such blather.

Teresa spoke at length and Maeve made soothing sounds. Finally Maeve said, "And how is poor Toss?"

A blast from the receiver. I had the feeling poor Toss was in deep shite, with his wife as well as the Gardai.

Having softened up her target, Maeve moved to her primary text. She wanted Toss to show her the entrance to the folly. She was sure he knew how to get into it, and equally sure he was oath-bound not to reveal the secret, but some things ought to take precedence over outworn loyalties. Saving Jay's life, for example. Maeve insinuated that Tierney cooperation in the search would sit well with the court when it came time to charge Tommy. Plea-bargaining is an American tradition. Clearly, the concept was not unknown in Ireland, either.

When Maeve hung up, I said, "Did it work? Will she get Toss to open up?"

"I don't know," Maeve said soberly. "I hope so. I can find the area where the entrance to the folly should be, but excavation's a slow process."

"And time is of the essence."

"It is indeed. At least now the word is out."

"Word?"

"That we need to know the way into the folly," she explained, patient. "Teresa will call her best friends and relatives to ask their advice and they'll call their friends. Every republican in County Wicklow of the right vintage will know what we need by noon. One of them should come through."

It sounded like jungle drums to me. I hoped Toss would remember Dad's Jameson's and weaken.

Maeve made another hurried call to her assistant, looked around for her handbag and coat, and took her leave. She meant to stop by her father's house and freshen up. She would leave the inquest as soon as was humanly possible, she said, but her assistant would probably arrive at the cottage before she did. His name was Johnnie Poole and he would be driving a Morris Minor held together with strapping tape. He would come as soon as the Gardai lifted the roadblocks.

Maeve's van rattled off as my father made his way upstairs. He was unshaven and still in his dressing gown, but his color was better than it had been at 3:00 A.M. While I brewed him a fresh pot of coffee, I reported my conversation with Ma. He allowed that he would call her, but not until he'd showered and shaved. He was downstairs with the hot water full on and the Rayburn gurgling away when Joe came in the door.

"What have you found?" The question burst from me.

Joe rubbed his eyes. He had been with us all night, so he was as tired as I felt, but he had been short of sleep, I thought, for several days. He looked his age. My age.

"Is that coffee?"

I possessed my soul in patience and poured him a cup.

He sugared and creamed it, sitting at the table with the ease of a friend. "They didn't find the folly, Lark, but I took Maeve's map with me and she's right. The mound extends northward. There are boulders and a tangle of briars on the north slope but we didn't find an entrance."

I swallowed my disappointment.

He took a sip, grimacing as the scalding coffee touched his lips. "Mahon's lot did find the place where Jay was captured."

My heart slammed into double time. "Where?"

"Past the rhododendrons on the drive to Stanyon. He was headed that way, apparently. We found American coins." He set his mug down and withdrew something from the breast of his smudged tunic. "Do you recognize that?"

It was wrapped in protective paper. He unfolded the covering carefully.

My tormented stomach churned. "That's the type of pen the college in Shoalwater stocks for professors. It's not exactly distinctive, though." The pens were cheap black ballpoints.

"I've not seen a pen like it here."

I gulped. "Then it's probably Jay's."

"So we thought." He drew a long breath and his blue eyes met mine with somber empathy. "There were signs of a scuffle, and shoe prints of a trainer in the earth beside the lane. We followed a trail of bent grass and scrape marks to the stone wall around the woods. Mahon is taking the idea that Jay may be concealed in the woods seriously now."

"Good. That's good."

"There's a gate on the far side of the woods, though, and a lane that connects with the Killaveen road. The abductor could have carried Jay to the gate and removed him by automobile. We're looking for signs of a car, though McDiarmuid's Saab was found this morning, abandoned in Limerick."

Limerick? That didn't make sense. Perhaps Liam and Tommy had stashed Jay in the folly and headed west together. If so, why had the Gardai not found Liam as well?

Joe watched me a moment, then said, "There was no blood where we found the signs of struggle."

"You're sure?"

"Positive."

A weight eased from my heart. "Jay's not a small man. Could Liam have carried him through the woods unassisted?"

"Only with difficulty." He cocked his head. "Your man is tall but not over-heavy. I could carry him." Joe was six feet tall and solid. Liam had to be three inches shorter.

"Was someone else involved?"

He gave a short laugh. "Tommy Tierney's neck deep, and he's a big bruiser, takes after his da."

"Has he talked?"

Joe shook his head. "They'll charge him this morning with burglary and flight to avoid prosecution. He may change his tune after another day in custody."

Another day. That was a long time to wait. I shivered. "Maeve called Tommy's mother."

Joe swore. "I'll have Maeve's ears on a platter, meddling with Mahon's witnesses. She's a damned interfering nuisance—"

"She's a good friend," I interrupted.

Silence lay between us.

Joe checked his watch. "I'm due at the inquest. The boys will be winding down their search of the woods soon, Lark. I told Declan Byrne to notify you when they've gone."

"Thanks."

At that point Dad came in and shook hands. Joe was so pressed for time he left me to explain to my father what the police had discovered. I could tell the lack of ceremony troubled Joe. At heart, he liked to do things by the book.

I poured Dad a fresh cup of coffee as I talked. "So Mahon has come around to Maeve's theory after all, but they didn't find the folly."

"Maeve will find it." Dad sat and sipped.

"Breakfast?"

"I am a bit hungry." He looked guilty.

I cut bread for him and scrambled a couple of eggs. When he had eaten, he phoned my mother. As I was pottering around the kitchen, tidying the table, Constable Byrne walked in from the woods. I brewed him a pot of tea. That seemed to be my role. I was beginning to resent it.

Byrne was finishing his "cuppa" and Dad had joined us when

a rusty Morris Minor pulled in behind the Toyota. Three students erupted from it, two young women and a very young man. All three wore jeans, sweatshirts, and wellies. They began unloading gear. It was surprising how much junk the tiny car could hold.

I invited the kids in and made some more tea. Then I rebelled. I was not some kind of skivvy. I intended to be part of the action. I announced that I was going downstairs to change into work clothes.

Dad and the students and the young Garda looked at me with so much sympathy I nearly threw the teapot at them.

Maeve returned before noon. She came in dressed in an Oxford-gray pantsuit, with her jeans and boots over one arm. She greeted her pupils, dashed downstairs, changed, and reappeared in the kitchen before the kettle boiled. She waved off my offer of tea, whipped out her ordnance map and the sketch she had made, and began briefing her team. I told her what Joe had told me of the mixed results of the search.

"Mahon's come over to my view? Good, good. Any word from Teresa Tierney?"

"No."

"Right." She looked disappointed but not daunted.

"Declan Byrne said Mahon left a couple of men in the woods. They can lead you directly to the north face of the mound, and they're supposed to put themselves at your disposal. Mahon will come to the site himself as soon as the coroner adjourns the inquest. Is it over yet?"

"I don't know. I left as soon as they'd taken my testimony. The Gardai will dig?" She made a face. "Mahon watching over my shoulder, obviously." She looked around at her team. "So let's do everything in textbook style. Ready?"

They were straining at the leash. So was I. So was my father. That presented a problem.

Maeve solved it by pleading with him to stand by the telephone in case Teresa Tierney called. Grumbling, he acceded and she went on with her briefing. Then we trooped outside. Johnnie Poole shouldered the theodolite, the young women lifted the chest of tools between them, and we headed for the stile. Before we reached it, I heard a car crunch on the gravel behind us. A door slammed. Maeve motioned us on, impatient, but Joe Kennedy hove into sight as we entered the woods with our Gardai guides.

Joe's arrival created a delay while he ranked Maeve down for telephoning Teresa Tierney. They glowered at each other. Maeve did not apologize. The students set their burdens down and listened to the ruction with their eyes wide. The two uniformed policemen shifted from foot to foot. I felt like screaming, but I didn't.

As the barbed exchange softened into a discussion of excavation procedures, I heard a further slamming of car doors.

"If we don't get into gear, Maeve, we'll still be standing here at sundown. That has to be Mahon." I waved my arm in the direction of the cottage.

Maeve and Joe exchanged looks. He made a gesture to the two patient Gardai and off we went.

In broad daylight the woods had lost their "airiness." I was again reminded of telephone poles. There was no birdsong—too many people, too much commotion. Occasional blotches of red paint showed like scabs on the tree trunks. The policemen led us north along the stone wall the full extent of the plantation before they turned west. They were taking us around the hill I had climbed the day I found my stone.

The north rim of the woods fronted a long, green slope dotted with sheep. The road to Killaveen wound past with the hills of Wicklow blue in the distance. A police van had been driven down what must have been a farm lane along the pasture wall. It was parked a few hundred yards from where the trees began. When I saw it, I understood why Mahon had to investigate the possibility that Jay had been carried through the woods and out the other side to a waiting car. My heart sank. Maeve was sure Jay was hidden in the folly. I hoped she was right, but my doubts stirred.

We walked along the bordering wall perhaps fifty yards. The sight of all that open country diminished the woods. The plantation was, after all, a small area. I could see how the mound rose up irregularly and that the trees on the mound proper were scraggly and stunted by comparison with the straight, sturdy growth elsewhere. Then we were among the trees again and I lost my perspective.

The silent Gardai took us directly to the area Maeve had designated in her sketch as the likeliest place for the folly entry. They stopped, and the shorter man gestured at an unremarkable slope, stone-studded and overgrown with vines, thrusting ferns, and briars. Overgrown with trees, too. I felt my chest tighten with panic. We'd never find the key to Jay's prison in all that tangled greenery. Even the students, who had been chattering among themselves as we walked north, fell silent.

Maeve surveyed the unpromising slope with narrowed eyes. "Right. We have secateurs in the chest. We're going to need axes and a saw, preferably powered. Meanwhile, we'll pace it off. And I want grid-lines, chaps. Johnnie, set up the theodolite over there." She gestured.

I'd forgotten the tedium involved at the start of a dig. I had once spent an amateur summer on an archaeological dig in northern California. That was where I met Jay. I thought back, trying to remember the site on my first day. It seemed to me the university had sent a reconnaissance team out well before the excavation began, that the site had been surveyed and marked before we set up our tents. This site was much smaller, of course, but if Maeve insisted on a textbook job it might be days before she dug through to the passageway into the tomb.

I sat on a boulder and thought dark thoughts. Joe sent one of the Gardai back in search of axes and saws—and permission from the Steins to fell their timber. By the book.

Part of my uncharacteristic funk arose from my uselessness. I could do nothing helpful until the grunt work began, so I sat there and brooded. A crow cawed. Every once in a while a car or lorry passed along the road and I heard the hum of its engine. Mahon appeared with his sergeant and constable in tow, and the police conferred in a clump while Maeve's team laid out the first of the grid-lines. They used metal stakes and heavy yellow twine. The assistant, Johnnie Poole, called out numbers from time to time. Maeve supervised.

They had worked a good two hours, sweating in the sun, cutting brush, marking their lines, before Maeve was satisfied. I had wandered around a bit, kicking the needles, brooding, but I kept coming back to watch. Now I could do something. I went over to the chest of gear, now nearly empty, and pulled out a shovel.

"Hi," one of the Gardai shouted. "You two. This is a crime scene. What're you doing here?"

All of us turned to stare as my father and the unprepossessing figure of Grace Flynn's escort, Artie, emerged from the forest.

Dad looked splendid. He gave me a smile, then turned to Mahon who had stepped forward, scowling. "Ah, inspector. This young man tells me his name is Arthur Sullivan. I think you should hear him out."

Mahon grunted.

Sunlight winked off the stud in Artie's nose. His eyes shifted and his cheeks turned pink under our combined stare.

Joe sighed. "Why did you come here, Artie? Speak up, lad."

He wiped his sleeve across his nose. "Grace sent me."

18 ❧

Amazing grace, how sweet the sound,
That saved a wretch like me.

—Hymn

"GRACE SENT YOU," Joe repeated in the calm, unthreatening tone I had once heard Jay use with a nervous gunman. "Can you tell us why, lad?"

Artie ducked his head, mumbling.

"You can what?"

"Show yez the way into the bolt hole, ye fooking idjit."

The breath went out of my body. Dad beamed as if a favored student had just passed his orals.

My heart hammered in my chest, and everyone began talking at once. I put my hands over my ears.

"Quiet!" boomed my father, with the weight of forty years of lectures in his voice.

"Do you truly know the way in, Artie?" Maeve asked.

"Sure, and didn't Tommy show me ages ago? He learnt it from his da. Old Toss." Artie snickered. "It was a secret we had, me and Tom. The captain didn't know."

By "captain" he had to mean Slade Wheeler.

"For God's sake, Artie, show us," I said hoarsely.

Mahon didn't wait for the moment of revelation. He whipped out his cellular phone and called for an ambulance. He also sent one of the uniformed men off toward the police van to direct incoming traffic, or so I supposed afterward when I was capable of thought.

While Mahon was giving the despatcher explicit instructions as to where the ambulance should come—by the lane through the sheep pasture—Artie surveyed the archaeologists' work. Shivering, I watched him.

A half-grin curled his lip. He was drawing out the suspense, showing off. "Where do yez think it is, then?"

Maeve pointed to a steep patch on the slope of the mound. It lay between two uninteresting rock faces, and her crew had cleared it of vines.

Artie giggled. "Close. It's the fooking rock, though." He strolled over, touched the lichened gray surface of the farther stone, slid his hand sideways, and tugged.

Slowly the entire rough-hewn slab pivoted to reveal a black gap about my height and twice as wide as a broad-shouldered man. In the open position, the "door" cut the space in thirds, with the slab taking up the middle segment. Needles and small stones sifted down from the mound above.

Artie spat. "It's a fooking fake, see. Tommy and me used to nip in and smoke our fags and look at the dirty pictures. The walls is covered with 'em." He snickered again. "And wasn't the captain and the lads hunting us the whole bleeding time? They never did find us."

I was halfway to Artie's side before he finished speaking. Joe intercepted me. "No."

"I want to go in. I want Jay."

"Let me enter first, Lark. He may not be there."

He has to be there! I swallowed the instinctive protest.

Joe raised his voice. "Did any damned fool think to bring a torch?"

One of the uniforms took a half-step forward, but Maeve strode to her bottomless tool chest and pulled out a long businesslike flashlight. Joe took it from her with a curt nod.

240

Mahon said heavily, "Mind the blood, sergeant."

I gasped and took another step toward the black opening.

Joe thumbed the flashlight on and shone it at the packed earth floor of the entrance. A brown stain had been trampled into the dirt at the opening. It had dried in ridges. Footprints trailed into the dark.

I was biting my fists.

"I'm going in," Joe muttered.

Mahon's morose constable forestalled him, pulled out a camera, and took at least three shots of the entryway before Joe said with quiet menace, "Move aside, if you please."

"Constable." Mahon jerked his head and the man stepped out of the way.

Joe inched sideways past the muddy patch, but he straightened at once, as if the passage had widened, and was soon out of sight. Mahon's camera-toting constable turned the lens on the hidden latch. His flash attachment strobed.

Maeve's students were talking in low voices, and I heard Artie giggle once, but I was so focused on the passageway the rest of the world receded. Dad walked over and wrapped his arms around me as he had done when I was a child. I buried my face for a moment in the tweedy shoulder. It seemed a very long time, though it was at most ten minutes, before Joe emerged.

He came straight to me. "He's there, unconscious but alive. I'm less certain of Liam McDiarmuid."

"Jay . . . oh, God, oh, thank God." I was half crying, half laughing and certainly not registering anomalies.

"Hush," Dad said. "Hush, darling, it's all right."

Joe turned to Mahon. "They're all the way in, at the end."

Mahon nodded. His constable took a step forward but Mahon waved him back without looking at him.

Maeve touched the sleeve of Joe's blue uniform. "Liam's there, too? I don't understand."

"He was bound hand and foot, like Jay, and he has at least

241

one serious knife wound. It bled a lot. His flesh is cold." Joe drew a breath. "They're both cold. I cut the ropes."

Maeve's hand dropped. I shivered again.

A klaxon sounded in the distance. Mahon must have had the ambulance crew on alert for his summons, the response was so quick. Either he had given Maeve's theory full credence or he was a man who liked to cover all his bases.

I leaned on my father and listened as the sound drew nearer and broke off in mid-hoot. Mahon was on the phone again, a little apart. I couldn't follow what he said. Maeve was frankly brooding. Her students exchanged looks.

Perhaps ten minutes later, the uniformed Garda and a team of paramedics bearing a stretcher made their way to us through the trees. Joe led the medics into the passage. Another interminable pause.

They brought Jay out first, wrestling the stretcher past the fake stone door. They had wrapped him in a thermal blanket and strapped him to the stretcher. The collar of his blue anorak peeked from beneath the blanket. His eyes were clenched shut and he didn't move.

I ran to him and stroked his cold, bristly cheek, but he didn't respond to my touch. His eyes must have shuttered in an involuntary reaction to the brilliant sunlight. He had been in the dark a long time. The area around his mouth was raw, smudged, his lower lip bleeding a little. He smelled of sweat and blood and fear.

Joe took my elbow and tugged me back so the medics could do their job. "His mouth was taped shut. I ripped the tape off. It may be I shouldn't have."

A third medic, probably the driver, reeled through the trees with a heavy-looking case. The others dived into it, muttering. Mahon was still talking on the cell phone while they set up an IV. A saline drip, I thought, or glucose. Jay was dehydrated, they said. He was also very cold. They told me his body temperature in Celsius degrees. My numbed brain refused to make the calculations, but I knew it was low. He had a knot on the side of his head, high in the hairline. They didn't think his skull was fractured.

I tried not to get in the paramedics' way, but I hung close to the stretcher. I was vaguely aware of noises. Maeve's team began to pack their gear. Dad and Joe conferred. Maeve was cross-examining Artie about Grace Flynn. How had Grace found out about the search for the folly, how had she known of the folly in the first place, and so on.

I heard all that and on some level registered it, but my full focus was on Jay. He might be bruised, filthy, unshaven, unconscious, and swaddled like a mummy in a gray thermal blanket, but I thought he was beautiful.

A crashing in the brush announced the arrival of a second team of paramedics. Mahon must have sent for another ambulance.

The new medics went in for Liam about the time the leader of the first team announced they could move Jay. One of the Gardai who had guided us to the mound hefted the back end of Jay's stretcher while a medic hovered over the IV. The apparatus stuck up like a flower stem stripped of petals.

"Easy does it, lads."

I followed on their heels.

Mahon's sergeant found his tongue at last. "You can't go with them, missus!"

I ignored him. Nothing and no one could have stopped me from riding in that ambulance with Jay. To the medics' credit they made no attempt to stop me.

Maeve trotted after me. "I'll bring your father to the hospital, Lark. Do you need anything?"

"Uh, my purse." I ducked sideways around a tree branch, my eyes on the Garda's solid blue shoulders, my feet scuffing fallen needles on the path. There was something I should say, something important. "Uh, thanks, Maeve. And thank Artie for me."

The jolting ambulance ride is a blur in memory. I squished

in near Jay's head. I could see marks on his exposed wrist from the rope that had bound him. The driver used the klaxon often, and we had at least one close call with an oncoming lorry. The medics made terse comments to each other. I was watching Jay's face. Once, when I touched his cheek, his eyelids fluttered.

The hospital was a new building, tastefully modern and full of light, with a sprinkling of bad religious statuary. I know that the Virgin has to wear symbolic colors, but why robin's egg blue? In the emergency room, the medics dislodged me from Jay's side, and a graying nun in semi-civilian garb came up with a clipboard to record vital statistics and insurance information. She asked if Jay had conditions the doctors ought to know about.

"Appalling nightmares." I stared at her round amiable face. Not to mention a flying phobia.

"Medical conditions," she said patiently. "Allergies, heart irregularities, and so on."

"He was shot in the stomach twelve, no, thirteen years ago."

The nun's eyebrows disappeared into her modified wimple.

I plodded on. "The doctors say he's all right now, but he has to be careful what he eats and drinks. Because of the possibility of ulcers." I had learned to cook thanks to Jay's balky stomach. I thought of saying something about a bland diet, then it occurred to me I was in a hospital in the Republic of Ireland. They were not going to feed Jay fajitas with *salsa picante*.

The nun bent to her form and scribbled. Then she thanked me and let me go.

I kicked my heels for what seemed like hours among the anxious and the curious before a nurse in full starch beckoned to me. "Mrs. Dodge?"

I nodded.

"You can join your husband now in the ward. He's been sedated but he's asking for you."

I gulped, sure I was going to cry, and followed her down a squeaky-clean corridor, into a lift, and up to the second floor. They had put Jay in a two-bed ward, but the other bed was

244

empty and a privacy curtain had been drawn. A uniformed Garda withdrew discreetly as I entered the room.

I poked my head around the edge of the curtain and startled a grizzled man in tweeds who was checking the dressing on Jay's head.

He turned. "Ah, you're the missus. I'm Seamus Hanlon. They called me in because of the head injury. He's doing very well now that we've warmed him up."

"Lark..."

I was at Jay's side in an instant, holding his free hand. The other was taped to an IV needle.

"Mmm," he said sleepily. "Year."

That's what it sounded like. I kissed his cheek. "Yes, I'm here."

"George?"

"Dad's okay."

"I le' tha' sucker whop me on the head." He licked his cut lip. "Howzat for incompetence?"

"Outstanding," I said unsteadily. I stayed with him, stroking his hand, until he fell sound asleep.

To my surprise, Dr. Hanlon was still waiting in the hall when I stuck my head out. He took me to the hospital tea shop over my protests—Jay wouldn't wake for several hours, he assured me—and fed me tea and scones while he gave me a thorough report. Much of what he said passed over my head. I was too dazed and tired to think, but I did gather that Jay was going to be fine. They were keeping him overnight for observation and I could take him home in the morning. Meanwhile, I was welcome to stay in the room with him. The orderly would bring a cot. I liked that idea.

Consequently, I was napping and my husband was still sleeping soundly when Maeve and my father, Alex, Barbara, Grace Flynn looking bilious, Artie, a silent Mike Novak, Mrs. O'Brien from Ballymann House, and Inspector Mahon all showed up in the corridor. Most of them seemed to be carrying flowers, and Maeve had brought my purse.

245

She handed it to me once I had staggered to my feet to greet them.

"What price folly?" she crowed.

We grinned at each other like idiots.

My father said, "I drove the Toyota."

"Dad!" I felt obliged to protest, but I was proud of him.

The Toyota was in the car park, he announced with satisfaction not untinged with guilt. "I followed Maeve." He beamed. "Jay looks splendid, my dear." How he could tell that from one glimpse through a crack in the privacy curtain I didn't know, but I wasn't going to argue. I kissed his cheek.

"The creature!" Mrs. O'Brien said in tones of utmost admiration. She thrust a magnificent bouquet of daffodils at me. She must have cut them from her own garden. Commercial growers don't stock that many varieties. "I promised me brother I'd see how Mr. Dodge is faring in hospital. Joe sends his respects. He's writing up a monster report this minute, or he'd come in person."

I thanked her. Strategic withdrawal? Evidently Joe and Maeve were still at odds—or possibly Joe and Chief Inspector Mahon. Mahon stood apart, quiet.

So did Grace and Artie.

I went over to Grace and hugged her. I also shook Artie's hand. His palm was damp and his eyes shifted. He gave a little giggle. Of such are heroes made.

"How did you know, Grace?"

"Sure, everybody knows there's a cave in the woods. Teresa Tierney called Mother, and Mam sent Ellen—that's me sister—to tell me there was a search on."

"And Artie admitted he knew the way in?"

She gave Artie a look compounded of contempt and affection. "Didn't Tommy tell me all about them dirty pictures? I know Tommy. He'd have to show off to somebody. So I chased Artie down at work and told him to nip along to the cottage."

Just like that. I thanked both of them again and so did Dad, and they left looking pleased with themselves. Mrs. O'Brien slipped out during Grace's tale. The crowd was thinning.

Barbara and Alex thrust hothouse mums into my arms. I juggled the mums and the daffs to a table that looked like a small altar. A not-too-gruesome crucifix hung above it.

Barbara said they were on their way to Wexford to see Liam, who had been airlifted to the county hospital to undergo emergency surgery. He was bleeding internally.

"Then he's still alive? I'm so glad." I was glad—and puzzled. "Does anyone know how he came to be shut up in the folly with Jay?"

"That's the million-dollar question." Mike Novak's face was grim.

Silence. Mahon cleared his throat.

"Do you know, inspector?"

"I do not. We're waiting until Hanlon lets us interview your husband."

That explained the Garda on duty at Jay's bedside. The man was standing out in the corridor as he had been since my arrival, patient and silent. I wondered what he was thinking.

Barbara said, "We'll have to destroy the folly."

Maeve gave a muted shriek. "You will not. It's a National Treasure and I intend to excavate it."

Alex's mouth curved. "What about the Victorian porn?"

"Regency porn," Maeve corrected, prim. "When I've done with the dolmen, set up a turnstile and charge admission." Everyone but Mahon laughed.

I said, "I think I missed something. Did you enter the folly?"

Maeve looked smug. "Chief Inspector Mahon kindly allowed Professor Dailey and me a glimpse."

"When the crime scene lot had finished their work," Mahon said with the air of a man confessing mortal sin to a cardinal. I could see he was embarrassed, either by the dirty pictures or by his concession to Maeve's curiosity.

"That's what took us so long, Lark," my father explained. "We didn't hurry. We knew you'd want time alone with Jay. The megalith is perfectly splendid!"

If I looked at Maeve I'd fall into uncontrollable giggles. "Never mind the dolmen. What about the pictures?"

Maeve gave an impatient shrug. "The usual. Gentlemen in starched cravats and naked women. I daresay the artwork is well enough in its way. The stone at the entrance reminds me of the architectural oddments in those huge display rooms at the Victoria and Albert."

I ransacked my memory. "The rooms they set up for art students?"

"Precisely. The Victorians were clever at reproduction. When I was an undergraduate I could never tell the real stuff from the plaster casts without reading the labels. Not that our door is plaster. Some native craftsman shaped a real stone and mounted it on bearings. I fancy my colleagues in industrial archaeology will find the workmanship interesting."

"Clever," Mahon muttered. He was still embarrassed.

"This is all very well," Mike Novak grated, "but Liam's in post-op by now. We'd better head for Wexford."

The Steins took a subdued leave of us and went off with Mike in the lead.

While Dad and I said goodbye to Alex and Barbara in the corridor, Maeve had taken a long look at Jay. "He'll be out for hours yet," she observed when I joined her at the sickbed.

I touched Jay's hand. He frowned a little and made a vague noise, then settled into his form like a hare. His breathing came slow and easy. The frown smoothed.

"Come with us," Dad urged. "We're meeting Maeve's students for pizza. You need sustenance."

I explained about the scones. "I want to be here when Jay wakes up." Mahon looked disappointed.

Dad and Maeve left, promising to return for me, and Mahon and I settled in to wait each other out. I had no intention of permitting the police to interrogate Jay unless I was there to run interference. He'd undergone a horrifying ordeal. I would have trusted Joe Kennedy to question him, but not Mahon. I didn't know Mahon well enough.

I sat on the cot and the chief inspector sat on a visitor's chair by the impromptu flower stand. He said polite things about Jay and I said polite things about Garda responsiveness. Finally he gave me a small, wry smile and stood up. "I'll return in an hour or so, Mrs. Dodge. We do need answers, you know."

I rose, too, and said I understood. God knows I had a few questions myself. As I drowsed on the cot the questions chased each other through my mind. If Liam hadn't abducted Jay, had Tommy? Why? How had Liam come to be in the folly? Had Tommy knifed him? Who killed Slade Wheeler? And so on.

Since I didn't have any answers I let my thoughts drift. An astonishing afternoon. I would have to call Mother and the dean. I'd forgotten the dean. I hoped he hadn't watched the eleven o'clock news. I wondered what Ma would think of Grace Flynn.

Grace and Artie. I thought about Artie, whom nobody except his mother and my father would ever call Arthur. Artie was a born henchman. He had been Tommy Tierney's henchman. Now he was Grace's, a step in the right direction. As for Grace, she might not be the Grainne of Maeve's legend, but she was a personality to be reckoned with.

Grace was the kind of woman men burn cities for. I thought of lines Yeats wrote about his own peculiar Grainne.

> *She thinks, part woman, three parts a child,*
> *That nobody looks; her feet*
> *Practise a tinker shuffle*
> *Picked up on a street.*
> *Like a long-legged fly upon the stream,*
> *Her mind moves upon silence.*

Grace didn't yet know her full power. I wondered what would happen when she found it out. The old stories about the Grainnes and the Helens are always told from the male viewpoint, but Grace was not going to adopt anyone's purposes but her own. I had never had her kind of power and never would, but I respected it.

19 🙚

Even the wisest man grows tense
With some sort of violence . . .

—William Butler Yeats, "Under Ben Bulben"

JAY WOKE WITH something like a yell. I jumped from the cot and ran to his side, tangling myself in the curtain on the way. It was a good thing they'd removed the IV. I would have knocked the pole over.

"It's all right, Jay. You're going to be all right." I started the mantra and held his hand—or he held mine. His grip hurt.

After a while he opened his eyes. "That was a winner. How long have I been here?"

I checked my watch. It was, unbelievably, only half past eight. "About five hours. Listen, Chief Inspector Mahon is coming back soon, and he's going to want to interrogate you. Are you ready for questions?"

He licked his lips. "Jesus, I suppose so. Is Liam . . . ?" His eyes squinched shut.

"Liam is in Wexford, in the county hospital."

"Ah, he's alive." He lay very still, eyes closed. "He kept talking. I couldn't say anything, nothing at all."

"Joe said your mouth was taped shut."

He shuddered and opened his eyes. "I don't know why that was so awful. It was dark and cold. I didn't like that." His voice thickened. "I wanted water. My wrists and my head hurt, and I was afraid it would take you a long time to find us. But the worst part was not being able to answer Liam. He thought he was dying."

I sorted through the dozens of questions that sprang to mind, but before I could ask any of them Mahon pulled the curtain aside.

He didn't yank it open. He was tentative, polite. "Sorry to intrude. Ah, Dodge, I see you're awake."

Jay nodded, frowning. His grip on my hand had eased. Now it tightened again.

"As you may imagine, I have questions for you. Are you up to answering them? I spoke with your physician."

"It's okay."

Mahon cleared his throat. "Mrs. Dodge . . ."

"Lark stays."

"Hmm." His face flushed and he looked at the floor. "Well, then, before we begin, I owe you an apology, Dodge. Sgt. Kennedy relayed your feelings about the press release. By and large, you know, we let the public relations types handle the media. There were questions in the Dail over my conduct of the case, though, and your foreign service people were asking questions, too, because the Wheelers were US citizens. The chief superintendent suggested I give the reporters your name as a consulting expert. 'Twas stretching a point, and I'd reservations of my own, but it flat didn't occur to me that I might put you in jeopardy, lad. I hope you believe that."

Jay sighed. "You exposed my wife and my father-in-law to harassment by the press. That was my main objection, though the fact that the cottage is isolated worried me, too. After the break-in . . ."

Mahon said heavily, "What's done is done. I don't mind admitting I've had a very bad twenty-four hours."

Jay's mouth twitched. "Not half as bad as mine, friend."

"True, but *your* conscience is clear." Mahon gave a short laugh. "Shall I call in my man? I want a record of what you say."

Mahon went out for his constable and I brought a chair for myself. The Gardai seemed to think that was a good idea, and as there were other chairs in the room, the three of us were soon seated around Jay's sickbed—they on one side and I on the other, like opposing diplomats at a bumpy truce table. Jay decided he wanted water, and we waited while the nurse fetched a covered thermos carafe with a bent straw. Finally, the constable put a fresh cassette in his machine and pressed the record button.

Mahon identified himself and got Jay's statistics into the record. "Now then, sir, can you tell us the name of your abductor?"

"Tommy Tierney," Jay said without hesitation. "He hit me over the head while I was walking down to Stanyon. He was waiting just beyond the rhododendrons that mark a split in the graveled drive leading to Stanyon Hall."

"Did you see him as he attacked you?"

"No, but I regained consciousness while he was dragging me over a stile into Stanyon Woods. I struggled with him, kicked him, but my hands were bound. He hit me again with a sap. I saw it coming. The next thing I knew I was in the . . . that tomb."

"The Stanyon folly?"

"Is that what they call it? It was cold as a tomb." Jay's grip tightened on my hand. "I thought it had to be somewhere in the woods but I wasn't sure."

"You were found in the Stanyon folly. Were you alone when you regained consciousness?"

"No, sir. Tierney had propped me in a chair and was tying my feet. I kicked and yelled at him. He bound me, then he whipped out the adhesive tape."

"And you saw him clearly?"

"Yes. He had one of those big electric flashlights. I think it was already in the chamber. He couldn't have carried it and me, not very far."

"A torch," I supplied when Mahon looked blank.

"Ah, I see. Go on."

Jay rubbed his forehead. "He set the light down so it shone on me. The battery was starting to fade. Still, I saw him face-to-face, and I'll be happy to identify him when you take him."

"He's in custody, charged with the break-in at the cottage."

Jay expelled a breath. "Quick work."

Mahon gave a gracious nod. "Go on."

"Tommy told me his name after he'd gagged me. He slapped me around, taunted me. Then he went off and took the flash-light with him." Jay fell silent. I handed him the jug and he sipped from it. His hand shook.

When he set the water down, Mahon said, "How did Mc-Diarmuid come to be in the folly with you?"

Jay took my hand. "I can tell you what he explained to me, but you ought to ask him. All I saw—and this was some time later, maybe an hour later—was that Tierney had brought in an-other victim. The light hurt my eyes at first, but when they ad-justed I could see it was Liam McDiarmuid and that he was bleeding."

"You know McDiarmuid," Mahon interrupted—for the record.

"Yes. I met him at Stanyon Hall."

The constable jotted something in a notebook.

"So young Tierney brought him into the folly."

Jay nodded. "He tied Liam to the other chair. There were these two chairs like short-legged thrones, with armrests and moth-eaten cloth back-rests and cushions. They smelled moldy."

If they were nearly two hundred years old they were enti-tled to smell moldy, I reflected, but the smell must have added to the horror.

Jay was saying, "He'd tied me to one chair and he tied Liam to the other."

"That's clear. Go on."

Jay swallowed more water. His voice sounded rough, as if he

had a cold coming on. "Liam had fainted. Tierney was ranting, laughing. I couldn't make much sense of what he said, but I gathered he'd fought with Liam. My head ached. Maybe I passed out, too. I was fading in and out. When I regained consciousness, Tierney had gone and taken the light with him. I could hear Liam breathing."

Mahon opened his mouth to ask the next question, but Jay said, in a less certain voice, "You're sure Liam's alive?"

"Yes." Mahon had had plenty of time to call the Wexford hospital.

Jay closed his eyes. "Okay. As I said, you should ask Liam what happened. He was out for quite a while. When he came to, he sounded weak. He wanted to know if I was all right and I said mm-hmm. Then he apologized."

"Apologized!"

"He said he'd tried to rescue me and failed."

Mahon made a skeptical noise.

Jay went on, dogged, "When he heard I'd disappeared, he was afraid Tommy had abducted me."

"Wasn't that a leap of logic?"

"Tommy'd seen the news stories."

"And they put the wind up him? I see." Mahon sounded depressed.

"Tommy called Liam at Stanyon and said he needed a getaway car. Liam agreed to help him escape to Shannon Airport and arranged to meet him in the lane west of the woods. Liam took a knife, drove there, and waited. He intended to force Tommy to take him to me. They fought and Tommy won." Jay's voice kept fading like a bad audio. "Tommy took Liam's cash and car keys and brought Liam into the tomb."

"The folly," Mahon corrected, absent. "That had to be before we got the telephone message saying you were being held hostage."

"There was a ransom demand?"

"We have it on tape. The laboratory think the voice was

255

Tommy's." Mahon explained the phony political message, then burst out, "In God's name, why? Why would a respectable man like McDiarmuid agree to such a thing?"

A considerable silence ensued. "Because Liam killed Slade Wheeler on Easter Sunday, and Tommy witnessed the killing." Jay drew a ragged breath. "And I wouldn't be telling you that if Liam hadn't also admitted he killed Wheeler's sister. I don't think the first death was murder. The second was."

Mahon raised a heavy hand and the constable shut off the recorder. "You're saying Liam McDiarmuid admitted he was responsible for both deaths?"

Jay nodded. He was tiring rapidly and I didn't like his color. "Liam thought he was dying. He wanted me to know what had happened because he believed I was going to die, too. Tommy meant to leave the country."

I said, "Tommy abandoned the two of you to die of thirst?" Jay was silent.

I felt a wave of nausea. It could have happened. If we hadn't known of the folly's existence. . . . No, surely not. Too many people knew of the hideaway. Someone would have come forward, but would they have come forward quickly enough? It doesn't take many days for a human being to die without water.

I gripped Jay's hand almost as fiercely as he had held mine.

"Well, well, my money was on young Stein." Mahon heaved a huge sigh. "I'd best make a telephone call. We'll have to put a guard on McDiarmuid's room and bar visitors. Tommy Tierney's in custody, but we were set to release him on bail Monday."

A nurse bustled in at that moment and ordered Mahon out. Perhaps she'd been eavesdropping. It was time, she announced, for Jay to eat. I was astonished I hadn't thought of feeding him. I'd been feeding people compulsively since I arrived in Ireland and here was my husband starving. I expressed myself.

It seemed they had fed him toast and broth earlier, before they called me to his room, and were about to administer cream of asparagus soup. Jay doesn't like cream of asparagus soup. I noticed that he ate it to the last drop. And drank a glass of juice. And ordered a steak, medium-rare, when the nurse returned. She laughed as she whisked the cart from the room and promised a midnight snack.

I was rather hungry myself by that time and thought longingly of pizza. However, Mahon would return at any moment and I was not going to leave Jay with the story untold. In fact, I was not going to leave him at all. I was explaining that to him in a low voice because I didn't want Gardai witnesses, when a crash sounded in the corridor.

Jay's muscles contracted. I turned.

Toss Tierney ripped the privacy curtain aside and stood swaying at the foot of the bed. He was drunk but by no means incapable of mayhem. I could see that in his eyes. I stood up slowly but Jay kept a hard grip on my hand.

"Liar!"

Jay said nothing.

"May God damn ye to hell telling lies about my son."

"What lies, Mr. Tierney?" Jay's voice was cool, almost detached.

Toss blinked. "And that hoor, Maeve Butler, wheedling and telling the missus she ought to betray Tommy. She's a traitor herself, the wee sassenach bitch. We know fine how to deal with traitors." He smacked the foot-rail and the bed shuddered.

I said, "Teresa didn't betray anyone, Toss, and neither did Maeve."

He called me unsanctified names in a spray of spittle. Jay squeezed my hand harder, holding me at his side.

I softened my voice. "I know you love your son. That's probably why you showed him how to enter the folly. He showed—others." I started to say he showed Artie and bit back the name. Why get Artie into trouble?

"Others? What others?"

"Does it matter? *You* were the one who betrayed the secret."

His lower lip stuck out, I swear, like a pouting baby's. His eyes shifted, and he let out a baffled roar, shaking the bed. "Liar! I say he's innocent. Tommy's innocent."

"He didn't kill Slade Wheeler," Jay murmured.

Toss caught himself in mid-roar. "Whazzat?"

"I said he did not kill Slade Wheeler."

Toss shook his head like a fly-tormented horse. "Ah, shite, wasn't he after telling me he *did?*"

I held my breath.

Jay shook his head slowly. No. He held Toss's eyes.

"Jaysus!" Toss sank onto the constable's chair. Great wrenching sobs shook his body. I don't think he noticed when Mahon and the constable, nightstick in hand, reentered the room. They handcuffed Toss and led him away, still sobbing.

Jay flopped back against the pillow.

I sat with a *thwack.* "You can let go of my hand."

He released it finger by finger. "My dear and darling wife, do not ever try to reason with a drunk. He was ready to tear the limbs from your body."

I shook my aching hand. "I wasn't trying to reason with him."

"Then what did you have in mind?"

I rose to my feet. "System overload."

He squinted up at me. "Say again?"

"I was trying to paralyze his central nervous system."

Jay let out a long breath and wriggled his shoulders. "You came fairly close to paralyzing mine."

"Anyone for pizza?" My father stood in the door holding a flat, grease-blotched carton. The smile that wreathed his features faded. "What's the matter?"

I said, "Just Toss Tierney. He's gone now."

Jay said, "Hello, George. Did somebody mention pizza?"

Dad's smile came back full force. His laid the carton on the bed and took Jay's hand. "My dear boy, we were so worried."

Jay's cheeks reddened. "So was I."

Maeve poked her head in from the corridor. "Is it safe?

Grand. We brought clothes and a razor, Jay." He needed a razor.

He smiled at her. "And pizza."

So Jay and I shared the pizza while Dad told Jay about Maeve's campaign to enter the folly and Artie's last-minute rescue.

I munched bland, cheesy pizza and watched my father. His voice was clear as a bell, no slurring, and his motions vigorous. Considering Dad had done every possible thing he shouldn't have done since I arrived, including breakfasting on scrambled eggs, I thought Ma was going to be pleased when she saw him. I was more than pleased. The session with Maeve's students had been a tonic, clearly. He liked students. They kept him young. Maybe he needed to teach a class now and then. I'd suggest that sometime—some other time.

"Sure, it's a council of war," Joe Kennedy said from the doorway.

"Join us." Jay licked a bit of mozzarella from one finger. "It's good to see you. I hear you pulled the tape off my mouth. Thanks, buddy." They shook hands.

Joe was blushing. "Ah, I couldn't help myself. Yon evidence johnny would have photographed you from a dozen angles and taken blood samples before he touched the tape—or the ropes."

"No sense of priorities."

Joe rubbed the back of his neck and grinned. "That's it." He was wearing jeans and a heathery blue pullover, so I gathered he was off-duty.

"Pizza?" Jay lifted the carton, which was balanced on his stomach. Dad and Maeve had brought the largest pizza in the province of Leinster.

Maeve handed Joe one of the paper plates Jay and I had ignored, American style. "Don't tell me you're hungry."

Joe helped himself. "I can never tell you anything that you don't already know, Miss Butler."

Maeve's eyes glinted and her jaw thrust out.

"Hey," I said, swallowing pizza. "Truce. You two have been at daggers drawn for days now. It's exhausting to watch. Besides, you make a splendid team even when you're quarreling. Think what triumphs of archaeology and criminology you'd achieve if you cooperated."

Both of them looked sheepish, so I pointed out Mrs. O'Brien's daffodils on the pseudo-altar by way of distraction, and told Joe I appreciated the gesture.

We chatted about one thing and another. Maeve was taking her team to the motorway site the next morning. Joe was going fishing. Dad said he'd called Mother and the dean. Ma was flying in to Dublin the following Saturday. Jay lay, eyes half-closed, yawning from time to time but obviously comfortable and interested.

However, when he heard I intended to stay the night, he told me point-blank to forget it. My feelings were hurt. I'm afraid I had been romanticizing my role as noble wife ministering to sick husband—and sleeping at his feet, more or less. It's easy to create foolish self-images.

Jay said, "Mahon's coming back. After that they'll knock me out again. I guarantee it. Come in the morning, Lark."

"But . . ."

He jabbed a thumb in the direction of my father who was asking Joe something about trout fishing.

"Oh." I am sometimes slow on the uptake. Jay didn't want me to leave Dad alone in the cottage. Tears stung my eyes. I bent down and gave him as thorough a kiss as I should have, given his sore lip. "Well, if you insist. Dad and I will come for you right after breakfast."

So we went away. Dad let me drive home. Maeve and Joe were standing in the car park talking when we left.

20 ❧

Oh, when my back began to smart
'Twas like a penknife in my heart,
And when my heart began to bleed,
Then that was death, and death indeed.

—Children's song

LIAM MCDIARMUID DIED early that morning. Alex called at half past seven. He told me the news, his voice trembling, and asked if he and Barbara could come to the cottage to talk to my father. Dad was in the shower, but I said yes. A week earlier I would have tried to shield him.

I brewed a fresh pot of coffee. When he came upstairs, I told him what had happened. Though he was sad, he was not as devastated as he might have been. We had talked for a long time the night before, unwinding, putting things in perspective, and I had told him of Jay's revelations. He agreed to let Alex and Barbara know, if Mahon had not told them, that their friend and colleague had probably committed murder. I thought it would come better from Dad than from me.

So I fixed him a quick breakfast and went downstairs for my own shower. I dawdled afterward, making the beds and running a batch of laundry. The *swoosh-swoosh* of the washer was oddly comforting. The spin cycle whined away, and I had set up a drying rack in the hallway, when I heard the Steins' knock.

I took my time festooning the passage with a week's worth of damp underwear. When I had tossed a colored load into the washer and set it going again, I crept upstairs.

Barbara was sniffing into a handkerchief and Alex gave me a dispirited flap of the hand by way of greeting as I entered the kitchen. I poured myself a cup and warmed the coffee in the three other mugs.

Barbara blew her nose. "I can't believe it. Not L-Liam. Jay must be mistaken."

She was very properly upset, so I didn't leap to Jay's defense. Dad kept quiet, too.

"It's horrible."

It was horrible. It was also puzzling.

Alex said hesitantly, "I think the Bosnian experience was more traumatic for Liam than he was willing to admit. He was taken by one of those roving bands of Serbian guerrillas, you know. They kept him prisoner awhile."

I sat down. "You mean he was a hostage?" That was an irony, and not a nice one.

Barbara plopped a second lump of sugar into her mug. "They didn't hold him for ransom or anything like that, and he got away from them after a week or ten days, but they confiscated his camera equipment and forced him to travel with them."

"He said they made him witness their atrocities."

I frowned. "I thought that sort tried to conceal their activities."

Dad said, "The senior military officers would."

Alex said, "This bunch was on its own, roving the country-side, chasing down Moslems and beating them to death. Lee said they were proud of what they were doing. They enjoyed it, and they believed in 'ethnic cleansing.' " His mouth twisted. "As far as Lee was concerned, those so-called patriots were a bunch of teenaged thugs." He pushed his mug away untouched. "And the business of digging up other victims for the UN commander, that haunted him."

"The Serbs who captured Liam made a game of killing." Barbara began to cry again. "Poor Liam. We liked him so much."

I had liked him, too. He was a charming, witty man and a fine photographer.

I said, "I didn't stay to see the paramedics bring him out of the folly, Alex, but last night Mahon seemed to think he'd survive. What happened?"

Alex sighed. "Pneumonia. He was running a high fever by the time we left the hospital, and they pumped him full of antibiotics, but I guess the combination of blood-loss and hypothermia were too much. The doctor who called me said Liam died around dawn." He shivered. "I still don't believe it."

Barbara turned to her husband. Her frizzy red hair crackled with earnestness, as if emotion had given it an electrical charge. "We knew he'd had a hard time, Alex. We should have been more sensitive to his feelings. We should have stopped Slade's stupid games."

Dad took a reflective sip of coffee. "But the war games were already well under way by the time Liam came to work for you, weren't they?"

Barbara scrubbed at her eyes. "Yes, and he knew they were. He made wisecracks about them all along. You know his style— it was hard to tell when he cared about something."

"Humor can be a defensive weapon," Dad murmured.

Barbara leaned forward. "Do you think we should move the company, George?"

"Heavens, no. You like it here, don't you?"

She gave a snort. "I wish I was in California cursing the smog. At least American violence is familiar."

"But violence is everywhere. You can't run away from it." Dad meditated over his cup. "And you have an obligation to the community, don't you? Your employees rely on you. I don't think you should give up and go home. I think you should find Irish partners, if possible, and hire other Irish artists and technicians."

"Make amends and mend our fences." Alex was smiling at him. "I told Barb that's what you'd say."

"Ask Maeve," I said. "She'll know what to do."

They left shortly after that, saying they knew we wanted to get to the hospital as soon as possible.

The news of Liam's death had shaken Jay. I was conscious of the weight of his silence in the back of the car as I drove home. In fact, I was so preoccupied I forgot to disable the alarm system when I unlocked the door. Jay and Dad must have been distracted, too. They didn't remind me in time to stop the hideous clangor. I shut the device off while Jay called the Garda station.

I plugged in the electric kettle. "Would you mind if I took Jay off for a drive, Dad? If he feels up to it. I need to talk to him."

He smiled. "An excellent thought. Maybe I can get some work done on my notes today."

"You have had an interruption or two."

Jay wandered in. "I talked to Joe. He said Mahon didn't reach the Wexford hospital in time for a formal interview before Liam's fever ran out of control. Still, Liam said enough while he was delirious to satisfy Mahon that my version of things was accurate." Mahon had talked to Jay again early that morning and broken the news of Liam's death.

"Then the Gardai are closing the Wheeler cases?"

"There are loose ends, and they'll need to take a deposition, but I probably won't have to return until they bring Tommy Tierney to trial."

The kettle shrieked. I unplugged it. "Another intercontinental flight? Oh, Jay, I'm sorry."

He took the steaming kettle from me and gave me a peck on the cheek. "You can come with me, help me hold the plane up."

The kiss was very promising. I asked him if he felt well enough to take a drive through the countryside.

"Absolutely." He wiggled the still protesting kettle. "Does anybody want tea?"

None of us did. I had boiled water reflexively, as a response to men in the kitchen—a habit I'd have to break.

Jay and I piled into the Toyota and took off. I wasn't aiming anywhere in particular. Jay didn't talk. I thought he deserved time to brood. When I'd driven some distance through the Vale of Avoca, I saw a sign for Avondale House and followed a coachload of German tourists to the car park.

"The guidebook says the grounds are extensive—lots of exotic trees. The Forestry Department runs a school here." I was chattering. "The house is supposed to be a museum. It was Charles Stewart Parnell's ancestral manor."

"Let's go for a walk." Jay got out, locking the door on his side.

I slid out and locked my side with the key. "Where to?"

"That looks like the path."

The mostly elderly tourists milled on the asphalt. We cut off through the trees, avoiding the house, and were soon alone in a quiet glade of tall evergreens.

The sun, though not warm, shone fitfully, and the ground was dry. Jay removed the anorak the hospital laundry had cleaned for him and spread it on the needles. We sat down, holding each other, not talking.

Finally, he said, "I thought a lot about you while I was stuck in the dark."

"I thought about you."

"I know. I wanted to tell Liam not to worry, that my wife was organizing our rescue."

"You're making fun of me."

"No," he said. "It kept me sane, believing that."

I touched the white dressing on the side of his head. "I didn't do anything. Maeve was the one who figured out where you were and forced the Gardai to let her dig." My hand dropped and my eyes filled. "She was the one who thought of calling Teresa Tierney."

He stroked my hair. "You mean that wasn't just Toss's imagination?"

Sniffing, I explained about the jungle drums.

Jay chuckled. "I'm damned."

"You never met Artie."

"Or the inimitable Grace. I'll have to thank them in person."

I sat up and dabbed my eyes with a tissue. "Artie you may meet. Not Grace. She's far too dangerous."

He touched my face. "Not to you, love. Will you listen to me while I confess my sins?"

I blinked at him. "Confess?"

He nodded. "You were right. I made a very dumb mistake coming here. I knew it the minute I saw your face at the airport, and I've been driving myself nuts ever since trying to figure out how to retrieve my error."

"But Jay—"

He touched my lips, hushing me. "When you didn't call me after you found the body, I panicked. That's the truth with no bark on it."

"Panic? You don't panic."

He kissed me. "My sweet innocent, I freaked out. I couldn't teach, I couldn't grade papers, I couldn't sleep. All I could think about was that our marriage was in danger and I wasn't doing anything about it. I need you, Lark. Believe me, only the thought of losing you would compel me to sit in a jumbo jet for eleven hours with little bits of Greenland breaking off into the Atlantic thirty thousand feet below me."

"It wasn't anything you did. It was the baby."

"Yes, I know."

"What if I can't give you a child?"

"A child is not a box of chocolates. If we can't have a baby ourselves, we'll adopt one. Or not. Your choice."

"But . . ."

"When the miscarriage happened, I thought I could help you. I knew you'd grieve. I did, too." His voice roughened. "I wanted to see your daughter, Lark. She would have been something wonderful."

I burst into tears.

Jay held me close and said other good things. Gradually I grew calmer, but I was still sniffling.

"Entschuldigen!" A bespectacled tourist backed hastily away

from our haven. We watched him until he disappeared behind a clump of white-blossomed rhododendrons.

Jay squeezed my shoulder. "Come on, let's walk. The damp's seeping through this jacket." He stood up in stages and pulled me to my feet.

"You said you thought you could help me." I took his arm. "You did, but I couldn't get past the awful feeling of failure. I guess I had to deal with that on my own."

He gave my hand a warm pat. "Maybe so."

"It's like Dad and the car." I explained my fresh insight into my father's state of mind. "I think I'm okay now. I think I worked through it before you were kidnapped. I never seriously thought of leaving you, Jay. I love you too much. But it made me sick to think I'd failed you."

He squeezed my shoulders and said my failure to conceive for so long was as likely to have been his problem as mine.

"Yes, but losing the baby after all that . . ." I shook my head. "I knew my reaction wasn't reasonable."

"But you're reasonable now?" He was half-teasing.

"I have," I said with dignity, "regained my sanity. And my sense of balance. And maybe even my sense of humor. Let's go back before Dad writes a monograph."

I'm afraid we didn't do justice to the Parnell estate. I drove away from it with cheerful abandon, scraping past a coach on the highway and zipping by a petrol tanker without flinching.

Jay flinched. "Thank God I don't have to drive."

"It's easy." I slowed for a curve. "You just have to trust the other guy."

Jay grunted, skeptical.

"Can you tell me about Liam or is that too raw to talk about?"

"No, but I feel clumsy."

"Clumsy!" Startled, I glanced at him and veered onto the shoulder. Gravel flew.

Jay winced. "Liam was an eloquent guy and I don't remember his exact words. I tried to tell Mahon the gist of what he said this morning and made a hash of it. My own judgment kept interfering, skewing his ideas."

"Give it a try. Did he tell you why?" I geared down to follow a tour bus. "Or maybe you could start with how. I still find it hard to believe a slight man who wasn't five-foot-nine could kill Slade Wheeler."

Jay shrugged. "Duck soup."

"If Liam had sneaked up on Slade from behind and administered a choke hold, yes, but you said he confronted Slade directly, that they actually fought."

"It's not all that surprising. Slade was a lardy loudmouth, not a fighter. Before Liam went out to the Balkans he took a couple of unarmed combat classes. He said he wasn't good, not a black belt or anything, but Slade was no good at all."

I thought of Slade's combat fatigues and polished boots. "I'll never understand men."

Jay said patiently, "Slade talked tough. Liam was tough. Mentally, I mean."

I was getting tired of dawdling. The road, though curving, seemed clear. I flashed my lights, the coach moved left, and I passed. I missed an oncoming sedan by a good yard. "So what happened?"

Jay had flung up his arm to protect his face from the inevitable collision. He lowered it. "On the evening of Easter Sunday, Liam met Slade in the woods by appointment. He— Liam, I mean—brought Tommy Tierney with him because he wanted a witness. He knew Tommy had clashed with Slade."

"I suppose Liam was trying to get Slade to discontinue the games?"

"There was an element of self-righteousness, too. He wanted Tommy to see him challenge and defeat Slade. I'm reading between the lines, of course. Liam didn't say that."

I was stuck behind another coach, this one French. I geared down. "Did he expect expect hand-to-hand combat when he went to meet Slade in the woods?"

"I don't think so. Slade made the mistake of attacking Liam verbally."

I brooded over that. Liam was clever with words.

Jay eased the shoulder harness. "He could have talked Wheeler into a disengagement. They didn't have to fight, but they did and Slade died. It was that simple."

"Not murder."

"The courts would have had a hard time proving intent. I think Mahon would have settled for manslaughter. Liam could have pleaded self-defense. If Tommy—and the jury—had co-operated . . ."

The coach pulled onto a lay-by. I shifted up and pressed the pedal. "He might have got away with it."

"Probably not entirely. The disposition of the body was too . . . peculiar."

"Symbolic."

"Yes. Jesus, a one-lane bridge with a pub attached. Outstanding urban design."

I had reached Avoca. It was Saturday and the pub on the bridge was doing land-office business. Pedestrians out for a look at the river had turned the bridge into an outdoor meeting hall. They stood there, beer glasses in hand, chatting. Some of them waved. I crept across the bridge in first gear. On the east side of the river, I had to make a right turn on a blind corner.

Jay was as still as a mouse while I negotiated the passage. As we wound out of the village, he said, "I didn't see Slade's body, but it sounded like an artistic composition, a last satirical comment on Wheeler's war games. I thought that when you described it to me, and what Liam said confirmed my opinion."

I turned onto the Killaveen road. "Then you suspected him?"

Jay nodded. "And Novak. I'm not the only one. Joe Kennedy suspected Liam, because of the daub of paint and because of Grace Flynn. They were cousins."

"You know that?" I felt a twinge of resentment I immediately suppressed. Jay was never going to tell me all he knew of a case.

"Joe told me."

Old boy's network. What a bore. *I* was not going to be secretive. I told Jay Maeve's theory about Diarmuid and Grainne and the mark on Diarmuid's forehead.

He listened intently. When I wound down, he said, "Yeah, there could be some connection. The love mark would have appealed to Liam's sense of humor."

I drove slowly through Killaveen. The car park of the pub was jammed. I didn't see anything funny about the legend. "Maeve said the disposition of the body was poetic."

"Imaginative, anyway." Jay craned for a glimpse of the trout stream, then sank back in the seat. "The hell of it is I kept fading in and out and so did Liam. What I heard was pretty disjointed."

I waited for a car full of kids to turn onto Suicide Lane ahead of me. "I suppose Liam despised Slade for corrupting the game-players."

Jay nodded, but he was pursuing his own train of thought. "I wish I could have answered him. There was a lot of self-serving rationalization in what Liam was saying. He told me about an experience he had in Bosnia."

I thought of our early visitors. "Alex said the Serbs forced him to witness atrocities."

"Yes. He came away from that convinced that the terrorism in Ulster—on both sides—was the same kind of stupidity, and he hated Wheeler for feeding into it."

That fitted with what Liam had told me at dinner the day I met him. "I can almost respect that . . ."

Jay touched the dressing on the side of his head. "He kept saying Wheeler had perverted the meaning of war. I wish I could have argued with him."

War was a subject I avoided discussing with Jay. I had no experience of it and he had too much.

After a moment, he said, "Liam liked the Steins. He kept saying they had European minds. Whereas Wheeler was a real

Yank icon, a violence junkie with no principles and no traditions."

"You disagreed with that."

He waited while a petrol tanker flashed past before he spoke. "It seemed to me that Wheeler boiled the structure of combat down to its essentials, but then I'm an American. I think like one."

"Maybe Liam was right."

"Come on, Lark," he snapped. "Wheeler's the victim here. He was a game junkie, if anything. He was dumb, and insensitive to local complications, but he understood one thing. The violence was already there in the kids. He choreographed it. To some extent he defanged it. The gamers didn't kill anybody and they didn't kill each other."

"Well, okay, but . . ."

He was intent on making his point. "The fact that Slade didn't pour a lot of windy ideas about freedom and justice and fatherland into their heads is to his credit, as far as I'm concerned."

I was coming up on our turnoff. The lot at the church hall looked empty so I pulled into it and stopped. "You sound as if you approve of war-gaming."

"No. Wheeler was a schmuck, but I don't see how attaching principles to what the gamers were acting out would have made it better. The violence would just have perverted the principles. Liam didn't see it that way. He saw a wicked American corrupting Irish youth. He read me a real sermon on Yank ignorance. I think he saw himself as some kind of hero for ridding the country of Wheeler's influence."

"A hero? Surely not."

"Even cynics can con themselves. If Liam had been honest with himself he would have called the Gardai and told them the fight got out of hand. Instead he desecrated Wheeler's corpse to show the world how clever he was."

"Isn't 'desecrated' a strong word?"

"You thought Slade had been shot in the head, didn't you?"

"For a few seconds." We sat silent. The scene in the potting shed was sharp in my memory.

Jay cleared his throat. "Liam and Tommy moved Slade's body twice, you know: once to conceal it and once to display it. It's the display part I find disgusting. That, and the killing of Kayla Wheeler. I told Mahon to check the trunk of Liam's Saab. I'll bet there's a camera there with undeveloped pictures of both corpses."

Liam as snuff artist? My mind rebelled, but the insight made too much sense to dismiss it out of hand. "Let's hope the press doesn't find the film."

Jay gave a wry grin. "A gruesome thought."

With the engine off, the car had begun to cool. I shivered. "Why did Liam kill Kayla? That doesn't make sense to me. You said it was murder."

"Yeah, he got cocky. He thought, wrongly, that he wasn't a suspect in Slade's death and decided he might as well get rid of Kayla, too."

" 'Get rid of her'?"

"That's what he said. He planned the second killing in detail. It was pretty nauseating. He went on about his cleverness, how he had flopped Kayla's dying body around to make it look as if she resisted."

"My God." Nauseating was right. My stomach clenched.

Jay leaned back against the headrest and closed his eyes. "He counted on Kayla's solitude and her alcoholism. He killed her in cold blood and faked a fight scene. He was good at stage settings and he gloated over that one. And he bragged about how he hid out waiting for Kayla in the bathroom, how he got rid of the nylon rope he used as a garotte, even how he laundered his clothes and showered afterwards, at home, to make sure there would be no physical evidence to incriminate him."

"But why?" I burst out. "What had she ever done to him?"

Jay opened his eyes and turned his head. His eyes were dark. "Nothing, but Kayla was a non-person to him, a gross inconvenience. He wanted the company to succeed, and he decided

Stonehall would run smoother with Kayla dead. She stood to inherit Slade's shares."

"Did he do it for Grace?" I was looking for comfort, or logic.

Jay shook his head. "Only in the sense that he thought he could manipulate Grace and Grace's child easier than he could deal with Kayla. Mind you, he didn't spend much time talking about Kayla or Grace. They were women and peripheral. He was too busy making sure I understood why he challenged and fought Slade. Kayla didn't interest him."

I was shaken. I had liked Liam. I said so, adding, "I must have lousy taste."

"He had a lot of charm—and some conscience. I think he did suffer post-traumatic stress over the Bosnian experience. I suspect he could have used that as a defense, even for Kayla's murder. But in all the elaborate explanations he gave me—mind you, he thought he was dying—he never once saw a connection between the Serbian atrocities and the atrocities he committed himself."

The irony of that made me writhe. I started the engine.

Jay said, "Nobody except you and George has tried to present the viewpoint of the victims. The Steins thought Kayla was tacky, and Slade was, at best, a convenient source of funds."

I eased the car onto Suicide Lane and headed for Stanyon. "Mike Novak loathed Slade's interference and thought he was stupid. So did Tracy."

"The Wheelers are dead. They didn't 'ask for it.' " Jay said the phrase with contempt. "As far as I can tell, neither of them committed a crime worthy of capital punishment."

I said hesitantly, "Slade did make a game of war."

Jay snorted. "Slade made a parody of war." His voice softened. "He was an overgrown kid, but he didn't kill anyone himself, and, unlike his Serbian counterparts—the ones Liam kept comparing him to—he didn't egg the kids on to kill anybody, either."

That was true. A motorcycle roared past and I thought briefly of Artie. I turned onto the graveled drive.

Jay said, "I don't think Slade was a saint or even an innocent. I don't doubt he was hard to put up with on the job. If he was anything like his sister, he must have been an unhappy man. As for Kayla, when I saw her I was reminded of the profile of victims of child abuse, especially incest."

He had to be right, though it would have taken me a long time to reach the same conclusion. "Her drinking?"

He nodded. "And the ponderous flirting and the eating disorder. She needed help. She sure didn't need what she got."

I had come to the Y. I stopped and looked down at Stanyon. A fairy-tale castle. Most fairy tales, I reminded myself, are grim. I turned right and passed beneath the blood-red blossoms of the rhododendrons.

Jay said, "You asked me how I felt about Liam McDiarmuid. Sad, I guess. Angry. Maybe relieved that he's dead."

I crept toward the cottage in first gear. "He tried to save your life."

"So he said." Jay gave a short, unamused laugh. "I guess he decided I was an acceptable European-style non-tacky Yank. If my mouth hadn't been taped shut I could have set him straight. I hope I would have said something about Kayla."

I hoped he would have, too.

When we entered the cottage Dad greeted us with sandwiches and tea. It was almost like coming home.

Epilogue ❧

And think of my happy condition,
Surrounded by acres of clams.

—American song, sung to the Irish air "Rosin the Beau"

JAY CALLED THE dean, who *had* watched the eleven o'clock
news. The dean was very solicitous. Jay had been hospitalized?
He should by all means recover completely before he tried to
fly home. Sick leave was something the dean understood. Since
Jay never used it, he had accumulated nearly a term's worth, so
he invoked it and stayed until Saturday. I flew home with him.

Mother's flight from New York arrived before our flight to
Seattle took off, so all four of us had a nice reunion in Dublin
airport; Joe and Maeve showed up before the plane left, too.
One benefit of Jay's ordeal was that Maeve and I were now
good friends, and Jay's hormones had decided he didn't need
to challenge Joe to a duel.

We had spent our six remaining days in Ireland very happily,
though the press hovered, and Jay underwent two intensive in-
terviews with Chief Inspector Mahon. Whenever Jay was free,
I whipped out my itinerary and we took off. We did see Glendalough with its round towers and Celtic crosses. When we
weren't dawdling around Quaker villages, we visited neolithic
sites. We even drove north to Newgrange.

We walked in the Stanyon Woods, too, partly to exorcise

Jay's demons. He thought the wall paintings in the folly were hilarious and wished he'd seen them before Tommy incarcerated him under the dolmen. I never did find my incised stone, though I looked for it.

Maeve called me from Dublin a couple of weeks after Jay and I got home. She'd introduced my mother to the Wicklow poets, and she also wanted to tell me that Grace was doing well. The lawyer was pressing for the child's rights. The Steins were mounting a retrospective showing of Liam's photographs. I suspected that the idea for the exhibition came from Maeve herself, though she didn't claim credit for it. Stonehall Enterprises had hired an Irish MBA to replace Slade Wheeler.

In September, Maeve called me again. She sounded shy.

"Joe and I have decided to do it."

"Do what?" My mind tossed up images of Regency porn.

"Get married."

I was delighted and said all the appropriate things. "When?"

"After Easter."

"Wonderful. Why don't you fly west and honeymoon on the Pacific? We'd love to see you both and it should be reasonably peaceful here by that time."

The honeymoon idea startled her, but she didn't reject it outright. We discussed the possibilities. Finally she said, "What do you mean peaceful? Are you expecting civil disturbances?"

"Only in a manner of speaking." I felt shy, too, and I shifted my enormous bulk on the kitchen chair. "The twins should be sleeping through the night by then."

"Twins?"

I cleared my throat and tested an Irish phrase I had overheard in a pub. "I'm up the pole."

"Pregnant?" Maeve cackled like a moorhen. "Don't put it that way, idjit. It's very rude language." Her turn to ask when.

"Early December. Little Sagittariuses. Two of them."

"Aren't you overdoing it?"

"Overcompensating maybe. Uh, Maeve . . ."

"What is it?"

"That double-spiral design on the megaliths. Does it have any significance?"

A crackling pause followed, but Maeve is not slow. "If you'd found a sheela-na-gig I could tell you it was a fertility symbol. We're not sure about the spirals."

"I'm sure."

"Are you happy?"

"As a clam."

In mid-December, at about the solstice, I gave birth to healthy fraternal twins, a boy and a girl. We called our son George James after his grandfather and his father. Our daughter we named Erin.